Bringing Abundance Back

BARBARA G. TUCKER

Barbara G Tucker

July 4, 2015

DEDICATION

To Tessie

Barbara G. Tucker

ACKNOWLEDGEMENTS:

Cover Photo: Mary Sheetz

Chapter 1

January 1998

The first and only memory Virginia Mae Foster had of her mother was the smell of chicken and dumplings, heavy with what she would eventually learn to recognize as onions and celery. Yes, now, fifty years later, it was the smell she remembered most, more than color or sound or facial expression or clothing or touch or temperature or furnishings. Over the years she had constructed a scene around that smell, a scene she knew was ninety-five percent imagination. The other five percent came from the photos of her youthful mother in a 1940s shirtwaist, hair curled in that wartime fashion the stars in old movies wore.

The scene she had created over the years was a kitchen, of course. Her mother, Hennie, must have been cooking, using that old-fashioned blue enamel cookware that looked like it was covered with white paint-spatters—what *did* they call that type of pot? And the general interior decorating scheme consisted of red gingham—curtains, her mother's apron, the plastic tablecloth, sometimes even the dish towels. Hennie was silent, not singing or telling a story or instructing her young daughter how to cook. Virginia had no recollection of her mother's voice, so silence made sense in this ragged-edged world.

In her constructed memory it was spring outside; she knew because the windows were open and a breeze puffed out the curtains, but no fans buzzed yet, and heaven knows that in the forties no one but the wealthy had anything like air conditioning in Abundance, South Carolina. The kitchen was spotless; the table was set for three: herself, her mother, and her father. Perhaps she had placed some of the silverware there herself. She would have been three or four at the time, old enough to set a table, and old enough to have a memory. She couldn't have been older than four, since that was

1

when Hennie left her and Daddy. Four-year-olds could understand the concept of setting a table, but not a missing mother.

Virginia--Virgie to her daddy, Virgie Mae to Aunt Zadie and Miss Topie, Gee-gee to her husband Mack--was indulging in this memory as she and Mack drove to the Abundance's bi-monthly city council meeting, the first one of the year. Tonight they, or at least she, would join others to deliberate on the newest idea for Abundance: a yearly town festival. Why the memory of her mother in that kitchen came to her now, as they passed dormant soybean fields, several strip malls, and the county's largest peach orchard, all clothed in darkness, she didn't know. Perhaps because she had been rummaging around in her mind for a theme for the festival and her thoughts kept going back to that old sense of comfort mixed with dread that the memory always gave her.

The town had been knocking around the possibility of a festival for about six months now. The idea had first come up at a council meeting right after Dublin Cotton Mill announced it was laying off 300 workers at its Abundance plant—reducing the payroll to 500. That scared everyone, especially Mack Foster and the five employees of Foster King Realty. Fewer workers at the plant meant less money for people to buy homes and property. Even though some would try to sell their homes to leave town for other work, the lack of new residents meant homes wouldn't sell and prices would shrink.

Foster King Realty. Humph. That name always got under Virginia's skin. The "King" was from Mack's cousin, Lee King, who had owned all that old farmland north of town that was really no good for anything but cheap subdivisions, not much better than trailer parks. But that's how the realty company got started, by selling that land to developers and then helping the developers sell the houses. Lee still owned half of the company even though he was about worthless when it came to selling real estate. It was Mack who built the business into the most profitable independent real estate firm in five Upstate counties. Lee King did little besides showing up at Chamber of Commerce luncheons, playing golf, and occasionally selling a house for a friend.

Oh, well. She and Mack weren't hurting. Certainly not. He was busy. And he kept saying that something big was coming down the road. Something really big for Abundance and all of Turling County, into Davis County and to the Georgia line. Maybe beyond, like for the whole Upstate. Clemson would even be involved. He'd even brought up the governor's name. Mack wasn't saying what it was, but he didn't overstate things. If Mack claimed it was big, it would be huge.

Tonight the council meeting would go long, because the main topic was picking a theme for the festival. That promised to be a catfight. The high school crowd was going to want something related to education or sports or the mascot or the arts. Coach Zachary would weigh in with something about how the football team had won the 2A state championship last year. That young drama teacher, Jenny Lucey, would want to push musical theatre, somehow. The principal, Ben Jenkins, her old nemesis, would want something too local like "Mustang Freedom" or something bland like ecology.

The cotton mill managers would want to start the Annual Cotton Festival. But there were already at least two dozen cotton festivals, cotton balls, or cotton parades in the South. Missy Franklin would claim a Tommy Franklin Festival would save the town. Tommy Franklin was Missy's daddy, the hometown hero—he'd won the Medal of Honor for service in the Pacific. But the town already had a Tommy Franklin week. Missy needed a life beyond fanning the flame of her daddy's war service, bless her heart.

And then there was that crowd who was buying up storefronts on Culver Street, the longhaired young people from Atlanta who had started a restaurant, bookstore, art gallery, and bakery. Some of the locals thought they were part of a religious cult, but they were just sweet kids who had all gone to college together at Emory. They wanted people to buy coffee from poor farmers in South America rather than from Maxwell House, and they refused to sell white bread. They'd probably want an art festival, but not art like in the galleries in the big cities. They would want about the art they called "native" or "primitive" or "outsider," the kind they sold.

The folks in this town just didn't understand that none of those would work as topics for a permanent festival that would bring in enough people to make a profit and maybe, just maybe, attract other businesses. Any town could run festivals on those themes, any town with a Mustang as the high school mascot, that is. No, those wouldn't do. She knew because she had investigated the whole science of town festivals. She had gone to the library in Greenville and found back copies of *Southern Living* and read through them all. She had been to Hendersonville, North Carolina, and to Fort Valley, Georgia, and to Burkeville, Alabama. Apples, peaches, okra. Agricultural products. Towns all over the Southeast hosted festivals based on some vegetable or fruit or flower. That was old hat. If Abundance, South Carolina, was going to have a festival that rescued it from the economic doldrums, it would have to be based around something unique, cultural, Southern, and edible, something that boldly said, "Abundance, South Carolina."

She knew exactly what would do the trick. Her theme was rooted in the history of the town she had lived in fifty-five years. And no one else was doing it—she'd checked. At least not so far in 1998.

It started to rain. Not heavily, but light raindrops hitting the windshield. It wasn't quite cold enough to turn to sleet, even in January. "Did you bring an umbrella, Mack?"

"There's one in the backseat."

She paused before responding. The location of the umbrella wasn't what she really wanted to know. "Are you going to stand behind me when I present my idea tonight?"

"You know I will, darlin'." Now he paused. "But that doesn't mean your idea will win. It may not be the best, or most popular. It may not be what these folks want."

"That doesn't sound like you're going to stand behind me."

"Now, Gee-gee, let's not get started with this. I do think your idea is great, hon. But that's no guarantee of anything."

"You don't even think the festival's a good idea."

"There you go again. It doesn't matter what I think. But no, I don't think it is. Or I don't think it's going to save the town, like some of y'all do. The town needs more than a weekend of tourists."

"And you're missing the point, Mack. A festival gives the town name recognition. It will draw attention to it. You're a business man, for goodness sake. Don't you know about advertising?"

"What I know about is people having jobs that they can get real paychecks and buy real houses."

"I don't like this conversation. Why are you even going to the meeting if you feel this way?"

"Because I'm not stupid. Because sometimes you get in front of a crowd to look like a leader."

"You sound like a politician."

"Not in this life." They drove for a while. She *didn't* like this conversation. It just brought up what they'd been fussing about for weeks, what was stretching into months—his secretiveness about the "next big thing," and her excitement about the idea of a festival.

"I believe in it."

"I know, Gee-gee. And that's good. The town needs you."

She only responded in her mind. "And he's thinking that I need the town. I need a project," she mused. "I need to find a way to displace this energy. I need a place to put my thoughts."

Because my thoughts have become constant wanderers. Yes, scattered thinking was a sign of the change, but that was already taken care of, three years ago, thank goodness. Scattered thinking was also a sign of stress, but the excess stress levels, like menopause, were behind her. Those months of dealing with Aunt Zadie's mild stroke and seeing to her, and then her aunt and Miss Topie both being moved into an assisted care home where they would get decent treatment and live out their days together. And the months leading up to her retirement from the Turling County School District, and getting Bethany off at Clemson and pushing and pulling Matthew through his high school math classes.

Now 1995 and 1996 seemed like one long hospital visit, tuition payment, and struggle with the health care profession and government. She thought she'd be glad to see the day when she could stop balancing teaching and Medicare paperwork and college visits for Matthew and Bethany's late-night calls from breaking up with that boy whose name Virginia couldn't even remember now. And on top of all that, breaking out in cold sweats five times a night. In October of 1996 she and Mack took that cruise through Canada's Maritime Provinces to celebrate thirty-two years of marriage and her first fall outside of a high school classroom in as many years. At least the Nova Scotia climate helped when her inner thermostat malfunctioned.

Two years later, it seemed as if life was a boring stretch of nothing compared to those eighteen months. Zadie and Topie had rooms next to each other at the Saint Ambrose Community. Topie was starting to show fairly clear signs of dementia, but Virginia had yet to see any mental change in Zadie. The stroke had impaired her walking for a while, but never her speech or memory, miraculously, nor her prolific bossiness. Topie was the only black resident in the Community, and Virginia had to smile when remembering how she had threatened to call in the "A" organizations—AARP, ACLU, NAACP—to get the reluctant director to take in an 83-year-old black woman with no children or siblings and a tiny Social Security check.

But Virginia was willing to go that far for Topie. First, because Zadie and Topie had been together longer than anyone could remember—over eighty years—and because Virginia considered Topie as much an aunt as anyone could fathom. Anyway, Zadie was for all reasonable purposes Virginia's momma, in every way but name and genes. When Zadie moved over into the role Hennie Cullins left, Topie scooted over into the aunt position. And they both fit pretty fine for a confused little girl.

Just as they did now for an energetic, retired, slightly bored, empty-nested, educated, strong-willed, and affluent fifty-five year-old mother of two. She was a woman whose husband, sitting beside her, seemed mightily preoccupied and whose two children were off discovering the world without their parents and with no intention of presenting her and Mack with grandchildren. She was the only woman in her mid-fifties she knew without grandbabies. "Well, I take that back," she thought. "I'm the only mid-fifties woman with an intact marriage and children and half a brain who doesn't have grandchildren."

They were pulling up to the Abundance City Hall-Conference Center, built in the '80s. That was back when the cotton mill was booming, the window factory had just moved to town, farm prices were high, and former leaders of the Turling County Democrats were screaming for more Reagan. The Center was starting to get that "not taken care of too well lately" look. Parts of the interior could use a coat of paint, and if it were spring the landscaping would be behind schedule, as it always was from April to September. Not that the rest of the country was doing so poorly that year. Mack's investments on the stock market were making it possible for Matthew to enjoy the College of Charleston even without a scholarship and without Virginia working. And all that Internet and dot com and tech boom jabber she heard on the news was making California richer than ever. Too bad someone around here didn't invent the next big electronic thing.

The Conference Center consisted of four smaller meeting rooms, a large auditorium that seated 500 and allowed them to listen by a modern p.a. system, and a wing of offices for the city government, police, and Chamber of Commerce. The city council was to meet in Room A. About fifty local folks were expected to show up to "politely dialogue" about the festival. Virginia snorted to herself when she read that on the invitation, sent out by the Chamber president, Carl Dillard. Carl did not hail from Abundance. He obviously didn't know that some of these folks were incapable of polite dialogue. The gloves could come off at Abundance City Council meetings over how often the public hedges should be trimmed, much less over the theme, time, and particulars of a festival that was supposed to change the town's fortunes.

Virginia really wasn't two-faced. She wasn't one to share things with female friends unless the opportunity presented itself and someone needed to be set straight and if it was the truth and it mattered. She thought that gossip was just plain tacky. She did have a right like anyone to her private opinions, but she knew when and where to let them out. So even if she did think Jenny Lucey needed to get off the dinner theatre kick, and if the high school principal's wife didn't have a clue about how to dress, and if Carl Dillard just hadn't been around long enough to know how to deal with the people in this town—she was not going to trot those opinions out right now. Anyway, she had an idea to sell tonight, and she'd better start working the room.

"Missy!" She called as she was approached by a short, plump, graying woman with an unlined, circular face and pale blue eyes. *If she would just do something with her hair,* Virginia thought. *She's not so heavy that she couldn't get a man interested. She's got the most pleasant face, when she doesn't have tears on it.* "Missy, so good to see you!" She hugged the shorter woman's neck. "How are you? And how's your daddy?"

Missy Franklin was one of those women whose tears lay just beneath the first layer of her skin, and they appeared on cue. Mack, not knowing how to deal with a crying female other than his wife, nor wanting to, had shaken Missy's hand and smiled and moved on. He found seats for himself and Virginia, leaving his wife to calm, comfort, encourage, or whatever it was Missy needed. But even if this was not a good time, Missy, ten years younger than Virginia, deserved at least a few words and half a minute of sympathy.

"Oh, Virgie, he's OK." Missy sniffed a bit. "His blood sugar is just so high. We're having such a time getting it down. He had to go to the hospital last weekend."

"I am so sorry to hear that, Missy. Is he doing better now?"

"Yes, ma'am, it's gotten down to somewhere closer to normal. But you know, I think he sneaks sweets. I cook him meals just like the *Diabetics' Handbook* says, and somehow it still goes up, way up."

"Oh, my goodness. How do you think he's getting sweets?"

"I just don't know, but he might be paying a neighborhood kid to go get him Coca-Colas when I'm at work. Daddy always says that is what he loves more than anything. When he was a prisoner of war in Burma, that's what he says he craved more than his momma's cooking or even liquor, not that Daddy's ever been a drinker, you understand."

"Of course, not, honey. He's the finest man and daddy anybody can imagine. You might just have to talk to the neighbor kids and tell them that if they bring him candy or Cokes it might mean bad things for your daddy, and they wouldn't want that to happen. Put the fear in them. It never hurts a kid to be a little scared, I don't care what they say."

"Yes, Virgie, I think I will do that. . . ." Missy was clearly thankful that someone had spoken to her for a few moments. "Well, this meeting is gonna start soon . . ."

"And I see Mack over there giving me one of those looks of his." She touched Missy's arm, allowing herself to think that she may have just won a vote for her festival theme. "I'll see you later." And she moved on from a satisfied Missy Franklin, who *would* look so much better if she tried contact lenses.

Mack had saved her a seat on the second row. He had marked it with the stack of the manila folders she had prepared and he had carried in for her. Each folder was stuffed with a stapled, eight-page handout documenting her research and supporting her claim on the festival with statistics, historical facts, and photos. A carefully prepared folder would end up in the hand of every attendee tonight. Virginia had paid the copy shop good money for these copies; they were even full color. But Mack could write it off as a business expense. Normally Mack would have been working the room, but tonight he was keeping his own counsel, still not convinced that tourism was the answer for the town's doldrums.

She slid into her seat just as the gavel landed, aided by Bob Smallwood, city council chair. Bob looked like a chair of a city council. Bob also played Santa Claus at Christmas, growing out his white beard every October during deer season to prepare for his role

and shaving it every New Year's Day. His scalp, cheeks, and neck were usually pink, but they could turn red quickly, a sure sign to everyone that he was either displeased with how the meeting was going or that he was about to erupt in laughter.

"This monthly meeting of the Abundance City Council is called to order. Reverend Hackett, would you lead us in prayer?" It was the turn of the minister from the local Church of God to pronounce the invocation, and everyone stood without being asked and bowed their heads as he asked God to bless the meeting and the future of the community.

He emphasized "in the name of Christ Jesus" at the end, in case anybody might think he was trying to be too ecumenical. Nobody in that room would raise a fuss. Even though a handful never entered a church but for weddings and funerals, all of them would admit to an affiliation. The room included a good cross section of Baptists, Methodists, Pentecostals, Episcopalians, and two or three Catholics.

After the prayer Carl Dillard led the meeting in the pledge of allegiance. The secretary of the council, Gail Mims, who was also by day the administrative assistance for the Chamber of Commerce, read the minutes of the last meeting. They were approved, as always, since no one really could stay alert through the reading because of Gail's soft, sugary voice. She could have said in that voice that she and Carl were having an affair and no one would have batted an eye. Everybody thought they were, anyway.

Some other preliminaries and obligatories were waded through until fifteen minutes after the hour, when Bob Smallwood said the old business was finished and now the meeting would move on to the new business. The agenda included just one item of new business: the discussion of themes for the festival and based on the theme, dates; and based on that, the choice for the leadership. Virginia had asked to go last. Last had its advantages: if all the other ideas were as pathetic as she expected them to be, she could surprise the audience with something much better. The disadvantage was that people would be tired after listening to several presentations; on the other hand, that might make them more likely to make a decision without prolonging the debate. She would know what she was up against before speaking and could respond. Yes, going last would work out all right.

Jenny Lucey had paired with the young crowd from Culver Street to propose an arts festival called "Arts on the Square." Music, theatre, dance, painting, sculpture, the works, spreading out from the town square. Abundance did have a really nice square, more than just another one of those old Southern standbys. Virginia admitted to herself that Jenny and her associates did a nice job on their presentation.

Then the high school principal and his staff presented an idea, but not at all what Virginia had expected. They argued for a Southern Heritage Festival, but it ended up more of what Virginia would have called a Bubba Fair. NASCAR, football, and bass fishing seemed to be the highlights. Granted, there was an annual NASCAR race not far from Abundance, and Lake Wonder was a center for bass fishing, and of course football ruled, from PeeWee League to Clemson. Still, the whole idea lacked uniqueness.

Youth organizations—the Boy Scouts, Girl Scouts, Little League, and some church groups—worked together to present "Young at Heart," a festival for children. Virginia had to admit the idea had appeal, but limited. The 4-H Club put in a brave but undeveloped effort to present a "Products of Turling County" Festival which could morph into an emphasis either on peaches, cotton, soybeans, or okra. Virginia concluded the presentation must have been some sort of project for a badge or competition. The child responsible must have just read *To Kill a Mockingbird* and plagiarized some of the last chapters.

Finally, it was Virginia's turn. She was not affiliated with any organization and was flying totally solo tonight. And her nerves felt as if she were sitting in a cockpit.

"Let me start by thanking all the participants before me. A lot of work went into those presentations." She could hear her teacher-speak coming out and modulated into a voice that sounded like an adult talking to other adults. "Before I begin I have a handout that I'd like to pass out to everyone. Missy, could you help me, and Mack?" Missy Franklin approached her to pass the packets to her side of the room, and Mack, with a slight grimace, got up and cooperated.

"Every one of us here tonight is concerned about the town and how we can draw attention to what it has to offer. Competition is a fact of life in business, and the world economy has made it clear to us that we can't take the security of the past for granted. We are rightly worried when we see layoffs at a local mill. We want to keep that from happening and find ways to strengthen the opportunities for our children so they won't think their only option is to move off to Charlotte or Atlanta. Yet, at the same time, we look to the past for comfort and direction and inspiration. Our roots are in the past and we want to celebrate that.

"Now, in thinking about the past, I got to wondering about the name of our town. Abundance. Do you know why it's called that? Some of you older folks know. Up until 1963, this was the headquarters of Abundance Mills Flour Company. It had been since 1901. For sixty-two years flour was milled here and Abundance Mills Flour Company was the second biggest employer. In 1910 the name of the town was changed from Rosy Dew, which is beautiful but not very modern, to Abundance Mills, and sometime later the Mills was dropped.

"In 1963 the Abundance Mills Flour Company was bought out by Double-Dutch Baking Products Company, which has since been bought out by some huge food conglomerate. That corporation still makes Double-Dutch Flour in Arkansas, but it sells in limited markets. Abundance Mills Flour was advertised with the slogan 'Abundant baking, Abundant flavor, Abundance Flour.' I have included a sample of an old advertisement for Abundance Flour on page two of your handout.

"I propose we have a festival centered around that wonderful staple of Southern cooking, the biscuit. It fits perfectly with the history of the town, so we can do re-enactments and turn-of-the-century dress-up. It lends itself to the Southern cultural angle. We could have a cooking competition, and best of all, no other town in

America right now has a biscuit festival, which you can't say for most agricultural products. I have taken the liberty of getting in touch with the Double-Dutch Flour Company and they would be very interested in using the festival for promotion and advertising. You can see a copy of the letter on page four."

She paused. She knew it was late. A couple of folks glanced at their watches and didn't try to hide it. But many more were nodding their heads or reading the letter from the Double-Dutch Company. "In the packet you will also see some ideas for a schedule of activities, some ways to use various parts of the town square, and some quotes from vendors who would want to come and sell crafts and food. It's fairly standard material if you are planning a festival of this size, but you need to know about it before you make a decision. Thank you for your time."

And she sat down. The audience could not deny which of the presenters had done the most homework. The arts crowd, the high school staff, the 4-Hers, and the young people had ideas, but no facts, no data, no maps, no letters from sponsors, no tie-in to the history of the town.

Virginia knew, though, that she had something else none of the rest of them had. History in Abundance--long history. Cleeland history, on her mother's side, going back to before the Civil War. That history was a point of pride for her, but she knew some of her fellow citizens didn't necessarily see her heritage that way. Most other families in town didn't have a branch of the library named after them, or a street. So she wasn't entirely surprised when Coach Zachary stood up.

"I just want to interject something here." Coach Zachary was the kind of man who used the world's worst grammar in the same sentence with three-dollar words. He rose from his seat two rows back of Virginia and Mack as he spoke, his hand raised. Then he hitched up his trousers and belt before going on. "We got to keep in mind the whole town here, and the future. Let's not make a decision based on just what happened in the past. I love history and biscuits as much as the next person, but what's going to attract the most people?"

Virgina noticed he said nothing about art, agricultural, or bass fishing. The comment was directed at her. She bit her lower lip; she could sense Mack looking at her and then felt his hand on her wrist. Was he comforting her, or getting ready to restrain her from jumping up to say something quick and hurting to defend her family's honor and contribution to the town. But he didn't need to. Virginia predicted this kind of comment; she was not even surprised it came from Zachary, with whom she had graduated from Turling County High so long ago.

"All right," Bob Smallwood began, as if ignoring Zachary's warning. "We've heard five ideas tonight. Do we need to give ourselves more time to think about this, or are we ready for a vote?"

"I move we vote tonight," Les Tolliver offered. He managed the local branch of Carolina Natural Gas and served on the council. He stood to his whole five-feet-five. "And that we get to work on whichever idea we pick if we plan on having this festival in the next year."

"I second that motion," Donna Hatfield, raised her hand. Donna, also on the council, ran her own beauty shop. More than once a letter to the editor of the *Turling County Messenger* had called into question a beautician's political skills, but Donna achieved re-election whenever she wanted it.

"Does anyone else have anything to say?" Bob asked. "That is, is there any discussion of the motion on the floor?"

No one spoke. "Let me ask this," Bob proceeded. "This decision is going to be made by the council, but we want to know the wishes of the people assembled here. Would anyone object to us taking a ballot to see what the room thinks? It wouldn't be binding on us, though."

The other eight city council members looked back and forth at each other, and all but Bob shrugged in a "why not" sort of way.

The 3 X 5 cards were distributed and the fifty-seven people present wrote their choice on a card. The cards were collected and counted by Gail Mims, who wrote the vote down and handed it to Bob, who passed it on to the others.

"Well, what does it say?" a voice in the audience demanded.

"Out of fifty-seven people who voted in this room, thirty-nine prefer the biscuit festival; ten the arts; and so on." Bob's voice indicated that the audience's preference was not his own. "What do the members of the council say? All in favor of the biscuit festival idea, raise your hands."

Seven of the nine raised hands. "The biscuit festival it is, then," Bob announced. "Now, dates."

Jacks Pierce, a retired chemistry teacher, raised his hand, "It's getting late, Bob. Can we appoint a committee to investigate dates for this thing and let them make recommendations next month? We could be here all night wrangling over weekends."

"Is that a motion?" Bob asked.

"Yes. I move that we table the discussion of dates until next meeting." The parliamentary procedures took their course and volunteers were solicited. By the end of the night, a committee was formed, with five members under the leadership of the biscuit festival proposer, Virginia Mae Cullins Foster.

Chapter 2

With all the preparation she had done for the city council
meeting, the one aspect Virginia had taken for neglected was the
actual date of the now-approved South Carolina Annual Biscuit
Festival. She could make a case for any time in the months of April,
May, September, or October, but nothing in between--too hot and
too much competition from the peach, okra, squash, Confederate,
and whatever festivals in a 100-mile radius. If the town—and more
specifically, her committee--was going to schedule, organize, and pull
off a festival of any credibility in less than four months—they had
better get kicking. Virginia called their first meeting for ten o'clock
the Thursday after the council meeting.

Virginia's five fellow committee members volunteered for
this duty. She had to take what she could get, but they were a group
she could work with. They were energetic, and they were committed.
She just wasn't sure they had the skills and the wherewithal she
needed. More leaders would have to be recruited, and soon. But for
today, she had to make the five people sitting around the table at one
of the conference center's workrooms feel that they were capable of
anything a festival could throw at them.

She looked around at the eager faces. Three men, two
women. Audrey Pike. Daryl Washburn. Melody Hamblin. Frank
Templeton. Ted Sneed. Like her, they were all retired, and therefore
had plenty of time. But each was still young enough and healthy
enough to stay up late and come in early if needed. All but one,
Melody, were married, although Audrey's husband would likely not
be much help, since he traveled most of the time for his job with
Duke Power. Audrey used to be a hospital administrator, and she
had the best organizational skills; the problem was, she could be
prickly.

Daryl Washburn had been a loan officer at Upstate National
Bank for so long that he could remember what the bank was called

three buyouts ago. Frank Templeton had only lived in Abundance for ten years. He had run a department at the community college in Greenville, something like computer repair or electronics, so he could take care of the technical end of things. Ted Sneed used to be n radio and still filled in on local stations occasionally. He was the town comedian. A little too much of one for Virginia's taste, but he was extremely well liked by almost everyone and would be great for running publicity. And Melody. Well, Melody was another issue.

Melody and Virginia had a history.

Melody and Virginia taught together at Westmoreland High for fifteen years. Virginia had spent all her professional life—over thirty years—there, but Melody had moved to Turling County in, oh, something like 1979, bringing in credits from another system so she was able to retire a couple of years before Virginia. Melody had been the cheerleading coach, and if anyone ever fit the description of a cheerleading coach, it was Melody Hamblin. Melody could have been a model for high-end tennis outfits. Her "girls," the cheerleaders, worshiped Melody. They weren't alone. A few of the male teachers did, too, and there was talk.

But Melody's personal appeal was not the source of the tension between Virginia and Melody. Virginia taught business courses: typing, accounting, basic computer skills, shorthand (back in the old days), and she led the school chapter of Business Achievers of America. In a school like Westmoreland High, there was never enough money for everything. Committed teachers competed for the best, most efficient, most lucrative fundraisers so their students could go to state competitions, or regional, or beyond.

So, cheerleaders or future businesspersons? Bake sales or carwashes, selling candles or greeting cards? Money for uniforms or money to attend a seminar on job interviewing? Who got the best rooms for meetings? And who, Virginia always wanted to know, would be helped ten years from now by having cheered in high school, and who would be able to get a better job because they learned marketable skills? Where does a young person put cheering on a resume, anyway?

More than once the two had to meet with the principal to "discuss" some timing, resource, event, student, or parent conflict. More than once Virginia thought she lost. More than once she had to wonder if Melody was sending too friendly signals to Principal Jenkins even as the three of them were trying to hash out a compromise. It was probably all her imagination, but . . . back then Melody *was* known to go through rough patches with her now ex-husband Larry, the popular pediatric dentist.

Virginia's reputation was secured when one of her BAA students won the national competition in public speaking in 1985 and then two went to nationals in 1987. Nothing like that had ever happened in the Turling County School District—national recognition. The closest was state championships in sports, occasionally, but they were an AA school, and the competition was usually not seen as very tough. This was Virginia's *coup de grace*, and Melody just never recovered.

The tension between Melody and Virginia never stretched so far that it snapped back on them, like a taut rubber band. But even now, it sat like a seventh member of the committee that only the two of them could see. Virginia just had to wonder if Melody would try to wrestle the festival out of her hands, somehow, just to make sure the score was even.

"Let's get started," Virginia began. "We all know each other, right?" Frank, Melody, Audrey, Ted, and Daryl nodded, acknowledging those they hadn't actually greeted yet. "I want to start with this task list of everything that must be done and when. I've already put this together." She handed each member a stapled stack of papers. "I compiled it after writing to five or six festivals in the Southeast and asking them if they had such a task list. They were real nice about helping me out, I must say. I took what they sent and tried to include everything and only delete what wouldn't apply due to the theme of the festival, and things that were repeated."

She gave them time to look over the sheets. "Now, as far as the agenda is concerned, the first thing we need to decide is when, so we can report that back to the council as soon as possible. Then we'll get into the other two main matters." She paused. "So, what do you think about dates?"

"I think the question is, Virginia, when do *you* think we should hold the festival?" Daryl ventured in after a fifteen-second silence.

"No, no, my opinion is not the final one. We need to get all the ideas on the table." Surely these smart professional people were not going to be sheep following her around, she thought. "I don't have any strong thoughts on it, except that July through August is too hot and will conflict with some other festivals in the state."

Audrey spoke. "Absolutely. We don't need people passing out from heat stroke the first time. And I have to say, I've thought about this, and whatever we decide should be permanent. If we go changing the date every year, we won't sustain any interest."

Virginia saw heads nod all around. "Good point, Audrey. So . . . where do we go from here?"

If Virginia had thought her committee members' silence meant an unwillingness to argue, she soon learned how mistaken she was. After her opening comment, a lively discussion began, where every date in April, May, September, and October was put under a microscope of scrutiny. Finally, the third weekend in May won the day. That weekend fell after Mother's Day but before high school graduations and Memorial Day. The weather would be hot but not unbearable yet. Virginia could live with that. She had originally favored an April date, but that would collide with Easter, at least sometimes, and the Masters' Golf Tournament—something Mack would never forgive her for.

They settled on the second weekend of September as a backup date, knowing that would never satisfy the city council because it conflicted with football and with some big Winston Cup race. Although Virginia could not abide car racing and remained intentionally ignorant of all things NASCAR, she knew football and stock car racing would always beat out a festival for the locals.

"All right, great," Virginia concluded. "We'll submit that May date to the council at the next meeting, and pray that they don't get any wild hares about changing it." She ran her fingers through her hair, thinking that running these meetings was going to be harder work than she had originally thought. "Now, let's look at these materials again. What do you think I missed, is the first question, and what do each one of you want to, well, run?"

The five members looked at each other. Melody, of course, spoke up first. "I don't know if you've missed anything. We might not know that for a while. But I'd like to be the one who contacts food vendors. I have some definite ideas on that. I mean, we want to have diverse cuisine."

Virginia wondered where Melody picked up that term. "That's a good point, Melody, and I think you'd be great at that. Food is the center of a festival. People come to these things to eat, or at least they expect good food. But that takes us to the next question—if this is a biscuit festival, because of the mill, where does that come in? How does the Double-Dutch Flour Company fit in?"

"I've been thinking about that, myself," Audrey piped up. "I am assuming they would want a bakeoff or contest or something, right?"

"That's a great idea," Ted added, always the optimist. "Virginia's right. We can't have a Southern festival without food, and plenty of it. Bake-offs draw crowds. And we need to do something more than corndogs and fried turkey legs. Since it's a biscuit festival, we need food based around biscuits."

"That's a thought, although I am not sure what you could do with biscuits or biscuit dough as far as variety," Virginia said.

"Oh, lots of things. Cobblers. Dumplings. Comfort food. I am surprised you haven't thought about that," Audrey answered.

Virginia started to speak, but Melody jumped in. "Oh, I can see you don't know something about our Virginia, Audrey."

"Excuse me?"

"Virginia doesn't cook."

"Melody, what a thing to say about someone," Audrey had a scolding look in her eyes, as if Melody had just said Virginia didn't wear appropriate foundation garments. "Of course she cooks."

"But it's true, isn't it, Virginia? I heard you say many a time in the faculty lounge that you stay as far away from the kitchen as you can, that you worked if for no other reason than to have someone else do your cooking for you."

Virginia could feel the heat rising up her neck. Melody was getting even, already. Virginia's attitude about kitchen duties didn't belong in this conversation, but Virginia couldn't let Melody think she'd scored a point. "And it's a philosophy that's worked just fine for me so far, too."

Frank spoke up firmly to stop Melody from taking it any further. "Why not let that flour company decide? That would take the pressure off of us to work on other matters, and shoot, it's their company, they're getting a lot of free advertising, why can't they figure it out?"

"I'll be the liaison with them, though, and do the work on this end for whatever they want. How would that be?" Audrey volunteered.

"Great. Thanks, Audrey." At this point, the men distinguished themselves by having avoided a job. "I'm going to stick my neck out and say I'll be the tech guy." Frank would work hard, but not leave his comfort zone, Virginia knew. "That's great, Frank." She paused.

"If we're volunteering," Ted jumped in, "I want to do publicity with the local media. The papers, radio stations, and TV."

Virginia had a vision of Ted re-living his career as a broadcasting personality. He liked the limelight, but that would serve the festival well. Ted used to have his own morning drive-time show in the Upstate, so he'd have no trouble with connections.

"That'll be wonderful, Ted. You *are* the one to do that. And let's see how much free advertising you can get with newspapers." She paused. "Looking at this list, what about you, Daryl?"

Daryl, Virginia was soon to find out, liked to sit back and only interject comments when the rest of the group had begun to make decisions. "You know, Virginia, I'm concerned about the funding for this festival. We are assuming that it will make money. But don't we have to, like the old saying says, spend money to make it?" Everybody knew that old saw. Virginia wondered if a lecture on finance was coming.

"The town agreed to a budget of $50,000 dollars seed money, Daryl, at the first meeting back in September when the festival idea first got proposed and accepted. It's all in the packet here. . . . So, whatever expenses up front we have, we have some money to work with. But you are the one to understand that part of it best. Why don't you serve as the accountant and bookkeeper for the festival?"

"I guess I could do that," Daryl said. He looked a little bit as if he'd been sent to the corner by the school marm. "But here's another thing—are just the six of us doing all the work?"

"No, and that's just it. We are the committee who makes things happen—but we need lots and lots more volunteers. We need music acts. We need a car show—or something like that. We need somebody to run the crafters, and we don't want a bunch of grandmas hawking aprons and decorated jelly jars. We need gatekeepers, car parkers, security workers, cleanup crew, water distributors, a person to oversee the street performers—well, it's all here."

"Then we need to engage the people who have expertise." Melody had that voice—that take-charge voice she used even when she didn't know what she was talking about. But right now, Virginia had to admit, the festival could easily overwhelm everyone and be a flop. As it stood, Melody was right. "Look: crafters and artists—who's going to know more about that than those artsy kids on Culver Street, the ones from Atlanta. They've got connections all over, and could invite decent craftsmen and artists. And we can ask the security company—what's its name, the one that provides rent-a-cops to the malls and all—maybe we could get volunteer help from them."

"I think Melody's right," Daryl said, seeming a little too ready to take sides since he'd been corralled into a responsible job a few minutes before. "We need to decide who would be the smartest person to head up each of these areas. For example, who could get musical acts? Who could get together a car show?"

At this point it seemed wisest to follow Daryl's line of thought, so the six spent the next half hour with plans for delegation. When every possible activity or venue or exhibit or show had a possible delegated volunteer and a back-up, Virginia sought to bring the meeting to a close. She was getting a headache. "Looks like we've made progress. And it looks like we've got plenty to do."

The other five leafed through the papers, consulted their lists, and looked at each other for five seconds. "Virginia," Frank finally said, "do you really think this is going to work? In less than four months?"

"It's a mighty tall order," Ted added, ending the sentence with his voice trailing off.

"Yes. It's huge. I know we're asking a lot, I'm asking a lot of you all. I'm going to commit every waking second, and most of the sleeping ones, to this festival." And to herself she added, "I will pull this whole town kicking and screaming into a successful festival no matter what. This town needs a boost. This town needs to know we can do it." She shined her most charming smile. "Think how great it will be for Abundance to be called the home of the Annual South Carolina Biscuit Festival."

That first planning committee meeting took a lot out of Virginia, but at the same time she felt invigorated. If others wanted to douse a little cold water on her spirits, it didn't work. Despite the possibility that Melody might be in it to take some glory, Virginia could tell Melody was the most committed to the festival; the men seemed to take an amused interest in the project compared to Melody's passion for "diverse cuisine" or whatever it was she was going to do with the food vendors. "Make a foe a friend, I guess," Virginia reminded herself.

She was glad she scheduled lunch that day with her two best friends, Tally Bryson and Leah McKamey. They could debrief her, she could feel a little superior to Melody, who really had kept her figure awfully well over the years, and they could have a little mid-day refreshment to help her headache. And Tally and Leah would stay totally out of her plans for the festival. They loved Virginia as much as any old-girl-friends-from-elementary-school could, but their version of retirement—Tally from an accounting job, Leah from a career as administrative assistant for a large insurance agency—had nothing to do with community involvement.

Abundance didn't actually have a country club set, but it did boast a respectable golf course and accompanying restaurant. Tally played golf every other day when the weather permitted, and it was sunny today, even in January and 45 degrees outside. She recuperated on the off days. Leah was a grandma. For some reason Leah's two daughters had multiplied exponentially into eight grandchildren—five and three, respectively. For Leah, retirement meant spending as much time with grandchildren as possible, since she had worked during her own children's upbringing. Maybe she was trying to make up for something. She claimed to love every minute of babysitting but set her foot down about sleepovers.

Despite the fact that Virginia, Tally, and Leah had very little in common on the surface—Leah never touched a golf club, and Tally and Virginia found themselves a long way from being grandmas—they were fast friends. Virginia never liked the phrase "best friends," because it made friendship into a contest. But the two women she most wanted to be around, other than Zadie and Topie and Bethany, were Tally and Leah.

And today they would meet at the 19th Hole Restaurant. Tally had played nine holes this morning and said she might consider finishing the back nine later that day, if she didn't imbibe too much Zinfandel at lunch. Leah had also put boundaries around today, to keep her grandchildren out. For two, maybe three hours, the three could eat too much, drink a little too much, laugh far too much in a public place, and reminisce just enough to keep biscuit festivals and golf and grandchildren and boredom away for a while.

The great thing about lunch with Tally and Leah is that they could go back over the same territory and no one cared. It wasn't the white wine; it was the sweetness of the memories. Tally and Leah's daddies were the two lawyers in town, and money was never a problem. They reached out to the little girl being raised by her aunt, the little girl whose grandfather was the town legend, Governor Rufus Cleeland. He had to be a legend—his parents named him "Governor" and he never spent a day in elected office, but everyone deferred to him because of his land, his demeanor, his traditional manners, and his fine suits. He also was held in esteem for his service in Cuba in the Spanish American War, a war no one really knew about but that sounded important. The legend was worth a lot of respect and awe and deference but not worth much in terms of cold cash, at least not after the '30s and the War. Tally and Leah's friendship rescued Virginia from the Governor's shadow and the whispers that could surround a little girl whose mother disappeared when she was four and was never heard from again.

When it came down to it, Tally and Leah thought the festival was a crazy idea. If Virgie wanted to make Abundance the biscuit capital of South Carolina, or the U.S., or the world, that had nothing whatsoever to do with either of them. So, other than tacky comments about Melody the cheerleading coach and Ted the radio guy, they preferred not to have their lunch be disturbed with talk of biscuits and bakeoffs, of car shows and tap-dancing five-year-olds.

"You are welcome to play golf with me any morning," Tally offered. "The course is going to look pretty nice in about three months. The almanac says spring will come early."

"Oh, Tally, you know I'd only embarrass myself on the golf course. People can only improve at golf if they make it a life commitment, and I'm just not there, yet, darlin'."

"Virgie is going to save this town from itself, Tally," Leah remarked. "I think she wants us to be the silicone valley of the Piedmont."

Virginia and Tally looked at each other and tried to stifle a laugh. They were unsuccessful, and Virginia thought something would come out of her nose when the laugh erupted. Leah, as smart as she was, confused words at the craziest times. "I think you mean silicon, Leah. The festival is not about boob jobs."

Chapter 3

At the second January meeting of the town council, the third weekend of May was submitted as the date of the festival. Although the meeting almost got out of hand with contributions that often had nothing to do with the festival or the date, the council voted unanimously for what the committee suggested. It felt less like a vote of confidence than a vote of apathy, as if the committee would now carry the sole responsibility for the success or failure of the festival and that the council members would wash their hands of it, unless the whole event flopped. Virginia steeled herself and determined that failure, flop, and disaster were not in her vocabulary, or at least not for the next four months.

Virginia also knew one thing couldn't change because of the festival. No matter how busy or distracted she became, her twice-weekly visit to Aunt Zadie and Miss Topie had to anchor her week. Virgie Mae, as Zadie still called her after all these years, wanted the caretakers at St. Ambrose Community to know her very well, and to know that she would be superintending her aunt's and her aunt's companion's care permanently and frequently.

Visits to the elderly could be tedious. Not with Zadie and Topie. Even if Topie, a woman who had always been slight and wiry and now seemed almost elfin, sat silent for long moments, looking into space to distinguish a memory from yesterday from one in 1945, the two women always had plenty to say.

Zadie occupied room 207 and Topie room 209 at St. Ambrose Community. That meant climbing a flight or taking the elevator, and Virginia usually walked up the carpeted, wide, winding stairs. Every effort had been made to create an atmosphere of comfortable classiness, perhaps more for visitors than for the residents. Yes, this was a perfect place for the ladies she privately called her two mommas.

Because from that day in Spring of 1947 when Hennie, Zadie's much younger half-sister, disappeared and never returned, Zadie stepped in, bringing the weeping, wide-eyed, and confused four-year-old into her home. That sprawling Victorian in the middle of town was still occupied on the top floor by Governor, a man whom the town still spoke about but who had retreated to daily solitude because of his lost splendor and faded good looks. That quasi-mansion, with five bedrooms and no indoor bathrooms until 1929, would now house a middle-aged widow, a very old Southern gentleman, and a preschooler recently removed from her parents' modest house outside of town. And every day they would be cared for by Topie's mother, Lula, the housekeeper since Zadie's childhood, and every evening Topie would join her mother after a hard day at the cotton mill and walk Lula home.

Virginia's daddy, Buddy Cullins, came to see her once a week, on Saturday mornings. He drove a truck for a textile mill, taking rolls of cotton off to the northern cities he said were dirty and noisy and filled with—and he had the intelligence to say this out of hearing of the women who cared for his only child—"coloreds." He lived in the house he and Hennie had occupied, alone, a house on the outskirts of Abundance in a converted mill village, one that developed a haphazard, tired, and neglected look over the years.

As she grew older Virginia suspected, and then finally knew, that he had a woman in at least one other city, probably Cleveland or Detroit or Columbus, whom he stayed with on his trips and from whom he received what a wife would give. Considering his bitterness toward Hennie, usually unspoken but always clear, he wouldn't tie himself down to a woman who might run off leaving him with another child to support and raise alone. When Virginia learned to drive, she would visit him; she persuaded him to give her a key and she even cleaned his house for him, learning to keep down vermin and roaches and to scrub toilets and tile when needed.

But if Buddy Cullins expected a hot meal on the table when he arrived home from points north, it was not to be. No dinner or supper of cube steak and mashed potatoes and pintos and cornbread and slaw, his favorites, was ever going to appear on his Formica kitchen table. No feast prepared by his loyal daughter who looked so much like the vanished Hennie but had none of Hennie's moods and tantrums and none of Hennie's interest and talents with food.

Hennie had been a looker, no doubt about it, and no woman he had met before or since could fix a meal like Hennie. For all of Virgie Mae's qualities—she was top of her class in school, she carried herself like a debutante, she was planning on getting a degree from Clemson, she cleaned up his house faithfully, she had written him letters on the road when she was a child, and she was devoted to Zadie and those colored woman who helped her—cooking was not one of them.

Melody thought she was being funny and making a dig at Virginia when she brought up Virginia's well known aversion to the kitchen this morning. Well, good for her. She had made her little point for the day. "No, I don't cook," Virginia admitted. And she wasn't going to go to a psychiatrist to find out why, any more than she was going to hire a private detective to find Hennie—although she'd thought about it enough over the years, and even talked to one back when the children were little. There were just some things you were allowed to be and do or not do without excuse. The way some women acted, not cooking was like sleeping with another man or shoplifting, or at least like going to the Winn-Dixie in your nightgown and rollers. And Melody—no one could prove *her* virtuosity in the kitchen. The difference was, Virginia just admitted to it.

It wasn't like she sprung it on Mack after they got married. Mack knew she couldn't cook and wasn't going to waste her time doing something that they could hire someone to do when Virginia's talents and energy should be spent elsewhere. Why this was such a crime, she didn't know. Virginia didn't cut her husband's and children's hair, either, and nobody made a big deal about it. The children were perfectly healthy, Mack's and her cholesterol levels were good, and no one who came in the house starved.

Minnie Rollins, a third cousin of Topie's, was her current cook and had been for ten years. Minnie also kept the Foster house clean after she came home from her job at the John C. Calhoun Elementary School cafeteria. Minnie was paid well, knew it, and planned on staying with the Fosters until she could retire from the school system in five more years.

Oh, Virginia, she often reminded herself, *you are too old to be letting that Melody or anybody get under your skin about something like that. You've got enough on your plate, to worry about whether you chopped it or fried it yourself.* But it did get under her skin, sometimes. More than it should, because she knew where the aversion to cooking came from, even if she would never express it.

Hennrietta Cleeland Cullins, a very pretty and delicate and sad woman, had left her own child. Yes, she may have left her husband and the child just happened to be part of the package, but she had left. Vanished. Disappeared without a note or a letter, even after all these years. It wasn't like she turned a baby over for adoption, a baby she'd birthed and never looked at, because she was poor or unmarried. Daddy made a decent living once he came back from three years' service in the War. Their house was comfortable by the standards back then. And even if that wasn't enough, she was due to come into some money some day from what was left of Governor's estate, even though so much of it was lost in the Depression and his own bad money sense. What Mack could have done with that land and assets! Mack had ten times the business sense Grandpa Cleeland ever thought about having.

No, Hennie just up and left one day. Many times Virginia

33

had pried Zadie with questions, but Zadie, not one to be weepy, reserved her tears for whatever it was that made her melancholy half-sister leave town and never look back.

"Surely you had the police look for her," Virginia asked, time and time again. "She could have been murdered, or kidnapped." Criminal activity should have been the first guess and no expense spared in trying to find the truth. I mean," Virginia would say, "the family was well known, and the people in town thought we had lots of money, even if we really didn't have all that much." People thinking you had money had more power than actually having it, especially in a place like Abundance.

"Of course," Zadie said, with Topie nodding her head and then shaking it at the thought of what might have driven Hennie away. "The sheriff looked and looked. The best I can tell," Zadie would say, in a way that signaled finality and her desire not to talk about it anymore, "that when Buddy came home from Germany in 1945 and they set up family living again after three years of her being on her own, she just didn't want that kind of life. She did what women in my generation would never have thought of. She did what her own momma probably wanted to do but decided to take it out on me and Topie and Hennie herself. That woman, my stepmomma, you never knew what to expect out of her—other than not much."

"She was just plain crazy, that Hennie," Topie would say, matter-of-factly, feeling no need years and decades later to put a nice face on the erratic behavior of—of... what? An old employer? More than an employer? Because as long as she could remember, Topie was part of their lives, even lived with them after Lula died, and it was not a matter of pay or employment or even servanthood, like some of the more affluent people in town. Topie was Zadie's best friend, and in this case, Virginia didn't see the phrase as a matter of competition. The old saying about friends, "two souls in the same body" applied more to Topie and Zadie than any two humans

Virginia had ever known. Their friendship was deep and enduring despite the fact that one was of African descent and the other of Scots-Irish, despite the fact they lived in a time and place where such friendship was frowned upon if not forbidden.

It did not surprise Virginia that her mind was going over and over these old conversations. How many times had she and Topie and Zadie had that discussion, in some form or another, with no satisfaction and yet no hope or encouragement about the mystery being solved. When she was a teenager—before college—Zadie came close to reprimanding Virginia for bringing it up. After she married Mack, and then Bethany, and then Matthew came, Zadie talked a little more about the person Hennie was but revealed nothing that would explain how or why she left. As far as Zadie was concerned, there was nothing to reveal. Good Christian people didn't do what Hennie did, and it didn't do to talk about it much either. Virginia always tread carefully now. Zadie and she shared a certain disregard for the foolish opinions of other townspeople, but some things were just plain shameful.

Virginia knew why these memories were rolling over in her head today as she drove from the golf course after a heavy lunch and two glasses of wine. She was thankful for the disturbing memories, since she could stand a nap right now and couldn't afford one. The old concerns and mysteries that put her on edge helped her stay alert. She was losing Topie to Alzheimer's, for one, and that meant one tie to the past was unraveling. And the festival was making her more aware of her hometown, its history, and its secrets.

***

The staff of St. Ambrose Community had decorated each resident's door with something representative of January, mostly some craft made by the senior behind the door. Zadie and Topie complained about the silliness of craft-making, but still participated and appreciated Virginia's praise for their efforts. A snowman hung on Topie's door and a mobile of snowflakes from Zadie's. Virginia knocked first on Zadie's door and announced herself as she came in.

"Here I am, Aunt Zadie," Virginia spoke just a few decibels louder but with a little more articulation.

"Hello, there, Virgie Mae," Zadie answered in her best Minnie Pearl voice, upbeat and exaggerated. "You don't have to ask, I'm fine today, so how are you?"

"I am exhausted, ma'am," Virginia allowed herself to flop down on Zadie's Queen Anne chair in her sitting room. The apartment of three rooms—no kitchen needed—enveloped them. It was as inviting as an institutional facility could be. The warm gold carpet, the mellow walls with daisy and fern wallpaper, the familiar antique pieces of furniture from their old home, the balcony with window boxes. Virginia would have preferred that Zadie and Topie stay in the once-impressive home on Clive Street. But that neighborhood wasn't what it used to be, and the crime rate, tiny by big city standards, alarmed Virginia. The house needed many repairs and updates, and the steps were too much for women in their eighties who had undergone hip (Zadie) and knee (Topie) surgeries.

"You are supposed to be retired, young lady!" Zadie pretended to correct her niece. "Didn't you know that retired means you're not allowed to be exhausted? You can take a nap any time you want and sleep 'til ten."

"Oh, Zadie, I wish that were true. I don't see myself sleeping or napping much at all until this festival is over."

"Pooh! Festival. Whoever heard about celebrating biscuits? That's like celebrating salt pork or iced tea. Or green beans. Or kitchen dish rags."

"I hate to tell you this, Aunt Zadie, but except for the dish rags, there's probably a festival somewhere in this country for all of those, and a whole lot more than you'd think. I know there's one for green beans, I forget where, though."

"People have got too much time and money on their hands if they can come to Abundance to celebrate a biscuit."

"Aunt Zadie, this is a country that has a day for a groundhog, so why not a party for biscuits! Anyway, if they have the money, better they spend it here in Abundance than somewhere else."

Zadie smiled. Arguing like this—what she called fussing— defined their relationship. Virginia believed it taught her not to back down when she was a child, and not to be too eager to take Mack's opinions quickly and uncritically as a young wife. "It's good to see you, baby," Zadie said.

"Aunt Zadie, I came in here and plopped down so fast that I didn't hug your neck," Virginia said, and promptly did. "What they serve you for lunch today?"

"You get one guess."

"Um, Broiled chicken, whole wheat rolls, steamed soggy frozen vegetables, rice, and a fruit cup."

"Close. Red potatoes instead of rice, pudding instead of fruit cup, and English peas."

"Not bad."

"You didn't eat it, Missy. The only thing I don't like about being in this place—"

Virginia knew what was coming. She'd heard it, if not every time she came, every other time, especially when the food's blandness particularly annoyed Zadie.

"It would be that you can't cook, Aunt Zadie," Virginia

finished her sentence for her. "I know, sweetie. Hey, I have an idea. It's been a while since I sprung you from this place." "This place" was what they always called St. Ambrose Community, as if the assistant living home was a rest stop on the interstate rather than an expensive care facility. It gave Zadie and Topie a small sense of rebellion.

"What's your idea?"

"I'll pick you up Sunday morning. You can go to church with us, and then come home and you and Topie can have the run of my kitchen and cook whatever you want for dinner. Then I'll get you back here before 8:00 that night. Y'all need a day out of here."

Zadie thought about this for five seconds. "I'd rather have the run of my own kitchen."

"I know that, darlin', but remember, we sold the home place. We couldn't keep it up now that you're in here, and even if it still belonged to us, you wouldn't want to cook on that old stove when I've got bright shiny Whirlpools."

"It's bright and shiny because you don't use it yourself," Zadie was thinking, but she figured Topie's cousin Minnie got enough use out of those new appliances. "You think you can handle Topie?"

"Topie's no trouble, Aunt Zadie. As long as we keep an eye on her from running off, looking for the home place, she'll be all right. What do you say?"

"What am I going to cook?"

"That's up to you. You make a list, I'll make sure all the ingredients are in the kitchen, and you can run the show, although I'm sure Topie will have a few things to say about that."

"Let's go ask her," Zadie suggested. At first the idea of

leaving St. Ambrose for a day tempted her, but two years spent there had made her forays out, occasionally to the doctor and even more occasionally to visit Virginia and Mack, very tiring and tense. She'd gotten good rehab or therapy or whatever they called it after that stroke in '95, but Zadie doubted she was really up to standing on her feet for an hour frying chicken.

"Sure. Where are your shoes? Your walker?"

"I'll just wear these house shoes. And I'll hold on to you. I don't need that walker just to go next door." Virginia helped her aunt to her feet and held her arm as they rambled over to Topie's room.

Topie's apartment was a two-room—a bathroom and larger bedroom than Zadie's apartment had, but no separate sitting room. Virginia recalled it was $500 a month cheaper to forgo the sitting room. The costs of this care facility were really outlandish, in Virginia's thinking, even if meals, security, cleaning, and trips to the doctor were included. Topie's room had a similar décor but different color scheme, more blue than gold.

The main contrast between the rooms was that Topie had every table top and almost every square foot of wall covered with photographs of her cousins and their children. The photographs varied from 3 X 3 Brownie camera snapshots to Technicolor school pictures to old sepia and black and white photos of Topie's ancestors that almost looked like daguerreotypes. All the large ones were framed in brown metal frames from K-Mart; the snapshots were pinned to one of the three bulletin boards that hung over her bed. Topie's family was huge. Her mother's mother had given birth to thirteen children; Virginia remembered that one of Topie's aunts had produced sixteen children herself. Back in those days when Topie's memory was sharp, she could call all the names of her first-cousins— 47 of them. Now, Topie sometimes could not remember her own name.

"Topie," Zadie called as she opened the door and walked in, not bothering to knock. "Topie, you up?"

"Yes, ma'am," they heard a weak voice. "Who is it?" As they came fully into the apartment, Topie turned her head around in her rocker, which was pointed toward the window so that Topie could look at the birds that frequented the three feeders she kept on her balcony. The sliding glass door, of course, was locked and bolted; the attendants were pretty good to put the seeds in when Topie remembered to ask them.

"Who do you think it is, girl?" Zadie spoke to her with a tone that some would think scolding and condescending if they didn't know the two women's histories. "I brought a visitor."

"Who? Oh, Virgie Mae," Topie recognized. Virginia breathed a sigh of relief to herself. *She knows us today. She hasn't gone away yet*, she thought.

"Miss Topie, I am here to hug your neck," Virginia settled her aunt into the overstuffed chair Topie had brought from home and approached Topie. She spoke even more loudly and distinctly than she did for Zadie, not sure how much Topie was able to comprehend. *How much longer?* Today must have been shower day. The old lady smelled of Dial Soap and the toilet water Virginia had given her last Christmas. Virginia leaned over and showed Topie all the affection she had showered on Zadie.

How she loved this old black woman. How every childhood memory seemed to include Topie, somehow. How her friends would never understand, her friends who pretended to be so enlightened, who acted as if they had never disparaged black people back in the '60s and '70s when the schools were being desegregated. How inseparable in her mind Zadie and Topie were, and how satisfied Virginia was to have no regrets about her own treatment of Topie or her family over the years.

Everyone, except for Zadie and Topie, had tried to tell her, in words or action, how to treat black people. Even her own daddy, knowing how much she loved and depended on Topie, expressed the same dismissive attitudes about the black men he worked with. She was implicitly taught to see the black people around her as less than, as undeserving, as not willing to put forth the effort, as people who did not take advantage of what was given them, as people who just didn't know how happy they should be to live in the other, rundown part of town and go to the schools with the third-hand textbooks.

Where did people, especially people around here, get those ideas? What fear or pride or spite or ignorance birthed and nurtured that kind of stupidity? Even if she herself didn't go to Mississippi and ride a bus to protest and register voters back in the early '60s, she could say with a clear conscience that Utopia Felecia Powders Jackson had taught her how to live. She had rewarded Topie by living that way in regard to every person.

"How are you doing today, Miss Topie? You smell real good. I see you are wearing your red muumuu with the parrots on it."

Topie looked down at her housecoat. "Will you look at that?" Topie liked birds. Virginia made sure that every gift of clothing had a bird of some kind on it. Topie smiled at the recognition that she was, indeed, wearing a bright red flannel housecoat that zipped up the front and that sported two big yellow parrots on both sides. It was loud, but fun. No need for an eighty-some-year-old woman to wear pink and blue every day.

"Miss Topie, can I move your chair around so you can look at us?" Virginia asked, getting ready to do it with or without permission. Miss Topie was small and frail. Zadie had always been a fleshier woman, taking after her mother Bonita, Governor's first wife, who had died in the flu epidemic when Zadie was seven. Zadie had survived because her parents had the prescience to send her away to family members in the mountains, where she was alone and isolated but safe until the disease had run its course.

Virginia read once that the Spanish influenza had killed more than fifty million people, an incomprehensible number. How people like Topie and her mother Lula survived was an insoluble puzzle. They were people who couldn't get away, who probably couldn't afford a doctor even if the doctor could have helped. When she looked at her aunts and they talked about that frightening time, what little they remembered after eighty years, Virginia always wondered if the disease had come up to their door, knocked, and found an unwilling immune system. Or if the disease had come in, altered their cells, and made them stronger. Zadie just laughed and said, "I had too much vinegar in me, and Topie had too much sugar in her, for those germs to live."

Virginia tugged gently to move Topie's rocker toward the other two chairs in the room, and seated herself in a straight-backed chair with cushions on it. Topie was not in a talkative mood, not today, so Virginia started in.

"Miss Topie, how would you like to get out of here and take a ride Sunday?"

"Huh? Where am I goin'?"

"You and Zadie are coming to my house. Zadie is whining about the food here and she wants to cook. Would you like that?"

Topie laughed quietly to herself, probably more at some loose memory than at the thought of her friend's complaining about the menu. "I'd like some greens and pinto beans. I haven't had any good beans and cornbread since I came in here." This was not exactly an answer, but she had heard and understood.

"Can you help her cook?" Virginia asked, knowing that Topie could still walk well but that her hand movements had grown clumsy and ineffectual. *She could stir something, maybe*, Virginia thought. *I'll ask Minnie to come in that day to help, pay her double if I have to. Topie would get a kick out of seeing a family member, anyway.*

"Yeah, I would like to take a trip," Topie answered. "What we gonna have for desert?"

"I don't know. Something easy. How about a banana pudding?"

"We get enough pudding here," Zadie said. "I'm sick of pudding. I want pecan pie."

"That's awfully hard to make, isn't it, Aunt Zadie?" Virginia asked. *And it's not exactly on your diet with your borderline diabetes, either.*

"I've got an easy recipe. Now, Missy." As always, Zadie changed subjects quickly. "If you are expecting me to cook, you are going to have to find my recipe box. Do you know where it is?"

"Yes, ma'am, I have it. It's worth a million dollars. It's locked in my safe deposit box at Upstate Regional Bank."

"It is not, girl. You shouldn't lie to me."

"OK, it's in my bedroom closet."

"What's it doing in there? Recipes are supposed to be in a kitchen."

"Not in my house, Aunt Zadie. That's Minnie's job, and hers are in her head, which I suspect yours are, too. I don't remember you using that recipe box very much."

"Never you mind, I still want you to get that out for me. Now, let's see. I want to fry some chicken, so go to the Winn Dixie and get fresh chicken cut on Saturday. It would be better if the chickens were killed Sunday morning, but you just can't do that unless you raise your own, and I know you don't have hens in your backyard."

"It's not allowed in my neighborhood," Virginia laughed. Back in the '40s and '50s, even in town, Zadie kept a gaggle of hens and a rooster in the backyard of Governor's home. After she had toget rid of them because of a city ordinance in 1962, she fussed for years about not having fresh eggs every morning and chickens to keep the bugs away.

"Get me two whole chickens, and have them cut up there on the spot. Make those butchers do it. They can. They'll give you a hard time about it, but that's their job."

"Yes, ma'am."

"I'll need about three pounds of Irish potatoes. I'll make cornbread, so you'll need to buy a bag of Martha White cornmeal. You won't be able to get fresh beans or produce since it's winter, so those will have to be canned. Buy a two-pound bag of pinto beans. And about a half a pound slab of salt meat.

"Get a bottle of dark Karo syrup," Zadie continued, "and at least a pound of pecans. I guess you have sugar already. I'll need lots of eggs and milk, and I just won't have time to make a piecrust on top of all this, so as much as I hate it, buy me one of those frozen piecrusts. They're awful, but I can't wear myself out. And have Minnie soak the pintos for Topie. You'll need to find some fresh turnip greens. Buy them with the turnips still on them. Be sure to have vinegar because I can't eat greens without vinegar. Topie can, but I can't. Now, I haven't seen you write any of this down."

"I've got it all in my head."

"No, you don't. Repeat back to me what I said."

"Two whole fresh chickens, cut up. Three pounds white

potatoes. Canned green beans. Dark Karo syrup, pound of pecans, eggs and milk, frozen piecrust, Martha White cornmeal. Fresh turnip greens still attached to the turnips. Bag of pintos for Minnie to soak. Salt pork. I already have the other stuff at home."

"How did you remember all that?"

"I know how to buy groceries, Aunt Zadie. I may not know what to do with them once I get them home, but I can buy them."

"All right."

"I'll be by 9:00 Sunday morning."

"No, don't come that early. I don't like Sunday School at your church. Just pick us up at 10:30."

"Topie, do you want me to take you to your church?"

"Yes, that'd be good." Topie was not only quiet today, but agreeable. Mack and Virginia attended Abundance First United Methodist. Zadie's momma had been Episcopalian and she still considered that her church, but she would consent to worship with the Methodists for the sake of family. Topie's Zion AME church was only three blocks from First UMC, so it wouldn't be a problem to let someone superintend her from 11:00 to 12:30 that day.

She and Mack would skip Sunday School, go out for brunch so they wouldn't be hungry at noon, and let her aunts control the kitchen until they managed to create their magic. It had been a long time since Zadie had fixed her a meal, and this would be a great treat after what promised to be a hectic week of festival work. Maybe she could get Bethany here, too.

The three chatted for a while. After about an hour, Virginia could tell Topie was tired, and she wanted a nap herself. She hugged their necks, kissed both on the cheek, walked Zadie back to her room, and shut the door. On her way out, she filled out the paperwork to take them both out for the day on Sunday. She, Mack, and Bethany were the only ones allowed to do so for Zadie, but a couple of Topie's cousins had that privilege as well. Yes, having Zadie and Topie out for Sunday would do them all good.

Chapter 4

As Virginia thought about her children--tall, self-assured Bethany and blond, charming Matthew--she found herself pitying Zadie and Topie for being childless. No, pity wasn't the word, but if it was possible to have regrets for another, that was the feeling she had for the two women who raised her. Zadie's husband Eddie McCann had died in Europe in World War II. They had been married five years already, though, and children had not come. Perhaps that was why Virginia was so readily welcomed. If Zadie had already been raising four or five children, where would Virginia have fit in?

And Topie. That was a different, much sadder story. Topie's children both suffered from a strange lung condition that kept them from living more than a few months. It might have been cystic fibrosis, or a susceptibility to respiratory infections. And she had miscarried twice. Four children gone! How brave of Topie. She was even braver when she told Lawrence Jackson, her husband of many years and a notorious womanizer, to get out. After years of working in a mill and living in the black part of town with her momma Lula, Zadie told her to just move in with her where she belonged, and Topie never left. That was in 1953, six years after Hennie's death and soon after Governor and Lula died. From then on, Virginia lived with her two "aunts" instead of a real momma.

Not the way most children get raised, especially in the South and especially in the 1950s. Thank goodness for Tally and Leah, who had three brothers each and lived in active, crazy homes with tolerant mommas who let the kids run in and out and squirt hoses and stay outside until ten at night in the summer. At least Zadie and Topie's independence, their intense willingness to live without men in their domestic lives, didn't deter Virginia from wanting a husband and children. Anyway, she always suspected both of them of having secret boyfriends. She found them laughing at times between themselves and showing each other Polaroids Virginia was not allowed to see. Virginia wondered where they really went when Zadie said she was playing bingo on Saturday nights, when bingo wasn't legal in South Carolina, and when Topie said she was going to a church retreat.

Colorful, it was. Unusual, yes. Secure, yes. Predictable, maybe not. Maybe it was the transfer, at the age of four, from the cottage with two parents to a huge, sometimes spooky house with a coughing grandpa upstairs. She remembered reading "A Rose for Emily" in a college English class and having a nightmare in which she opened grandpa's room and found a corpse. Every large home in literature from the past looked, in Virginia's mind, like the home place, what Zadie called it because of its age and its provenance. It had been built in the decade immediately after the Civil War when the Cleelands came up from Charleston to grow cotton instead of importing it. Land was cheap then because the planters were selling off their estates to pay taxes. The Governor's grandfather, Preston Cleeland, bought 500 acres, took over Rosy Dew, built the finest house anyone around there had ever seen, and fathered six children.

His own children, however, were not so prolific, and they and their offspring were not content to live in the backwaters at the foot of the Appalachian Mountains. The sons took advantage of their inheritances to be educated and move off. They liked law and medicine, made their own fortunes, and didn't fight it when Preston left everything to his oldest son, William, who was Governor Cleeland's daddy. Governor was the weak link in the family, though. It wasn't that he drank and gambled to excess, he just wasn't good with money. He made bad investments, and the fortune dwindled to something much less impressive than the almost $500,000 in 1910 dollars that he inherited. By the 1950s enough was left for him and Zadie and Virginia to live on and for Virginia to get through Clemson. When she married Mack, though, she was marrying up financially. She might have had the legacy, but Mack Foster had the business smarts.

No child has control over its upbringing; the best a child can do is pitch fits to get her way. Zadie may not have birthed children but she had a good sense about what it took to raise a willful child. When it came to disciplining a preschooler, Zadie was ahead of her time: no belt, no paddles. She figured out what Virginia wanted at that moment and denied her that desire as punishment when Virginia smart-mouthed or stamped her foot or threw something or slammed a door. Very effective. And neither Zadie nor Topie were yellers. Topie missed her own babies too much to hurt a child's feelings with a harsh, loud voice.

To his credit, Daddy never disciplined her. He didn't have the right to really, because he let her go live with her aunt without much of a fight. And Daddy didn't have a reason to spank her, either. When she was with Daddy, she could do no wrong. On those Saturdays he was home from driving the truck up north, Buddy Cullins took his pretty little girl with him to the barber shop, to the junk yard, or to visit his two brothers on their truck farms up in Spartanburg County. She sat next to him in the cab of his pickup, jumping around without a seat belt, wearing one of his ball caps and sucking down one Coca-Cola after another. Virginia knew just where to draw the line between being cute enough to get Grandma Cullins to laugh and being punished for mouthiness.

No, children didn't have much control, and when they tried to exert it, it usually backfired, at least at the Cleeland homestead. How she had wanted a normal family. She wanted a momma and daddy who tucked her in, a little brother or sister, a dog and a cat. Zadie didn't allow any predatory animals around the home place— they would bother the chickens. Virginia fantasized about siblings and pets anyway, of course. It wouldn't have mattered if the imaginary house were smaller than the seeming mansion on Clive Street. Normal meant siblings. Normal kept the schoolteachers from being confused about who was signing your permission slips or report cards. Normal meant you saw your daddy more often. She loved her aunts but dreamed of a life that she had more say in, that conformed to the TV show families and how her schoolmates lived.

Not that she was going to see a psychiatrist to know that she missed something in her childhood. That would be a waste of time and money. Weak people needed to pay doctors to listen to them whine. But what she didn't know as she grew up was how she would fill the hole that missing piece of her life had left. Not the hole of losing a momma. That happened to people. That wasn't something she could call an injustice. Mothers died; usually fathers died first, but her father was still alive, almost eighty, in Florida, rarely calling her, not estranged but not really interested in her affluent life.

Buddy acted sometimes as if Mack's and her lifestyle was an affront to his own. He had always accused Zadie of thinking Hennie was too good for him; Virginia had heard that rant from him more than once. Zadie never spoke poorly of Buddy Cullins in Virginia's hearing, but Buddy was convinced she did, and frequently. "Buddy was low-class, Buddy was just a truck-driver, Buddy wasn't a good husband, Buddy had other women, Buddy didn't come to see Virgie Mae enough." Those were the words Buddy would have put in Zadie's mouth but that she never truly spoke.

In the alternate universe, the real world that her upbringing didn't much resemble, mothers and fathers lived together with two, three, or six children. Mothers, almost always, stayed home with the children and loved and scolded and wiped their noses and felt their heads for fevers. Fathers saw their children every day when they came home to dinner on the table. If mothers died, they had graves the children could visit. Fathers found wives again and remarried and provided a mother for the orphaned children. Aunts lived in other houses. Grandpas were crusty and funny, not scary historical relics.

This kind of normal was what she wanted for Matthew and

Bethany. This was what she worked for, balancing motherhood and wifehood with a teaching career. This was what she fought for when Mack got a wild hare for two weeks at forty-five and thought he wanted out. She told him she would make it hotter than Hades for him if he pulled that, and if there was another woman involved (there wasn't), Virginia would find out her identity and put up a billboard on I-85 with both Mack's and the floozy's pictures.

The normal, committed, and stable was what she wanted to protect, and not just for the Fosters. She hoped it for her former students who stuck around Abundance, especially in this day of crumbling marriages and families. If she could help Abundance be a better place to live, to bring up children, to have jobs, to stay together, in a small way, she would have done her part. She would have had control over something.

She was so deep in her thoughts that she was surprised to find herself home now. She pulled into the driveway of 27 Apple Grove Walk, pushed the garage door opener, and drove the Explorer into her space. Later Mack would park his Volvo beside her. She liked the feel of the SUV; seated up high she could see better, for one thing. The garage door closed behind her and she left her car and her thoughts ticking away and cooling down in the garage. It was five o'clock.

She heard the bark and scurrying feet of BoJo, their Shitzu. BoJo came out of her doggie flap in the door between the garage and kitchen. "Hey little girl, what are you up to?" A dog greeting you when you came home had to be the one of the finest pleasures of life, Virginia decided. The children had always had a dog, but larger ones, Labs and Collies. This little one fit retirement much better, and BoJo didn't shed much. BoJo stood for Bonita Josephine, Zadie's mother and Mack's grandmother. She doubted those ladies would have appreciated a dog being named after them, but no disrespect was meant. Anyway, she could just as easily say BoJo was named after Jon Bon Jovi.

Minnie had created a pasta dish that was warming in the oven. Virginia could smell the garlic and cheese as she entered. "I'm home."

"Hey, I'm in here," Minnie called. She walked back into the kitchen from the living room carrying her purse, keys, and with her red wool coat hanging from her shoulder. Minnie, like Topie and Lula, was slender and energetic. She was about Virginia's age, or at least Virginia figured she was. "Dinner's in the oven. I did three loads of wash this afternoon. The dryer is still runnin'."

"Great. Listen, Minnie, are you busy Sunday? I'm picking up Topie and Zadie to come here. Zadie wants to cook, and they both need some fresh air out of St. Ambrose. Would you like to come and help them out? I really don't think they can handle the cooking by themselves."

"I don't know, Virginia, I was hoping. . . "

"I'll pay you double time for the afternoon. And you'll get to see Topie. She still recognizes me, so I'm pretty sure she'll get a charge out of seeing a family member. You can bring your momma if you want."

Minnie was doing the math in her head. "Momma was talking about Topie the other day. Sure, I'll do it. What about the food?"

"All you'll need to do is soak some beans, pintos, Thursday evening and cook them the next day."

"No, ma'am, that won't do. They need to cook all day to be any good, and I don't get in here 'til three."

"What can we do?"

"Virginia, you can make beans. There's nothing to it."

"You know I just don't cook, Minnie. I'd probably get it wrong. How about this, you get them ready Thursday evening, and I'll turn the burner on the next morning."

"You'll need to put a piece of fat meat in it."

"Ok, I think I can do that. I'll get all the other groceries Saturday. Zadie insisted on fresh chicken."

"She's right about that. Once you put it in the freezer, it's not half as good. Anybody knows that."

"Yes," Virginia answered, absently. But Minnie was thinking, "Silly woman. How can you get to be her age and not know how to cook a pot of pintos? Good Lord. But she is awfully good to Topie, so I can't fault her. It would be good to see Momma and Topie together. And double time will let me pay off that TV set."

"Well, I'll be gettin' on home'," Minnie said. "See you tomorrow. I'll ask Momma about coming."

"Good-bye." After Minnie left, Virginia checked the refrigerator, found the salad to go with the dish in the oven, set the table, and stretched out across the sunroom day bed until Mack came home.

Sunday felt like old times, like her childhood. Three black women and one white woman, stirring, chopping, bossing, looking into the sparkling oven and under lifted pot lids. Laughing and telling stories. Arguing about the merits of Martha White over White Lily flour and cornmeal. Complaining about . . . lots of things, but not about being together and sharing a kitchen. The smells kept tempting Virginia back into the kitchen that was getting hot with the extra bodies and the 400 degree oven. "Open a window, Virgie Mae," Zadie commanded about 2:00.

Virginia obeyed and sat down at the table to watch and listen. Zadie, despite her legacy, fit in seamlessly with Topie, Minnie, and Deedra, Minnie's mother and Topie's second cousin. Zadie acted as if there was no difference between any of them, fitting her behavior to reality instead of trying to do the opposite. *How did she learn that, living in the times she did, where she did?* Virginia wondered. *What an amazing person Zadiah McCann was to rise above, to not care about conforming to, what surrounded her. Where does that kind of backbone, and that kind of love, come from?*

When the meal was finally ready, at 2:45, they all agreed it was well worth the wait. Greens with chopped up turnips and tiny pieces of salt pork. Enough to flavor, not enough to create a film of grease. Now, that took artistry. Creamy, almost flawless mashed potatoes (Virginia found one pea-sized lump in hers) and milk gravy off the drippings of crunchy, pan-fried, egg-and-flour-and-cornmeal dredged chicken. Zadie and Topie never used a deep fryer, stemming from an accident years ago when it tipped over and gave Zadie third degree burns on four inches of her right lower leg.

The green beans were a disappointment, being canned, but the cooks weren't responsible for that. Moist cornbread. Pinto beans that made you understand why people craved them sometimes. And pecan pie, a different version, with pecans throughout instead of on top, with real whipped cream. Sweet tea, of course, but Virginia made sure there was unsweetened just in case someone wanted to watch their blood sugar level. But this was not a day for worrying about finger-pricks. It was a day to enjoy what may not be diverse cuisine—Virginia stifled a laugh when she thought about Melody pulling that one out of her hat—but the best cooking they'd eaten in a long time.

With women who could cook like this in her house, in her family, why should Virginia aspire to equal them? She wouldn't take up painting to create Michelangelos, or start learning piano to go on concert tours. She knew her strengths. She organized. She was a good mother. She was a great wife. And yet that niggling, little voice, always had to be silenced. No, she would not let that stereotype make her think any less of herself or enjoy this exquisite food any less.

Chapter 5

October 27, 1918

Zadie looked at the calendar, then the clock, then out the window. She repeated this action. Perhaps that is all she had done today. It felt that way. Of course, she wasn't quite sure how to read the clock. It didn't have numbers, but funny figures like Xs and capital Is. But there were twelve of them, like a regular clock. And this clock was big and stood in the hallway and struck bells a lot. Too much. It kept her up at night, waiting for the next one. And the calendar. She came here to Kings Mountain to stay with Uncle Lyons and Aunt Margaret Cleeland on September 20, and they crossed off the days until today, October 27.

Everybody said she was quick and smart in school, and that seven-year-olds usually couldn't tell time (that meant read the clock) and read books as well as she did, but she picked it up easily because Daddy read to her and taught her those things. She was supposed to have started school this year, but the sickness messed everything up. On September 18, the first person in Turling County got sick with the infooenza, they called it, and she heard the adults say that person was on the train and got off for the night and was carrying the infooenza. She wondered if he carried it in a bucket or maybe in a suitcase, since he was on the train, but he gave it to the stationmaster. Two days later people who had the money or the kinfolk were sending their children away in cars and buggies to families in the mountains and the hills.

Uncle Lyons and Aunt Margaret had five children, but the youngest was Merlin and he was thirteen and no fun. He had a tutor getting him ready to go to military school when the eplidimek was over. All of Uncle Lyons' boys, three of them, went to military school in Charleston and the two girls went to finishing schools in Charlotte. She wasn't sure what they learned in finishing school, but they were big girls, fifteen and seventeen now, and she had not met them. Zadie wondered how somebody knew she was finished, and what age a girl had to be to reach being finished. That must be something only grownups knew. Zadie thought about these kinds of things a lot here; she didn't have much else to do.

"You were sent to us for your protection, Zadiah Louise Cleeland," said her aunt Margaret when Zadie arrived at the big house in Kings Mountain. Margaret Cleeland was a very big woman, who wore lace-covered, fancy dresses that covered every inch of her body all day long and who never appeared in a wrapper or with her hair down. Margaret didn't seem concerned that there was no one for Zadie to play with. The only children were those of the colored servants and the white men who farmed their land, but she wasn't allowed to be around them, because they were skeptable to the infooenza, Margaret said. Even going outside was risky, but Zadie was allowed on the front porch.

So the days at Kings Mountain came and went very slow. Aunt and Uncle did have lots of books and toys they had not discarded, so Zadie had a new set of playthings and could look at the pictures and try to decipher words in the books. She liked the Bobbsey Twins and could almost make sense out of it. She didn't know anybody who was a twin and this family had two sets! She wasn't sure if that was confusing or wonderful.

She wanted to go home, to Daddy and Momma and Lula their housekeeper, and to Topie, Lula's little girl who Zadie played with all the time. Why Topie couldn't come to escape the infooenza, she didn't know. Well, maybe she did. Topie was one of dark-skinned people who surrounded them like shadows, who often did not speak when the pink-skinned people were around but who spoke lots, and loud, when they were by themselves, in the kitchen or out in the backyard. Topie told her she had one doll; Zadie had four in her bedroom. That must mean something about the dark-skinned people, the ones her daddy and momma called colored or darkies and sometimes another name that sounded mean, and that they said in a mean way. Zadie wasn't sure what it all meant, but she wished Topie was here. Topie was five, and little for five, but funny and sassy.

The clock rang its bells. She sighed. Outside it had started to rain. Not with thunder and lightning, just slowly. The trees had all turned yellow and brown and some a pretty orange. The clock rang its bells again.

"Zadiah Louise, I need to talk to you." It was Daddy's voice. She turned away from the window and saw her father. He was a tall man, taller than Uncle Lyons. He wore a gray flannel suit, double-breasted, with a pocket watch chain showing. But he looked different now. He had shaved his beard. And he looked like he needed to sit down, or sleep.

But what was Daddy doing here? "Daddy!" She ran to him and hugged his waist. Normally Daddy would pick her up and kiss her, and she would nuzzle against his beard. But today he just put his hand on her head. "Let's sit down, Zadiah Louise." He was calling her by her two names. He never did that.

He guided her to the loveseat by the window. It was made of a heavy gold and red cloth. She didn't realize she would remember it for a long time.

"I'm here to take you home in a few days. I am going to stay with Uncle Lyons until then."

"Is the infooenza eplidemick over?"

"It's influenza, Zadiah. People call it the flu."

"That's easy. Maybe it flu away like a bird." She thought her joke was funny. Daddy didn't smile.

"It's—gone, almost."

"Why didn't Momma come? Where's Momma?"

Governor Cleeland looked away from Zadie, focusing on something out the window. "She couldn't come, Zadiah. You see, she got very sick the day after you left. We put her to bed. Lula took good care of her. She called for you. She missed you and wanted to see you. But, you see, the flu was hard on her, and . . ."

"So are you going to take me home to see her now?"

"No, darling. Your momma died. Three weeks ago."

Zadie knew what died meant. She had even been to a funeral already. But—

"Daddy, is she in—the ground?"

"Her body is in the ground, in a nice coffin, you know, a big pretty box, and we buried her at the family cemetery plot. You know where it is, and I'll take you there when we go back. But your Momma is in heaven, darling. Forever and ever."

That was what people said in church, and she believed it only because she didn't have an alternative to believe. Three weeks was a long time to not know Momma was in the ground, or in heaven, or just not in the house. Zadie knew she wasn't supposed to feel this way, but if it had to be Momma or Daddy to die, it was better that it was Momma. Momma let Lula do what mommas were supposed to do. Momma rushed her off when company came. Momma didn't want to sit and cuddle and tell her stories. She loved Momma, but as long as Daddy was here, it was hard to think about Momma in a box, cold and still like a big statue.

Daddy sat there on the loveseat, with Zadie on his lap, through two rings of the bells in the clock. Zadie was getting sleepy in the warm room and listening to the quietly dropping rain. Daddy's breathing wasn't even and the same, sometimes he seemed to hiccup, and Zadie realized he was crying, a little. "Zadie," he sighed after the bell rung again. "We'll stay here and take the train home Saturday. But I need to tell you something. Lula is going to come live in our house. So is Utopia, I mean Topie. Would you like that?"

"Yes!" Zadie sat up, excited. Grief was gone. Now she'd have an all-the-time playmate and the happy Lula, who sang songs and danced with Topie around the house, there when she went to bed at night and woke up in the morning. That made the four days before they boarded the train seem as slow as Christmas coming. She was glad to leave Uncle Lyons' gloomy house.

They rode a buggy from the train at the Abundance station to their house in the middle of town. Zadie wondered if they were going to buy an automobile. She had only seen two, and one of them was Uncle Lyons', but she hadn't ridden in it. Surely Daddy had the money for an automobile, whatever they cost. Horses were slow, and they bolted; she heard that cars could go twenty miles an hour. She didn't know what that meant, but it sounded fast.

They arrived at their home, the house with two stories and porch that ran along the front and left side and the windows with green shutters. As soon as Daddy opened the door, she knew something was different. The windows' heavy curtains were drawn even though it was still light outside, and only the parlor had gas lamps burning. She smelled something new. Later she would learn it was a medicine that was supposed to keep the germs away. A scent of flowers lingered in the air. But she also smelled something cooking, and Lula knew how to make her favorite foods. She was glad to be home.

***

When Lula Powders saw her employer and his daughter, her big white smile widened as joyously as always, but then Lula greeted them, quietly, since this was a place where death had come. Lula was pretty, and she knew it, and recognized that others knew it, too. Especially Zadie—Zadie thought Lula was beautiful. She had really dark skin—some colored people looked just a little brown, or had freckles, or even reddish hair, but Lula was truly dark, with deep brown eyes, and a prominent mouth, and she wore her hair in what she called a turban, so Zadie didn't really know what her hair looked like. Lula was not big like Momma, and she moved quickly, making order, making food, making beds, making things.

Somehow, out of all those people who were meeting their Creator because of this flu, Lula and her baby Utopia had been spared. She would kneel by her bed and thank Jesus for that for as long as she lived. People had been dying on every street of the town. The funeral homes, colored and white, couldn't keep up with the burials. She'd say her people had it worse than the whites, but that wasn't fair. No one knew that. Out of all her brothers and sisters, all her nieces and nephews, cousins and uncles and aunts, only three died. Lula knew this was a grieving house, a house where the mistress was gone. A house where the demon of illness came in, rested on Miz Cleeland, and did its mean business, until the Lord released her soul from her hungry, hot, wretching body. A house where a little white girl would need help remembering, and maybe forgetting, her momma. And the house where she and her baby girl would live for a long time, protected from being out of work, from being pushed around, from being in a crowded house with Mammy and the rest of the family. The Governor would see to that. She knew he would.

***

The home place, as Governor Cleeland called it, had more rooms than they needed. Downstairs was a parlor, a dining room. A sitting room for women to have tea. A kitchen. One bedroom on the first floor. Upstairs, there was a nursery, four other bedrooms, and a room for bathing. The outhouse sat ten yards from the back porch. Grownups talked about how, in the big cities in the north, which meant toward the top of the map, people had outhouses inside that were clean, not stinky. The people with the inside outhouses didn't need slop jars by the end of the bed for when you had to go in the middle of the night and they didn't have to worry about snakes and rats. That was hard to imagine but nice to dream about on cold mornings.

Topie and Lula slept in the bedroom downstairs, the one behind the kitchen. Zadie still occupied the nursery. Daddy slept in the biggest room in the back of the house, the one that also had a desk and bookshelves. He called it his study, and he sometimes stayed there for long times, even when Lula went in there to clean. Zadie would have asked for Topie to come to her room to sleep, but something told her coloreds and whites didn't sleep in the same room, just like they didn't go to the same churches and they didn't live in the same part of town or go to the same schools. In fact, she wasn't sure the coloreds even went to school.

"They do in some places. In Atlanta and Columbia and Charleston and Charlotte," Lula told her one day. "There they have their own schools. They even have some colleges. I hear there's all kinds of colleges coloreds can go to. But not here in Abundance. Good sense ain't got to this part of South Carolina yet. I guess they figure a colored who's gone to school might just figure somethin' out."

Lula never talked like that before Momma died. In fact, Lula did a lot of things now that she had not done before Zadie went to Kings Mountain. Lula sang a lot more, songs about men and women and love, not just songs about Jesus, like she used to. When Daddy was in his study, she and Topie sat down to eat meals with Zadie—in the dining room. Lula bossed the tradesmen who came to the door—colored and white alike. Lula just plain acted like she was the momma. It didn't bother Zadie, but she sure didn't see a colored woman act like that anywhere else.

In January, the epidemic—Zadie finally figured out how to say those disease words—was over and school was open. Zadie started first grade again and found herself moved to the second by March because of her reading ability, even though the teacher was the same for both grades. The arithmetic made her head hurt, but she figured it out. She loved school. The teacher loved Zadie. Miss Lantrey was pretty and proper. Spending the day with the twenty other children in the first and second grade room agreed with her.

She only wished Topie was there, because Topie was smart. Topie couldn't play gin rummy with her if she couldn't read the numbers on the cards or add them up. Well, she could beat Topie all the time, but Topie had more sense than to play cards with her just to lose. So, on Saturday Zadie taught Topie, as best she could, everything Miss Lantrey showed them in class during the week. Then they could read to each other, those books about the family in the cabin out in the middle of the country and the little women and Bobbsey Twins.

Living with Lula and Daddy and Topie was a happy kind of life, being eight, and nine, and then ten, and then eleven, with Topie following just two years behind her like a real little sister.

"How come you have green eyes?" Zadie once asked Topie.

"How should I know? You get the color of the eyes you get," Topie responded. "What a dumb question."

"Colored people have brown eyes."

"How do you know? Have you met every colored person in the whole wide world? You don't know all of 'em in Abundance, much less all of 'em in the world. Maybe lots of colored people have green eyes, or blue."

"Humph." That was all Zadie could say. Topie knew how to win an argument.

"Where's your real daddy?" Zadie asked once, in a snit at Topie.

"He works on the train. He goes between Charlotte and Greenville."

"I've never seen him."

"He and Momma decided not to be married any more when I was little."

"Do you ever see him?"

"No. But Momma showed me a picture. He got married again to some other lady."

Zadie felt bad now for pointing out Topie didn't have a daddy around that she knew, so she never brought it up again.

In 1922, when Zadie was eleven and Topie nine, the Governor started going out at night to see a widowed woman who lived across the county line. He drove a car by then, and he left at four to eat dinner with her and came back after Zadie was asleep. Her name was Jessamyn Pritchett, and her husband had died and left her with a small general store but no children. Jessamyn was already forty. After two months of visits two or three times a week, he brought Jessamyn home.

Jessamyn was a tiny woman compared to Momma, and she was the same height as eleven-year-old Zadie. She was pretty, too, with very dark hair, thick eyelashes, and skin without wrinkles or blemishes, freckles or spots from the pox. She reminded Zadie of a cherished doll with a porcelain head. Her eyes were deep brown. Jessamyn seemed never to have been exposed to evil or tension, and she walked calmly into the room, extended her hand and spoke in a voice like nothing Zadie had ever heard.

"I am pleased to meet you, Zadiah," Jessamyn said. Governor must have noticed Zadie's furrowed brow.

"Don't make a face like that, girl," he scolded. "Speak up."

"Yes, ma'am, pleased to meet you."

"She probably hasn't ever heard anyone with a northern accent."

"Maybe not, but she knows her manners," the Governor's voice sounded displeased, something else Zadie was not used to. "Zadiah, Mrs. Pritchett has agreed to marry me. She is going to be your new mother."

"Oh!" the sound was out before Zadie could stop it, and she clapped her hand over her own mouth. But Jessamyn did not act offended.

"Governor, you have shocked the child. You could have broken it to her a bit more delicately." Now that Zadie could understand Jessamyn, she liked the even and precise cadences of her voice. "I hope you will be happy for us. We're getting married next Sunday, here in this beautiful house."

"That's right," Governor confirmed. He smiled down at his doll-like fiancée. Zadie saw that Jessamyn, now that she had confidently pronounced her future, had a far-away look in her eyes.

In the next week or so Zadie was to learn all the details that her father desired her to know about her new stepmother. Jessamyn and her husband had moved to Anderson County ten years ago to start a business. Its success had been, in her words, erratic. Jessamyn liked to use words like that. Jessamyn liked to read. In fact, she had gone to college for two whole years—this was the first woman Zadie had ever met who had gone to college and wasn't a schoolteacher.

Zadie held Jessamyn in wonder. Her husband had left the business to her, and now that she was to marry Governor, she would allow him to sell it and she would become a wife and mother, not a shopkeeper.

Two days before the wedding Zadie came home from school to find Lula in the kitchen slapping piecrust dough on to the cutting board with hard, pounding strokes. Lula made piecrusts like no one else, and in trying to teach Zadie to cook, had warned, "Treat the dough like a baby. It's not like yeast bread, that you roll and push, roll and push till you're sick of it. Mash down on the piecrust dough gentle-like." Lula was disregarding her own cooking advice, and all this time she was muttering under her breath, something about a man being worthless, all of them being no-count.

Zadie stood in the doorway watching her. Maybe she had heard from Topie's father; maybe Lula had a man friend nobody knew about. Maybe he was "treatin' her bad," like in the blues songs Lula liked to sing. Finally, Lula made one final chop with her hand on the dough, then picked it up and threw it out the open window as if she was trying to hit a buzzard in the backyard.

"Lula!" Zadie erupted, shocked but wanting to laugh. "What did you do that for?"

Lula turned around. "You shouldn't be sneaking up on a body, Zadie. What are you, a tomcat? I didn't like the feel of that dough, that's all. The chickens can eat of it."

"Are you mad about something, Lula?"

"Me, mad? What would I be mad about? What would I have to be mad about? He brings another woman in here after all these years, and she's gonna be wanting me to leave, and where is that gonna leave me and Utopia?"

"Mrs. Pritchett isn't going to throw you out, Lula. I don't

think she's wanting to keep house without help in such a big place. You won't be out of a job."

Lula looked at Zadie in a way that said Zadie didn't, and couldn't understand what she meant. "I don't mean I won't be cooking and cleaning here anymore, Miss Zadie. I mean we won't be living here anymore."

"Oh." Zadie hadn't thought about that. "Where will you go?"

Lula wiped her hands on her apron and sank into a chair by the kitchen table. She hid her face behind her hands. She didn't speak, and Zadie was surprised to see a tear go down her face. Lula's body trembled. Zadie had never seen Lula sad or weeping. Mad maybe, like a few minutes ago, but mostly always happy. Zadie depended on Lula to keep the home in good spirits.

"I know, I'll tell Daddy he has to pay you more, so you can afford a place to stay in town, all by yourself."

Lula used a handkerchief to dry her cheeks. "No, honey. Your daddy's already took care of that. He done bought me and Topie a house over in the colored part of town. It's right nice. There's a room for me and one for Topie. Think of that, she'll have her own room. He said he couldn't think of doing any less, those were his exact words."

"That's wonderful. Your own house! "

Lula smiled. Behind the smile Zadie could not know what she was thinking, that this little white girl who was not so little anymore, she loved her daddy. She'd have a lot to learn about men some day. Not today. She's had to get used to a new momma again and her daddy had picked himself trouble, whether he knew it or not.

Then Lula spoke. "I am just sorry I won't be here for you,"

Lula explained. "I'm so used to getting you up and turning your lights off at night."

Zadie blushed. "I'm getting too old for that, Lula. I'll be twelve in two months."

"Yes, you will, darlin'." Lula looked around, ready to get back to work. "Let me try that pie crust again. I've got to get started on that dinner for your daddy's wedding."

Jessamyn and Governor married in a ceremony held on the big front porch of Governor's home. Father Bragg presided, but not without first saying that a Christian marriage should take place within the walls of a church sanctuary. The fine spring sun warmed the twenty or so attendees who stood to watch them exchange vows. All were residents of Abundance; Jessamyn had no family nearby to witness her second marriage. Tally's and Leah's parents and siblings were there; a few fellow parishioners, Governor's banker and his wife, and the newspaper editor came.

Afterward everyone ate little pieces of sandwiches and pieces of pecan pie and drank what seemed like gallons of iced tea. Lula and Topie had prepared it all. They wore their best Sunday dresses for the wedding, even though before and after they had to run between the kitchen and porch to serve the guests.

When the guests had left, Governor kissed Zadie good-bye, Jessamyn patted her head, and they left in Governor's car for their honeymoon with a promise that they should be back in a week or so. They planned to begin married life in Greenville, at the Poinsett Hotel, the finest in town, and then maybe just go somewhere else. Governor winked playfully when he announced that. Zadie had never seen her father wink as if he were trying to hide a secret.

In five days Zadie received a postcard from Asheville, saying they would be home the next day. Zadie felt as if she were looking into a dark hole. Tomorrow she would have to start living with the reality of a stepmother, and she would have to live without Topie and Lula in the house. Lula would still come and work for them, but their servant and her daughter would move into a four-room house south of the railroad tracks, where almost all the colored people in Abundance lived. That house was tiny compared to the Cleeland home place, Topie told Zadie, but it would be all theirs and no other cousins and aunts and uncles would be allowed to live with them— that was part of the bargain. Just Topie and Lula, with a kitchen, sitting room and two bedrooms. Governor paid lots of money for it. Small it might be, but that house would be like a paradise for them after staying together in the downstairs bedroom of Zadie's house.

When she went to bed, for the first time in her life Zadie couldn't sleep. She had heard grownups say things about tossing and turning, and that's what she found herself doing. She couldn't stop wondering about what the next day would be like, with Topie and Lula moving out. Suddenly she felt a deep tug at her heart, and she slipped out of bed and down to Lula's room as quietly as she could. Lula was still up; Zadie could hear her listening to the radio in the parlor with the sound turned down low. Lula loved the radio— she didn't care what was on, she would listen anyway. Tonight a religious program was on, music and preaching.

Zadie crept over to Topie's bed and lifted the cover. "Topie, let me in with you."

Topie was fast asleep. "Topie, wake up."

In the shadowy room Topie squinted to figure out who was waking her up.

"Wha--. What you want?"

"Move over."

"You got your own bed. I don't have enough room for you."

"I don't care. I can't sleep. Move over."

"Girl." Topie scooted over as much as she could. Zadie made herself fit in what space was left. Topie was much smaller than she.

"What would your rich daddy say about you getting into bed with a colored girl?" Topie asked. She didn't appreciate being waked up and felt cranky, and she knew she could be cranky with Zadie. She and her momma would be busy tomorrow, with moving into their house and the Governor coming back, too, and there was no telling how picky Zadie's new momma would be. Topie wanted to get her sleep for the big day.

"I don't care. I feel like my life is ending," Zadie said.

"Oh, silly. You like to make things like they's a big show. You read too many books."

"Stepmothers are mean."

"How do you know that?"

"In all the stories they are."

"Stories ain't all true. Some are just stories. Stories sometimes is lies." Topie yawned after this pronouncement. She resettled herself to be more comfortable, hoping Zadie would take the hint.

"That's not the only reason. You won't be living here anymore."

"Shoot, girl, I'll still be here when Momma is. We just go home at night, to our own house." She liked the sound of that so much, she said it again and again in different ways. "Our *own* house. *Our* own house. Our own *house*."

Zadie was as hopeless over these words as Topie was hopeful. "Topie, I wish you were my sister."

"What are you talkin' about? Go to sleep."

"Jessamyn might have a baby, and she'd be my sister, half-way, they say."

"I think she too old."

"No, I don't think so. She'll have a baby, and if it's a girl, she'll be my sister, and I don't want her for a sister. I want you for one."

"Maybe she'll have a boy and you won't have to worry about that." Zadie didn't respond, and Topie hoped that had silenced her friend.

"Wouldn't you want a sister, Topie?"

"Sure."

"Would you pick me for a sister?"

For some reason, this brought Topie fully awake. "What in the world?"

"Would you? If you had to pick a sister, would you pick me?"

"I don't know what I'd be doing with a white girl for a sister, silly."

"But if that didn't matter, would you pick me?" Topie was only nine, but she knew enough in her short life that Zadie's question angered her. She sat up in bed, but didn't know what words to use. "If it didn't matter that she was white and Topie was colored?" Only a silly little white girl with a rich daddy to protect her would say such a thing. Didn't she get to go to school? Didn't she have more clothes and toys than all the other colored children Topie knew combined?

Yet Zadie was her best friend, the girl she played with the most, the girl from whom she got her clothes as hand-me-downs, the girl she fussed with, the girl who taught her to read and do numbers. "I guess you make as good a sister as anybody, since I don't have another one to do me," Topie said. "So will you go to sleep now, and in your own bed?"

"In a minute," Zadie said. Topie could hear the smile in her voice. Soon Topie was back asleep. Even in the crowded bed, Zadie managed to drop off to sleep herself, and Lula found two intertwined bodies when she entered the room after the radio station went off the air. She covered them up tightly before changing into her nightclothes.

Sixteen months to the day that Jessamyn Pritchett became Mrs. Governor Cleeland, she gave birth, at 41, to Hennrietta Mavis Cleeland. Hennrietta weighed in a five pounds, the tiniest baby the doctor in Abundance had ever delivered who was otherwise healthy and hearty. Zadie and Topie had never seen a newborn, and Hennie fascinated them. Zadie had long since given up dolls, but here was a doll with infinite possibilities.

As Zadie peered down at her little sister, something opened in her mind and heart that she didn't recognize at first. In thirteen years now of living, she had never had to think of anyone else's needs or wants. Her needs were what everyone else served. She tried not to take advantage of it, but she did take it for granted. They had enough money not to have to worry about it. If she asked Daddy, he would send her off to one of those finishing schools like Uncle Lyons' daughters attended. Not that she wanted to. Abundance High School might be tiny and limited, but it was home and her educational spirit was not adventurous.

What opened was not love. She loved Daddy, Topie, and Lula. She felt that Hennie was going to depend on her and that was as it should be. Yes, that was it: what opened was responsibility.

Before she knew it, she had reason to use her newfound sense of responsibility. Having a baby did not sit well with Jessamyn. And since Jessamyn had no family within 500 miles of South Carolina, and since Daddy was useless when it came to anything having to do with babies or housework or childbirth, something had to be done. Jessamyn didn't seem to have enough milk to feed the always hungry and squawling Hennrietta. That was what Jessamyn called the baby, while the other women decided that was too formal a name for a mite like Hennie. Besides, the way her little mouth went for a nipple looked like a baby bird's.

Lula found a friend who was willing to suckle Hennie until the public health nurse could teach them how to make clean bottles full of sterilized milk to feed Hennie. Zadie and Topie learned how to burp and comfort and rock the baby while her mother lay in bed with her face to the wall, eating only thin soup. Jessamyn was losing weight and talking out of her head, and she could only sit for a half an hour holding Hennie while the infant slept. If Hennie cried, she pushed her onto Zadie or Topie or Lula and left the room.

"What is wrong with her, Lula?" Zadie questioned.

"She got the baby blues, real bad," Lula said. "I seen it before, and I don't want to tell you what happens when a momma don't have someone to watch after her and the baby. Miss Jessamyn is lucky; she's got the three of us to make sure she don't do something crazy to that little girl."

Jessamyn did not improve for four months. The doctor told daddy to send her to the state asylum in Columbia. Governor drove her there himself and stayed with her until her mind cleared and she came home when Hennie was six months old. If Hennie's mother was distraught and ill, Hennie thrived. She was still smaller than most babies her age, but she was happy and hungry, giggled when tickled and frowned when her diaper was full. Yes, she was a doll with infinite possibilities and a fierce temper when placed in her cradle by herself. With three substitute mommas, she expected to be held and bounced and caressed and rocked as long as she was awake to know about it.

By the time Hennie was walking, Jessamyn began to take an interest in her. Zadie hoped for all of their sakes that, at 43, her stepmother did whatever married ladies do to keep from having babies. Apparently she did, because Jessamyn's first daughter was her last. Jessamyn never seemed to feel any remorse over her stepdaughter's devoted care for Hennie. And Hennie didn't mind it. She followed her older sister around, cried when she left for school in the morning, wanted to sleep in Zadie's bed, and called Zadie "Mommy" even though she was corrected over and over. She adored Zadie and would have worshiped Topie as well, but Jessamyn managed to convince Hennie that Topie was paid to be Hennie's friend while Zadie loved her as a true sister. If Jessamyn had slapped Zadie across the face, she couldn't have hurt her more than to say that about Topie.

However, after a while it was clear that Hennie didn't call Zadie "Mommy" because she forgot or got confused. She did it willingly, knowing that "sister" did not mean the same as "Mother." Because Hennie was, if anything, determined. Determined to be a sweet, obedient girl if it struck her fancy that day; determined to counter the Governor and Jessamyn at any turn if it got into her head and suited her to do so. And it often suited her.

Chapter 6

Special to the *Turling County Messenger.*
Columbia, SC, February 10, 1998.

Representatives of the Kyung Motors Company of
Seoul, South Korea, announced today in a press
conference in the South Carolina capitol that a city in
the Upstate has been named as one of the finalists for
the site of a fifty-five-million-dollar plant to build its
subcompact vehicles, the Quiara.

Vice President of North American Operations
for the Korean automaker, Jeffrey Kim, made the
announcement at 2:15. Accompanying Mr. Kim on the
platform were Ben Smithers, the mayor of Abundance,
the county seat of Turling County; Mr. Jin Pak and Ms.
Ann Gi, special assistants to Mr. Kim; Leslie Callot,
state representative from the district in which Turling
county is located, and Fred Hatfield, state senator from
the same district. Mr. Smithers was joined later by
members of the local Chambers of Commerce.

In his announcement, Mr. Kim stated that
Turling County is one of three candidates for the plant
in the Southeast. Macon, Georgia, and Jackson,
Tennessee are the other two cities. Mr. Kim stated that
Kyung Motors is especially interested in Turling County
because of its proximity to Clemson University and
major highways. The company is in negotiation with
state and local authorities for tax incentives.

If chosen, residents of Abundance and the
surrounding municipalities will see plant construction
begin in Fall of 2000. The construction phase is
expected to hire 450 workers, and the plant itself will

employ at least 900 local workers when in full operation.

The Quiara debuted in 1992 and was the number four leading subcompact in the U.S. in the last two years. It has been produced solely in Korea up until now.

In a phone interview with the mayor of Jackson, Tennessee, Mayor Tom Jenkins stated that while he wishes the Upstate well in its pursuit of the Kyung Motors plant, he believes Jackson is better situated for the company's project. The mayor of Macon was not available for comment.

Turling County is home to 60,000 residents. The population of Abundance is 35,789 according the recent estimates based on projections since the 1990 census. Its employment rate has decreased in the past few years due to layoffs in the textile industry.

According to Mr. Kim, Kyung Motors' management will make its decision about the new plant's location by June of this year. Delegations from the board of directors will be touring the Upstate and meeting with officials in May.

Written by staff reporters of the Columbia Times-Herald.

Virginia folded the newspaper she was reading over morning coffee. This was what Mack had been hiding from her. This was what he couldn't tell her or anybody else when he said something big, really big, might be coming to Abundance. This was why he scheduled a trip to Columbia to be down there for the announcement, standing in the front of the crowd, she knew, with the Chamber. Why he was still down there, meeting with the state representatives and senators. And he had been right. If a car company was going to build a plant and employ 900 people and bring in many others from Korea or other parts of the country, that would push Abundance into the new millennium. It would mean other businesses that supplied the car plant would relocate, too.

Land prices would skyrocket, and since Mack sold real estate, so would his business. Some people would have to give up their homes or acreage to build the plant. The roads would be widened and repaved, even redirected. Public moneys would be reallocated to improve the schools, just like they should. The tax base would rise accordingly, so the schools should be better. She of all people knew what the public schools were up against in this state. She saw it for thirty years, and she was one of those supposedly hypocritical public school teachers who sent their children to private schools. Let people criticize teachers who did that, she told herself: we paid the price, double, and got what we paid for.

But a car plant! The possibilities were endless. And the timing couldn't be better. "The article says they are coming in May," she thought. "If there is any way the delegation could be here for the festival! Can that be arranged? Can Mack do it? Can the Chamber?"

From that moment, priority number one for the First Annual South Carolina Biscuit Festival was to get the Korean carmakers there and let them know what the people of Abundance and their neighbors were like.

Mack got home late the day after the press conference in Columbia. He was tired, but keyed up. Mack had been a successful businessman because he knew when to hold his cards close to his chest with rivals and clients and creditors and banks, but what was the point of a marriage if he wouldn't tell her what she needed to know? Now that the news was out, he let it spill. How long this had been in the works. The bargaining chips the state and the counties played, what they might have to sacrifice, how much land would go

77

for, how many outsiders would probably be coming in, and the potential revenue enhancement from the plant over the next ten years. Now she knew why he had been preoccupied for the last six months. He seemed to have every fact and figure in his head.

She praised him and talked about how proud of him she was, and as always her pride in him was attractive. Even though he was tired, their old desires came back, and she treated him like she did back on their honeymoon, as a bride unleashed from her inhibitions. Why people strayed, she didn't know. As far as she was concerned, Mack was still-- what did the kids say nowadays?--"hot." He had his hair and all but two of his teeth still. He took care to get physical activity and wasn't one to plop in front of the television for hours on end, even in ACC football season.

Mack's only girlfriend had been the business, and only because he wanted to enjoy the fruits of success his parents never did as mill workers and because he wanted her and the kids to live well. And Virginia appreciated it and tried not to let herself go either. She only weighed fifteen pounds more than she did on her wedding day in 1966. Not that she would get her face worked on—she was pretty sure Melody had, and even Leah admitted to getting a little help. The thought of a knife on her face made her shudder. No, she'd stay with what God and genes gave her, and if Hennie had been the world's worst mother, she had at least passed on the Grandma Jessie's dark eyes, good skin, and delicate hands. The Cleelands contributed more-than-average height and a strong nose.

There she was again. Why were Hennrietta Cullins and Jessamyn Pritchett intruding into her every day thoughts so much? Didn't she have enough on her mind? It probably was because of Zadie and Topie. The reality that those two women may not be around forever had struck her, almost violently, when she drove them back to St. Ambrose last Sunday night. She was so glad, for their sakes, she had brought them home, although they would have preferred to be back in what they called the home place.

Thank goodness it was dark and she could make an excuse not to drive them by that sprawling house she grew up in over on Clive Street. They would have seen, and been upset by, both its condition and the fact that it had been converted into apartments. It had been beautiful at one time, but now—she doubted the current owner had done everything necessary to make it livable, and was probably charging outrageous rents for the folks who lived there, folks who were one step away from homelessness. Selling it helped pay for Zadie and Topie's care, though.

Zadie was 87, and Topie 85, and even though Topie was losing the dementia battle, Zadie could go any minute as well. The women in the family, Jessamyn and Bonita, had died early, but one was from cancer and the other from the epidemic. Maybe Hennie died young, too. Virginia felt her blood pressure go up when she thought about Hennie. Oh, yes, Grandpa Cleeland lived to 75, a decent age back then. And Topie's momma died in a fire, so that didn't count. Maybe genes were on their side, maybe not. Either way, she had to be realistic and ready for the time her aunts would pass. They at least had been practical, and had their funerals paid for and planned, including the music and preferred minister. Zadie's would be a formal Episcopalian service of Christian burial. Topie's would be a rip-snorting celebration. How odd that two women so inseparable for eighty years would have such different religious tastes. How odd that two women of different races would have been such close friends in the segregated South. How odd . . .

No, it couldn't be.

At the second committee meeting for the festival planners, everyone had good news to report and successes to recount. Melody had been working the phones with agencies that represented food vendors and with all the decent restaurants in the county. In one week Audrey had conducted three conference calls with the marketing end of Double-Dutch, a brand greatly in need of whatever the South Carolina Biscuit Festival could do for it. Daryl Washburn found a computer program that could track expenses and negotiated with the city treasurer to set up a bank account for the festival and obtain credit for purchases.

Frank Templeton had found a domain name, designed a website, and worked out an infrastructure plan for the electrical and communication lines for downtown. And Ted Sneed was the most excited of all. He had reconnected with all his buddies in radio and television from Columbia to Rock Hill. He had already scheduled interviews, public service announcements, and billboard for I-85 and I-26.

In the last week, Virginia had convinced the owner of TownSquare Gallery to engage quality crafters and artists. The young man, Daniel Perkins, who wore his waist-length blond hair pulled back with a scarf, claimed he knew every potter, glass-blower, painter, sculptor, and ceramicist in the Upstate and then some. He might be given to exaggeration, but his membership in the South Carolina, Southern Appalachian, and Georgia artist associations convinced her.

The real struggle was going to be "talent" of the musical kind because of their getting a late start on festival planning. Virginia knew she could go totally local and low budget. Swing Band from the High School. Miss Genie's Toddling Tots from the town dance studio. The gospel choir from Mt. Pisgah Baptist church. These folks couldn't be excluded. Meemaws and papaws would come to the festival just to see little Blake or Madison in her tutu. But that wouldn't do for the night life. This festival had to get a reputation as more than the locals showing off for each other. Maybe not this year, but in the future, she wanted visitors from every state west of the Mississippi. Yes, real bands—which would have to be paid well—had to be engaged, and three months lead time was probably going to make for slim pickings.

And then there was the issue of what people liked. Oldies. Bluegrass. Real country honky tonk. Definitely not any rockers, heavens no. And they'd have to have Stamps Baxter on Sunday morning for the ecumenical service, ecumenical in this case meaning major Protestant denominations. And what else? She would have to engage Jenny Lucey for this one, and the other music teachers at the high school, what were their names? Also some of the better music ministers.

As pleased as she found herself with what the other five festival planners had done, Virginia could have reported that she had accomplished far more. She had secured tax-exempt status for all purchases and established the festival as a nonprofit organization. The city attorney helped with that. But she wanted more for the festival than freedom from taxes. She wanted the businesses, professional firms, and agencies in the area—and she was willing to consider the "area" as broadly as anyone was willing to go—to see the festival as the deserving and willing recipient of services, products, and donations of any kind. The festival, which had its own bank account and was on its way to being incorporated for protection, should not have to pay for very much; all the entities of the Upstate should see it as the vehicle that would bring, well, would bring Abundance back from its recession and back to its economic strength. "Yes!" she realized. "That's the slogan I've been looking for: 'Bringing Abundance Back.'" It had that double-meaning that good slogans were supposed to have.

If the festival was the vehicle, the businesses, law firms, medical practices, schools, civic groups, and public agencies should provide the gas to drive the vehicle. That was their job. As far as she was concerned, the festival would only make a profit in one of two ways. One was charging lots of hidden fees to vendors and crafters and requiring a hefty entrance fee. She didn't like that, and could make the argument against it. If people were asked to spend $15, or $20 to walk down the street of a town they could walk any day of the week, there wouldn't be much incentive in that. Just a token entrance fee, so that lots of people would crowd the town square. The other option, the one she liked better, was to spend not a dime more of that $50,000 from the city council than was absolutely necessary, eliminating expenses by getting as many donations as possible and volunteers for every service.

And how was that to come about? By pride. Abundance, the whole county, the little towns around it had to feel proud of their region. And she was smart enough to know that pride didn't have to come from being able to point to great accomplishments. It could come from lots of small achievements and from perceptions, right and wrong. From now on, the folks around Turling County had to be reminded of who they were, and what their parents and grandparents and great-grandparents had done.

She proposed to get the local papers—the *Turling County Messenger* and the *Abundance Advertisor*—not a real paper, and not much on editorial quality, as the misspelled title showed—to run a series of articles about the history and accomplishments of the town. Perhaps Ted could reference these in his interviews, and maybe one of the TV stations would make a documentary out of the articles, since she knew as well as anybody that folks around here didn't read much.

The good news was that most of the work was already done by the County Library. She knew because students had been required to work on history projects over the years, and they used the repository. Although she really didn't have much time, she could get the librarians to help her write the articles so that the right spin would be put on the information. It was something she couldn't leave to chance.

Of course, the car company news that hit the town two days before the committee meeting dominated the discussion. However, as exciting as the news was, its only direct impact on the festival was whether the powers-that-be could schedule the delegation's visit for the date of the festival, even if just for a few hours of it. Otherwise, the festival preparation would have to go on as planned. And, yes, if the delegation was coming during the four-day festival, Thursday through Sunday, there would have to be some sort of welcome program la-di-da about it, and she'd have to make sure the people there didn't make some horrible faux pas about communicating with Asians. Oh, my, that would ruin it all.

Chapter 7

February passed. March came in, rainy, insurance perhaps against a drought that summer. Virginia noted every day because every day involved a long list of phone calls to make, letters to answer, meetings to attend with this committee, that band, this civic group, that church women's group. She hadn't worked this hard since . . . well, she hadn't even worked this hard as a teacher, and she got paid for that. She was earning no salary for running the festival, and if it failed—a possibility she didn't want to contemplate—if it wasn't successful, she'd get fired from doing it next year. Or the city council would decide not to hold it again. Would that be so bad? Yes, it would, because Abundance might go backward. Not going forward meant going backward nowadays.

Abundance had always been, if not a sleepy town, a town happy to let outsiders make the investments in it and reap those benefits as long as the citizens of the town had jobs and decent livings. That was the problem. The people of Abundance—and she knew them, could call at least half the town by name if she had to—let themselves be acted upon rather than take the reins and control what happened to their town. They complained plenty, but drifted.

It was against Virginia's nature to drift. She knew what happened to women who let themselves live without purpose, without will. Maybe some women drifted by choice, maybe because they didn't see their options. Maybe that's what Hennie did, found her life being pulled away from her and made a choice that seemed her only one, even if it meant never seeing her little girl again. And from the stories Zadie told about Jessamyn, her stepmother, the grandmother Virginia had never met, Jessamyn sounded like a drifter. What a beautiful name, though. It was a name she could have given Bethany if Zadie hadn't dissuaded her. Jessamyn succumbed to post-partum, maybe worse. She could have kept her husband's store and made something of it, but she chose to marry Grandpa and rest for the remainder of her days, letting Zadie and Topie raise her daughter and hiding behind mental illness and baby blues. That's why Zadie said not to give Bethany her name.

Zadie and Topie didn't drift. They worked hard. They kept live chickens in the city limits until the public health laws forbad it and raised a garden and canned up until a year before they entered St. Ambrose. They devoted themselves to the town and Zadie made sure Grandpa's dwindled fortunes were doled out to the right charities as much as possible. She made sure one of the library's branches was named after him. No, they didn't go to college, they didn't have professional careers, and they didn't travel the world, but they didn't drift.

Drifting was the unpardonable sin. If Abundance drifted any more, its name—already humorous really, like Seventy-Six and Ball's Field, the one the kids all turned into something vulgar—would become a total joke. Hope lay around the corner. If Kyung Motors had an interest in Turling County, that meant other big companies might. But Abundance needed to create its own wealth, and a festival could help do that. It wouldn't solve everything, but it would be a catalyst.

Virginia believed this. She had to believe it.

Did anybody know how they figured Easter? Virginia had learned once, but sometimes got it backward. Was it the first Sunday after the first day of spring after the first full moon? No, it was the other way around. Didn't Passover have something to do with it? This year Easter was earlier than usual—the last Sunday in March. It was a good weekend to take a break from the festival, which had consumed her for two months, to bring Zadie and Topie home again, for the children to be in, and for a catered meal this time instead of giving Zadie and Topie full reign of the kitchen.

Bethany came home from Charlotte. She brought her latest boyfriend, Roger. She wanted them to share a room.

"Bethany, you know better. I'm disappointed in you. Your daddy would skin you both alive. He might not know what you do in Charlotte, but he'll want to keep you four years old in his mind. So, no. We have five bedrooms in this house, and two guestrooms. Roger can stay there."

"Oh, Momma."

"Oh, Momma, nothing. What does Roger do, anyway?"

"He's an accountant. He works at the bank."

"He doesn't look like an accountant."

"What do accountants look like?"

"Not so tanned. They don't have tattoos."

"Oh, for heavens' sake, Momma."

"Does he stay at your apartment?"

"Sometimes, or me at his. But we don't live together."

"Thank goodness for that. When women let a man move in with them, they get the short end of the stick. Have enough sense to realize that."

"You're so old fashioned. This is 1998."

"And men haven't changed. I didn't raise you to be one of these women who men take advantage of."

"He's not taking advantage of me."

"I didn't say he was."

Bethany, a self-confident, 5'9" brunette who benefited from orthodontics and private school, knew her mother, like Aunts Zadie and Topie, would prolong this argument until she was sure she had won it, so Bethany changed the subject. "When is Matthew getting in?"

They were sitting in the sunroom, with glasses of white wine. Bethany loved this room, and it had all of Momma's touches. Momma did know how to decorate—well, she knew how to hire good decorators and make the right choices from what they tried to sell her. Roger was off with a friend from college who lived in Abundance, and Bethany was glad that for now she didn't have to entertain him and pacify her mother at the same time.

"He said by 5:00 this evening. I really wanted us all to go to the Good Friday service at 7:00. Then we'll all go out to dinner."

"Couldn't we eat in? Have sandwiches or something? You could at least fix that."

Virginia ignored that remark. "Bethany, do you ever talk to Matthew?"

"Me? Are you kidding? He's Mr. College of Charleston. He wouldn't call me, even if he does have unlimited minutes on his cell phone."

Virginia was staring out the window at the daffodils and tulips that had flowered in the side yard.

"Why, doesn't he call you?" Bethany asked.

"No. I can sometimes reach him. But he never calls me or your daddy on his own."

"Humm."

"Humm, what?"

"Oh, I don't know." Bethany set down her wine. "I think . . . Momma, did you ever notice that Matthew, well, did you notice that you would buy some wine, and drink some of it, and put it in the fridge, and then a new bottle, totally fresh would appear?"

"No. Should I have?"

"Yes. I think Matthew has a drinking problem."

"What are you saying, Bethany? We don't have liquor in this house. Wine doesn't count. Nothing hard, and Daddy can't abide beer."

"I know, I know. This is the thing," she leaned forward. "On his birthday, back in January, I forgot about it. I forgot to send him a card, and it was really late—like 11:30 when I called. It was a Tuesday night."

"Yes, I know. I called him that morning. I wanted to see if he got the present I'd sent him."

"Well, Momma, at first I thought, when he answered, this can't be Matthew. It didn't sound like my little brother. Then I said, 'Matthew, wake up, what's wrong with you?' His talk was all slurred and goofy. He didn't know who I was at first."

Virginia looked intently at Bethany, her brow furrowed, waiting for the rest of the story. Bethany regretted wading into these waters, but it was too late now. Anyway, Momma had to know. She'd been so obsessed with this festival, and trying to get over the empty nest, that she still saw Matthew as the skinny little boy in his soccer uniform from Washington Academy. Now a tear was forming in the corner of each of Momma's eyes.

"So I said, 'Matthew, are you drunk?'" Bethany went on. "And he said, 'No I've just been celebrating my birthday with my buddies,' but I could barely understand him. I mean, it was a

Tuesday night, at the beginning of the semester, a school night. It blew me away."

"Why didn't you tell me this before?"

Bethany sighed. She could have taken this as an accusation, but she chose not to. It would be hard for Momma to hear this. She was such a perfectionist, and expected almost perfection from Daddy, Matthew, and her. Bethany had to take an antacid to calm her stomach before she brought Roger home. "I wanted to. I don't know. I mean, all boys get a little wild about the drinking when they go off to college. The girls can be just as bad. But, he was drop-down drunk, Momma. He could barely put a sentence together."

Virginia looked at her watch. "It's 5:05 now." Bethany knew this meant she was worried. Worried that Matthew would even drive home under the influence.

"It's a long trip, Momma, four or five hours, and he had to come through Columbia on a holiday weekend. You can't get worried about it now. Not yet."

Virginia now started to pace. Fortunately, they soon heard a car drive up, and she walked to the front of the house to see that it was Matthew in his Subaru SUV. Unlike his sister, Matthew had inherited blond curls from his daddy's people, stood 6'1", and walked like he had no fear of criticism or scolding from anyone. Some people would have called it entitlement, and Matthew would have been a prime candidate for it. He could charm any girl he chose to with that perfect smile of his. He hadn't needed braces. He hadn't needed contacts or glasses. He had needed tutoring and help with a slight learning disability, but everything else came easily to him.

Matthew strolled in through the front door. "Hey, I'm here. Let the party begin." He strode though the house, threw his car keys and the ball cap that pressed his curls down onto the shiny dining room table Virginia, anxious, met him there with a hug. "Hey, Mom," wrapping her in a hug. "Bethany here? Dad home?" He had no inkling that he had been the topic of conversation, but wouldn't have been surprised. "Where's BoJo?"

"Do I smell something on his breath?" Virginia thought. "Glad you're home, Mattie. Bethany is on the sun porch." Meanwhile, Matthew was greeted with the sound of little claws scratching against the kitchen floor. BoJo was running from her "apartment" in the kitchen. She barked when she saw Matthew and jumped into his arms when he bent over and summoned her with a "Here, girl."

Carrying BoJo into the sunroom, he greeted his sister. "Bethany, Miss Wall Street." He let the dog free and reached down to hug his big sister.

"Ha, ha. How you doing down there in Charleston?"

"Pretty good. When's supper?"

"You can get a snack now," his mother said. "We'll have a late supper after Good Friday service at First UMC."

"Church? Man, I didn't bring any church clothes. Just jeans and khakis. Wanted to see if I could get a tee time tomorrow."

"Matthew, it's Easter weekend. Of course we go to church on Easter weekend. What were you thinking?"

"I can go out and get something at the mall tomorrow."

"Khakis will have to do tonight. You can wear one of your daddy's shirts and ties."

"Man, I hate ties."

"What kind of job are you going to have where you don't

wear a tie?"

"Ok, you guys," Bethany interrupted. Momma's worry was
moving over into nagging, and she could nag, especially Matthew,
with the best of them. Of course, Bethany got her share, but
Matthew, well, Matthew just seemed to be on the receiving end of a
lot more, especially since high school. Bethany always wondered if it
was because Momma was so perfectionistic, or an only child, or had
grown up with old women instead of a house full of brothers.

"I'm going to be a recreational engineer. I'll build golf
courses," Matthew liked to get the last word in, too. "It must be a
family trait," Bethany mused.

Virginia stopped. "Honey, if you're hungry, there's a doggie
bag plate from Cracker Barrel last night. Your daddy and I went
there for dinner. It's chicken fingers and such."

"That'll do." Matthew jumped up, steadied himself a bit, and
entered the kitchen. Bethany couldn't help wondering if that was the
walk of a sober young man, and Virginia looked worried--again.

Matthew was in Abundance for the weekend, but you
couldn't really say he was home. He spent six hours at the golf
course on Saturday, went out with high school chums Saturday night,
and needed three separate pounds on the door to wake up for
church. "I'll get to the 11:00 service on my own," he said.

"No, you won't. We're all going together and that includes
Sunday School."

Virginia had to get Mack involved, and Mack had a different
approach to rearing a son. "Get your ass out of bed, boy," was all it
took. Not appropriate language for Easter morning, perhaps, but
effective. He appeared with slightly wet hair in the backseat of
Mack's Volvo at 9:20 for the ride to First United Methodist. He
dozed off during the service. Bethany and Roger sat politely, rigid;

Bethany looked at her fingernails quite a bit.

Virginia wasn't going to admit to a sinking feeling about her children's spiritual health, but that didn't mean it wasn't there. She had done everything right in the way of Christian upbringing. Sunday School. Vacation Bible School. Youth group. Camps in summer. More than she had been allowed to do and more than was available when she was growing up. Back then children quietly attended Sunday School and church and didn't question if the stories made sense or if the minister was really worthy of the respect he received. She did go to Topie's church sometimes and enter into the festive singing. As a teenager , Virginia thought Zadie's church was formal and beautiful and stultifying.

Mack's church was the Methodists, and she liked them. They weren't anti-women like the Baptists tended to be, and didn't run the aisles like some, and yet they actually talked about the Bible and acted like it meant something. She believed "bring up a child in the way he should go," and she'd tried to do that, to the letter, well, maybe not as strictly as some would, but definitely enough to make the expectations clear. Bethany and Matthew knew the standards; they were just making their own choices. She should bring this up for prayer with her woman's Bible class when she started going back after the festival was over.

St. Ambrose Community had its own special Easter service, and Zadie and Topie opted for that. Topie was getting harder to move anyway. Not because of her size; she couldn't weigh ninety pounds now. More because of her lethargy, and at times her stubbornness. She oscillated between long stretches of good moods, and shorter but stronger periods of not wanting to do what she was asked by the staff members and just sitting, almost catatonically, in her chair, like dead weight. This was the progression of dementia. When she was in a good mood, her sassy, delightful, sly remarks lit up the room. Then there were the other days . . . like this one. Topie did not join them for Easter dinner this year.

But Zadie wanted an outing, so she consented to be picked up alone and brought to her niece's home for a traditional, if not home cooked, Easter meal for Southerners. Ham, sweet potato casserole, Parker House rolls, green beans, slaw, and coconut cake. Zadie pronounced it all eatable but far inferior to Topie's cooking in her prime. Zadie never bragged on her own cooking; anyway, the two women cooked for so long in tandem that it was impossible to tell where one's skills started and the other's ended.

The day turned out warm, too warm for so early in the year, and as they sat in the sunroom drinking tea and enjoying the moist cake, they chatted. Zadie told a story or two the children had not heard, she interrogated Roger about his interest in Bethany, to Bethany's mock embarrassment, and Mack proudly recounted the business coup of getting Kyung Motors interested in Turling County. Mack went on a bit too long; Virginia could see Zadie's attention faltering and offered as soon as possible to take her back to St. Ambrose.

"Before you do, I want you to drive me by the home place."

"Oh, Aunt Zadie, are you sure about that?"

"It's not out of the way, girl."

"I know, but, well, it's been over two years now, and . . . "

"Are you telling me they tore my house down, those rednecks I sold it to?"

"No, it's still there."

"Then I want to see it."

"Ok."

Zadie was right; the mansion on Clive Street was not out of the way, and actually missing it would have taken them longer. Virginia turned off McKenzie and eased the Volvo into a parking space in front of the sad-looking house, now badly in need of paint and for the porch to be propped up.

"I'm sorry, Aunt Zadie. I didn't want to bring you by here."

"No, Virgie Mae, don't apologize. I expected worse. It's old, just like me. It's an old house, you know. Over 120 years old. Built in the 1870s."

"We should have had it put on the registry of historic places when we had a chance."

"Nothing historic ever happened there. Not even a famous person coming to visit. Governor was a private man, not like the rest of the Cleelands."

"It doesn't have to be a place where something historic or important happened to be on the registry, Aunt Zadie. Just old, I think."

"Maybe. Well, it's too late now. It doesn't belong to the Cleelands anymore."

"Mack and I should have bought it from you. Looking at it now, I could kick myself over that."

"Oh, Virgie, don't go on talking like that. It's a house. Houses aren't meant to be worshiped. People live in them. People aren't their houses. You'd be stuck with it and having to make it look nice, just one more expense."

"It's hard to hear you say that, Zadie. I thought you loved that house."

"I did, but . . . it doesn't matter now. Take me on back to St.

94

Ambrose. Topie is going to be upset if I'm not there when she wakes up from her nap."

Virginia spent some time with Topie, who didn't recognize her today. This was not working out to be a blessed Easter. Not as far as family and circumstances were concerned. Yes, the service was nice, and she liked Easter's message. New life, God's love, hope after Jesus' death. But the message wasn't so visible, not today.

She cut her time short at St. Ambrose so that she could get home before Matthew left. He was going to want to leave by 5:00 to be back in Charleston for classes the next morning—at least she hoped he'd be in classes the next morning. She needed to talk with him before he left. He had managed to avoid any more than five or ten minutes alone in her presence since he pulled into the driveway Friday evening.

"Matthew, honey, sit down with me."

"Sure, Mom."

He landed in the wicker loveseat in the sunroom, the one with the extra thick canvas cushions decorated with yellow roses. "Mom," he thought, "likes yellow." He could take it or leave it. He pulled off his ball cap, ran his fingers through his hair, and readjusted his cap. "What's up?"

"Oh, I don't know. How are your grades?"

"Uh, you saw my first report card. I kept a 2.0."

"Those are just C's."

"Yeah, college is tough."

"Honey, you went to one of the best private schools in the state. You should have been prepared for college."

He didn't look at his mother. He really didn't want to have this conversation, but they *were* paying the bills. Pretty hefty bills, too. "I'll do better."

"So what about this semester?"

"I'll pull it out."

She paused. "Honey, Bethany told me something that worried me. She said she called you one night and that you—she thought—you were drunk. On a school night."

"She did?" He adopted an evasive tone; was he getting ready to lie about something? "Oh, yeah, I remember, that was my birthday. My buds and I celebrated a bit too much that night. I promise, that's not normal."

"Really? You don't usually drink to the point of getting drunk?"

"Well, not on a night before class."

"Not on a night before class?"

"Not very often."

"Not very often?"

"You're repeating my words, Mom." He hated when she did that.

"I'm just worried, darling."

"Don't be, Mom. I'm not an alky. Promise."

"I didn't say you were an alcoholic, Matthew. But you have to watch out."

"I know, I know. It's ok, ok? Let's not fight before I leave."

"Matthew, I'm not fighting. I can't keep you from drinking, but you are underage. And you've got to swear to me, with all your heart, you wouldn't get in your car when you're drinking."

"No, I don't do that."

"Never?"

He looked at her. Full on, no eyes roaming around the room. "No, never. I mean it. I know what happened to Dad's brother and his family. I would kill myself before doing that." Mack's younger brother Tommy had been hit by a drunk driver in 1985, killing Tommy and sending his wife and son to the hospital for weeks. Matthew was only eight when it happened, and it scarred him.

She didn't like his hyperbole, but she satisfied herself that he thought seriously about his drinking habits. "It's just that, you seemed, a little out of it Friday night."

"Oh, I was just tired. I promise." Again, she wanted to trust him, but she had the faintest feeling that he had learned to lie very well, something she knew was a great skill for people with drinking problems.

"OK, honey. I believe you." She hoped she did. She detested being lied to, and yet sometimes she felt that for so much of her life, she had been.

Chapter 8

Virginia had driven herself so hard with the festival that she wasn't surprised when she developed a scratchy throat and headache a couple of days after Easter. She had to take a day off to spend in bed, no car trips, no phone calls, and no committee meetings. She watched an old Bette Davis movie she found on cable but slept most of the day with the help of several extra strength acetaminophen tablets. Mack was back in Columbia anyway.

On Wednesday she felt like a new woman, and decided to modulate her work pace before she ended up in the hospital. At Thursday's festival planning committee meeting, the news spelled progress. The festival preparations had met very few speed bumps. One of them involved the Double-Dutch flour company, which wanted the festival to pay royalties for use of their logo and name. Virginia learned how staunch a negotiator Audrey could be; Audrey got better offers from two other regional flour companies and Double-Dutch backed down. The other blip had to do with bands. The festival just plain got started too Friday or Saturday night.

Perhaps that would be a good thing, in the end. The festival would save money with a country band on Saturday whose reputation was limited to the Piedmont area, and Friday night might pull in the college crowd with a slate of three bands, one from Athens, Georgia, one from the University of South Carolina, and one from Clemson. On the other hand, it wasn't difficult to find bands willing to play during the day; these wannabes all but lined up to play for an hour. Early on, Virginia decided to own up to her limited musical tastes and lack of connections and depended on the planners and volunteers to develop a musical program for the four days of the festival.

Half-way through the meeting, a knock was heard at the door to their designated room in the Abundance City Hall-Conference Center. Virginia glanced at her watch. "Oh, that must be Daniel Perkins." She rose to answer the door. She admitted a slender young man with waist-length blond hair, wearing a hooded jacket over a T-shirt and worn jeans. Part of the name of a rock band no one else in the room recognized could be seen on the chest of the T-shirt.

"I'm here," he said, smiling, not the least uncomfortable.

"Daniel, this is the festival planning committee," Virginia said. She introduced everyone and there were tentative handshakes all around. "Have a seat. Daniel's here to talk about an idea he had for the festival. Oh, maybe I should tell you who he is. Daniel runs the TownSquare Gallery on Culver Street. We've been talking about an idea for the festival."

"Uh, yeah," the young man started. Despite being comfortable in the meeting, he seemed to take an impromptu approach to public speaking. "I think the festival should have some sort of competition for local artists. They could submit completed two- and three-dimensional art, and it could be shown around town in businesses the two weeks before the festival. That would get more people involved, seeing the art around town, and free showing space for the artists."

Virginia looked around at Melody, Audrey, Ted, Daryl, and Frank. Their faces looked a little blank, neither approving or disapproving. Daniel decided to keep talking.

"Um, well, and like, every artist would pay $10.00 to submit a piece, and it would go through a jury before being accepted for display, and then there would, uh, of course, be a big prize at the end."

"How much of a big prize?" asked Daryl.

"At least $1000 for each category. That's pretty standard."

"Depends on how many categories," interjected Frank.

Daniel looked at Virginia, confused. "How many different

kinds of art will be in the competition?"

"Oh, uh, watercolor, oils, pottery, and sculpture. For this year. Next year we can do more."

The room was silent. "A thousand dollars times four seems like a lot. We wouldn't break even on that, unless you had, uh, 400 entries," Virginia spoke slowly, diplomatically.

"Ah, no, I don't think we'd have that many."

"What about insurance? What if somebody's painting or artwork got stolen or damaged?"

"Well," Daniel thought for a minute, "we wouldn't be putting them out in the street. They would be in businesses and public buildings that get locked up at night with security systems. The businesses have insurance, too. I guess it could happen, but . . . that's a risk somebody takes when they show anywhere, really."

The members continued to be silent for ten, then fifteen seconds. Virginia had thought the idea of supporting the local arts would go over well, but she could see the committee was debt-phobic about everything related to the festival. At the same time, Virginia knew that the festival committee already felt as overwhelmed as she did, so she began to understand their hesitation about adding another venue as large as a major art competition to the festival.

"Daniel, what if we just focused on one type of art, like painting, any medium, this year?" She felt a relaxation of tension in the room.

"Sure, maybe that would be best."

"I really like the idea, Virginia," Audrey started, "but do we have time right now? To get the entries and have the art put up?"

"Oh, that's not a problem," Daniel jumped in. "We use the

Internet and email to inform everyone in the Georgia, South Carolina, and North Carolina artist groups, and the artists who show at TownSquare are willing to help with installations around town. They see this as a good thing for them, get their name and work out there. Ten dollars is low for a submission fee."

Daryl finally spoke. "Virginia, I got to admit, I don't know a thing about art and art shows and art competitions. If the rest of the committee thinks this will be a good thing, a draw, and help the community, I can't argue with it. I'm just concerned about overdoing."

"I understand that, Daryl. I know we have a lot going on. But if Daniel and his associates are behind this, I think we should try it. One thing we discussed early on is that not one segment of the community would feel that the festival was excluding them, if we could help it. We didn't want it all about sports, or hot rods, or food, or music." *And I think giving space to quality visual arts would contribute a little class,* Virginia thought, but kept that part to herself.

"Then I say, let's let them move forward," said Ted, "but . . . maybe the artists could sign a waiver about damage to their artwork, that kind of thing?"

Daniel still looked a bit confused, but he nodded. "Sure. I have that for my gallery. The next big step is to get local businesses and public spaces to show the paintings."

"Oh, we can help with that," offered Melody. "We can put an announcement in the paper asking for volunteers."

"Uh, great," said Daniel.

"So, we're in agreement to allow Daniel and TownSquare Gallery sponsor the art competition under the name of the festival, and that entries can be hung in local businesses and places like the town hall and library?"

The other five members nodded, Daniel smiled and nodded. "Great. See you guys. I'll report back to you when I start getting entries and offers from the businesses." Daniel left the room, as comfortably as he entered. The breaths that seemed to be held were released, and the remainder of tension left the room. *Why were they so nervous about Daniel?* Virginia thought. *Maybe they are just getting antsy at this long meeting. It does seem to be going on a while. So much to do. They are probably thinking, what did we get ourselves in for? Oh, well, too late to turn back now.*

Virginia decided to be satisfied that the meeting was moving on successfully until an item came up that threatened to send her back to bed with a headache.

Maddie Flynn occupied the number ten place on the agenda. Maddie Flynn owned Pageant Babies, a local business that ran beauty pageants for children—and Virginia gasped when she heard this— starting at six months old. Maddie had first called Melody, who asked for the item to be put on the agenda: a request, and expectation, that a child's beauty pageant be part of the festival.

"Absolutely not," Virginia said. "Let's move on to the next item."

"Wait a minute, Virgie," Melody broke in, dropping back to the name Virginia preferred not be used outside of her family and closest friends. "I made a promise to Maddie that we'd look at her proposal." Melody started distributing single sheets stapled to the brochure for Maddie's business.

"All right." Virginia put her pen down, leaned back in her chair and folded her arms across her chest to signal clearly her disdain for what was coming.

"What she wants us to do," Melody began, not exactly enthusiastically but trying to fulfill her commitment. "She wants an hour and a half on Saturday on one of the main stages for a competition for the whole Upstate. She knows she can't get more than that—well, I told her that was the most she could possibly expect—so it won't be a full pageant, no talent, no bathing suit, just the little girls in evening costumes." Melody consulted the handout. "There will be four age groups, 3-4, 5-6, 7-9, and 10-12 year olds. She estimates between fifty and seventy little—uh, contestants. The hour and a half time slot will include the judging and awarding of trophies."

Melody finished. Since Virginia had already expressed her opinion, physically and verbally, the other four members of the committee averted their eyes and let someone else go on. No one did.

Finally, Virginia sat up and stiffened her spine. "Like I said, I don't think that's a request we can honor, Melody."

"O.K., but you're going to have to give her a reason."

"Why?" Audrey asked.

"Because, she's the only one we've—that we will have turned down."

Frank decided to jump in. "We turned down that tattoo parlor that wanted to have a booth."

"We didn't turn them down, not really," countered Melody.

"No, but they didn't want to pay for a vendor's booth. They wanted a free space because they said they were artists, not vendors." Frank seemed to have a photographic memory for conversations. "Then they tried to say they were a nonprofit, because we are letting nonprofits have a free booth if they provide volunteers."

"Yeah, that's right." Ted, as usual, was finding humor in the situation. "I remember them. They said they just wanted to advertise, not do tattoos at the festival, so that would make them nonprofit. Then they said they would design a special tattoo for the biscuit festival, for a discount price!" This got the other two men to chuckling, and Frank took off his glasses to wipe his eyes, obviously tired already from the haggling.

"Exactly," Virginia said. "No, we're not going to have a bunch of little girls cavorting on a public stage in inappropriate clothing and slutty hair and makeup. Period. We don't want that kind of reputation. Didn't the news coverage of that little girl's murder out West tell us that kind of thing attracts perverts? No, Melody. Tell her that . . . that . . . Help me out, here, Audrey."

"Me? I don't like the idea, but I can't think of a reason, not off the top of my head."

"Have we really been that picky before now?" Ted asked.

"He's right," Melody argued. "I don't like those pageants either, but they're popular and it will bring a lot of interest to the festival. We're letting the Dancing Tots have an hour, and I can't see a lot of difference between them. We don't know that being onstage for a beauty pageant at the first ever biscuit festival is going to wreak psychological damage on these little girls for the rest of their lives."

Virginia made a noise of disgust, almost a snort, and rolled her eyes.

"Now, Virginia, we don't," Melody had obviously figured out in the last few minutes that "Virgie" was reserved for her aunts and husband. "And, really, Virginia, weren't you in the Miss South Carolina pageant when you were in college?"

"That is beside the point, Melody." Virginia could feel her face warming and reddening. This was not the time to bring up 1964 and Clemson sorority silliness. "If for no other reason, I was twenty-one, not three, and no pesky stage momma was teasing my hair and putting trashy makeup on me." She paused to get her voice back to normal. "Tell her we already have enough acts for the stages."

Darryl, always the factual accountant, had to speak. "But we don't. We have some free time on . . ." He was looking at the schedule. "Saturday morning. Yes, an hour and a half on one of the side street stages."

"We'll find something else to go in there. I vote no. If you all want to vote against me—"

The rest of the committee was willing to argue, but not to present a divided front to the community. An uncomfortable silence settled in the room.

Audrey finally spoke. "I have to go with my gut. No. I would never want a child to do that. It's creepy."

The men, who had no emotional connection or revulsion about what silly mothers did with their little girls, found themselves nodding nonetheless. Melody gave in. "All right, but Maddie isn't going to like it."

"Just tell her we couldn't see how it fit into the mission of the festival," Virginia said. "Now, let's go on.

During the rest of the meeting, the tension returned to the faces around her at the table, but Virginia didn't regret being adamant. She did feel a little selfish about getting what she wanted and denying another's request, though. And that Melody, bringing up the past like that. At least Melody was working her head off for the festival. Virginia knew she was, even if she sometimes seemed to undermine what Virginia was trying to accomplish.

Yes, back in college Virginia had succumbed to vanity and let the other girls in the sorority talk her into running for Miss Clemson, a stepping stone to the Miss South Carolina pageant. Mack was thrilled. Well, his ego was at first, until he realized how much time it took from their dating and that the other guys got to ogle her in a white bathing suit. Zadie scoffed at her, but later admitted that she always expected the granddaughter of Jessamyn and the daughter of Hennie, both delicately beautiful women, to be "feted" for her looks. Zadie actually used that old-timey word. Daddy bragged on her.

Virginia came in third place, thankfully. No more of that nonsense. Now the episode was a humorous footnote to family history. One time Matthew showed an old photo album to a friend, who saw the picture of Virginia as a contestant and said, "Wow, your mom was pretty. But what's up with that hair?" At the time Virginia was in the next room and about spit out her iced tea in laughter.

The Thursday planning meeting adjourned with everyone grateful it was over and Melody promising to put a good face on whatever it was she would tell Maddie Flynn.

Chapter 9

After the weekend Virginia realized she had not kept up with her commitment to create a series of articles for the local papers on the history of the town. With only six weeks to festival weekend, she had to get started. Both of the local newspapers begged for content, so getting the space was not a problem, and both had given discount rates for festival advertising. These articles would be a form of marketing. She planned to spend Monday at the library and to begin her research.

She drove to the library Monday morning and arrived by 9:00. For the first four days of the week, through the illness and through the contentious meeting, she had tried to push out of her mind the image of a stumbling Matthew, a Matthew who might forget his promise not to drive under the influence, a Matthew whom she always thought was less susceptible to peer pressure than what she was seeing. Maybe she should call him on a Monday or Tuesday night at 11:30. Maybe she should talk to Mack about it. Mack might be busy with Kyung Motors, but he was supposed to help with the children, too. He and Matthew had been best buds until Matthew was sixteen. By the age of sixteen Mack himself was working after school and weekends to help his parents, and Matthew at nineteen had never earned a paycheck. In the past three years Mack and Matthew had less and less reason to play golf together, or fish, or even talk. Mack reprimanded Matthew vicariously through Virginia until she told Mack to do his own scolding.

Had she given her children too much? Yes, of course she had. Did they have a sense of entitlement? Probably, except they knew that after the educational years were over, Momma and Daddy's flow of cash would dry up. She and Mack earned what they had. Even if the Cleelands had been the town patrons forty or fifty years ago, she was a Cullins, too, people who drove trucks, grew peaches and corn, and worked in cotton mills.

She had learned that lots of money could slip through fingers when people took it for granted, when they . . . drifted. Bethany understood that without being told. Surely Matthew understood it and just wanted to take advantage of the free ride for as long as possible. If she had given her children too much, so be it. She wouldn't have changed anything in that regard, but she would have watched Matthew a little more closely.

She entered the library and asked to speak to the special collections librarian, Libby Walters. Libby was also the reference librarian and ran the children's programs. The Abundance branch of the Turling County Library only employed two other staff members: the head librarian and a part-time cataloger. Libby did not fit the stereotype of a librarian. She looked more like a girl's basketball coach. Big-boned, 5'10", long, sweeping, honey-colored hair pulled back with a Scrunchi, and energetic. She had to be energetic to juggle all those jobs.

"Hey, Libby," she greeted. The library was quiet with only a few people using the computers in the back.

"Hey, Ms. Foster. What can I do for you today?"

"Mind if I have the key to the archive room? I need to do some town history research for the festival."

"No problem." Libby reached into a drawer. "Here it is. Do you know how to use the microfilm machine?"

"Oh, yes. Back when I was in college, that was all we had, if that. We actually had to read books back then for research."

Libby smiled. "Do you and Mr. Foster have a computer yet at home?"

"No, Mack has one at work. If I need to use it, I go there. But I'm getting the hang of it."

"The library is asking for funds to put the archive on CDs. Microfilm is really out-of-date."

"I hope that works out for you all."

Virginia said she'd be in the archive room for most of the morning. She didn't want to have to come back and could print anything she really needed. The archive room was to the left, not much larger than a public bathroom, with a cabinet of microfilm, a reader, and a shelf of books local historians had written about the town and county and surrounding area. Some books of genealogy were also there, done by retirees in the Upstate who had the time to dig through birth certificates and parish baptismal records and to travel to cemeteries.

No one in the Cleelands that she knew of had ever bothered to trace the roots to England or Scotland or Wales or Ireland. Researching family roots was not her style; she knew who her family was, and as a child had scoured all the old albums and Bibles with birthdates to create a picture that satisfied her. Otherwise, all the stories she needed came down through Zadie. That Macarthur Cleeland came over from Scotland in the 1750s, at a time when the English were treating the Scots badly. Other branches of the family—the Lloyds, the Hanovers, the Bennetts, and maybe a Hugenot or two down in Charleston, melted into the pot, but the Cleelands always had enough sons to keep the name prominent. On the other side, the Cullins were descended from Irish who came during the potato famine, settled in South Georgia, and then moved to a somewhat cooler climate a few decades later.

Virginia settled down and started looking through the microfilm. She was mostly interested in back copies of the newspapers. The *Turling County Messenger* had been in operation for thirty years. Prior to that the paper of note was the *Abundance Gazette*, and before that the *Abundance Mills Gazette*. It went back to 1911, the year that the town changed its name and the year that Aunt

Zadie was born.

She loaded the microfilm machine and started with June 1, 1911. Aunt Zadie's birthday was in September, so maybe she would find a birth announcement. Virginia was mostly looking for information about the town, its government, and its accomplishments, not crime reports, sports news (precious little of that in 1911), or ads. However the advertisements for women's undergarments, farm tools, and cooking items caught her attention. How much had changed in eighty-seven years, the span of her aunt's life.

Virginia found news about the flour company being built and beginning operation, a report on the altering of the town's name, and a story about the first automobile being seen in Turling County (a feat since there were no decent roads). An article about a traveling theatrical team; an editorial about whether the dry conditions would turn into a drought and letters to the editor advocating that the weather was God's punishment for the presence of road houses down by Lake Wonder. A week after Zadie's birthdate she found a birth announcement about the first child being born to Governor and Bonita Cleeland, a healthy girl named Zadiah Louise. She printed several of these articles, including the birth announcement to show Zadie. She noted some photographs she might choose to use, and kept looking.

Microfilm is hard to read! she thought. But she plugged on. After forty-five minutes she took a break, rubbed her eyes, and went to the bathroom. She had progressed to 1920. In that time she read about the devastating flu epidemic, the list of names who died in it, finding Bonita's. Poor Zadie. She knew what it was like to lose a mother, one way or another. And yet she was such a good one herself, in her own manner. Zadie wasn't the most doting or affectionate mother figure, but she was a consistent, present, persistent one.

She decided to try to get from 1920 to 1930, take another

break, and then start in again. The 1920s brought stories of new businesses coming into town and of raids on taverns that tried to go underground during Prohibition. She found the wedding announcement for Governor and Jessamyn and a birth announcement for Hennie. After years of stories of a booming economy in Abundance and Turling County, with cotton mills to join the flour producer, the 1920s ended with reports of bank failures and photos of soup lines. No unemployment insurance back then. Small farmers like the Cullinses had it especially rough when food prices plummeted, but at least they knew how to grow their own food.

She had not come into the archive room this morning expecting to have an emotional reaction, only to get the information she needed. But all these old news reports were starting to have an effect on her. They instilled gratitude and sorrow and curiosity. It was also hard not to home in on stories involving the Cleelands. After her second break, she came back in ready to sift through the Great Depression and World War II.

The news about this period almost made her stop. Even the newspaper communicated hopelessness through those early days of the '30s. A little upsurge of optimism came with the inauguration of Roosevelt, since at that time a Republican would have been as hard to find in the Upstate as a polar bear. After 1934, projected public works were the highlight of every issue. Instead of photographs of gaunt men in shabby, oversized clothes standing in breadlines, she saw photos of energetic men with shovels and other gear working on roads and water lines.

By the early 1940s, she saw what she expected—lots of news about Europe and Japan, and of course the bold, shocking headline about Pearl Harbor on the edition right after December 7, 1941. Then reports of men heading out to army bases, of draft lines, and of what the wives and mothers and daughters who stayed home were doing.

She looked at the wedding announcements, wondering if she would see a photo of her mother. She knew they married in early spring of 1942, right before Daddy shipped out to England for three years. No photo on the society page, but since all marriages had to be reported, there was a short notice that Hennrietta Mavis Cleeland of Abundance had married Leonard Ray Cullins of Union, South Carolina, at the home of Pastor Calvin Jones of First Methodist on May 12, 1942.

Back then many couples did this. They found a minister, tied the knot, enjoyed a short honeymoon and then separated for as long as it would take. Hennie must have gotten pregnant right off, Virginia thought. At least she wasn't pregnant when she married. Virginia was born February 20, 1943, ten months after the wedding. She found her own birth announcement.

"Well, enough of this walk down memory lane, Virgie. Get back to town history and let's get out of here before next Tuesday," she berated herself. She read of the toll the war took on local families; of boys and men who died; of plans for monuments to honor them. She saw other bold headlines about D-Day in 1944, and Victory in Europe, and then the atomic bombs being dropped. She skimmed several articles about Missy Franklin's daddy. She noticed as the years passed that the photographs were clearer, the newsprint more modern and readable, and the prose less passionate and purple.

She took a break again. Maybe she needed to call it a day; her eyes were hurting, she wanted a cup of coffee, and she had enough material to get started. Then again, she didn't want to have to come back here. She locked the room and walked up to Libby, sitting at the circulation desk reading a novel. How *did* librarians decide what to read? she wondered quickly. "Libby, I'm going to go get some lunch across the street. I may come back in a bit. Depends on how my head feels."

"Ok, I'll be here if you need me. Did you find what you were looking for?"

"Oh, and more. It's overwhelming. If you don't see me again today, I'll be back in a day or two."

"Okie doke," Libby said in her everything's-all-right-with-me manner. She might look like a girl's P.E. teacher, but she was probably too accepting and calm for such a job.

Virginia walked across the street to a little restaurant that wanted to be an authentic tea room but only qualified as a lunch room. She didn't want tea anyway; she wanted a couple of cups of heavy-duty coffee to help her wake up. It was odd to eat by herself in a restaurant, and it was only 11:30 on a Monday morning, so the restaurant was almost empty. After a chicken salad sandwich and some fruit and yogurt, she paid her bill and went back to the library.

"I decided to come back. Too many meetings next week about the festival. Today is the only day I have to devote to this research, and I'm only half way through." This was probably more information than Libby the librarian needed.

Libby took this in, smiled passively, and handed her the key. "Good luck!"

In a few minutes Virginia was reading about the aftermath of World War II in Turling County. She found a posed photo of returning G.I.s and saw her daddy standing in the back, looking solemn. No pictures of sailors grabbing and kissing girls on the street in the *Abundance Gazette*. She discovered that the cotton mills were being re-fitted to produce fabric for civilian clothes, since they had been devoted to uniforms and tents and other military uses for three or four years.

She knew she was coming up to the time when Hennie disappeared. Would anything in the papers mention Hennie, say that the sheriff was investigating whether something criminal happened to her? Surely there would be a short piece if the daughter of a prominent, if eccentric, citizen had vanished.

Reminding herself that she was there to research the history of the town, she loaded the microfilm roll for 1947. The town seemed to be booming again. Abundance Mills was expanding. Their new slogan was, "This is the flour that makes you feel rich," presumably because it was ultrasifted and could make very light biscuits and cakes. *Cute marketing idea*, she thought. There was a report about the large, "modern" high school being built, and that the coloreds would be moving into the old one. *Typical. It's a wonder there wasn't more civil rights unrest than there was in this country, considering how the blacks were treated for so long*, she mused.

She rolled the film to the week of April 27. At that time the paper was printed twice a week, on Sundays and Wednesdays. On page three of section A she saw something that stopped her breathing.

Sheriff's deputies and firemen were called out to the area near the intersection of U.S. Route 29 and State Route 7 in the early morning of April 26 to put out a raging car fire on the side of the road. The car was seen skidding off the side of the road and hitting a large oak before starting to burn. The body was not extricated from the burned wreckage, but enough was left for the sheriff's department to conclude that the 1940 Ford was registered to Mr. Leonard Cullins of a Rural Route address near Abundance.

Daddy's car! Burned to the ground after a wreck. Who was driving?

She knew, of course. Who else would it have been?

Why? Why had they not told her? A mother dying in a car wreck was not a secret to keep from a child. No, they hadn't kept a secret. They had lied. All these years, Daddy, now living without a care in Florida, and Zadie, and Topie, had lied. Why in the world would they do that? How could they think that a child growing up believing her mother had abandoned her was somehow better than knowing the mother had died accidentally?

She sat there stunned. When she came to that thought—how they had thought telling her, for fifty years, that Hennie had disappeared was kinder than that Hennie died. Unless, Hennie's death was not an accident. Something shameful and frightening and horrible must have been the reason for the crash.

This was too much. She started to pace. Not only did her eyes hurt, but her head was pounding and her back stiff and sore from sitting in a straight-backed chair for so long. *I came in here to write innocuous articles, fluffy upbeat pieces for the local paper about the high points of history in the town, and I find one the answer to one personal mystery and another one opens up.*

She wanted to jump in the car and drive straight to Jacksonville Beach and find Daddy, now eighty-three years old but still in fine health and still just as lackadaisical as ever about her and Mack and the children. She wanted to look him square in the eye and not leave until she got a straight answer about why he acted like a man whose miserable excuse for a wife left him when he was actually a widower, or maybe worse. Her own father was the most responsible for this lie perpetrated for fifty-one years.

But she couldn't let Zadie off the hook. She'd get in Daddy's face soon enough, but Zadie was over on the other side of town. Zadie had lied about her own sister. And Topie. Well, Topie was a servant, really, in their home back then, with no family loyalties and no reason to be held accountable for what crazy white people did. It pained her to think of Topie that way, since Topie had been so good and kind and really thought of Virginia as a replacement for the four children she lost as babies, poor thing. No, this was a Zadie matter, and Topie was in no condition to deal with it anyway.

She sat back down. She wanted to see if anything else appeared in the papers. She looked at the obituaries in that biweekly issue. Nothing was listed for Hennie. She went to the next issue. Nothing there. How odd. She moved back through the film to the issue before, thinking that perhaps the police had not finished the paperwork in time for the April 27 edition. No obituary for her mother. She rolled through a month's worth microfilmed pages. No other reports, no other mention of Hennie Cleeland, or of the fiery wreckage.

What did that mean? Was she wrong, and someone else was in Daddy's car? A drinking buddy who had too many and lost control? Could someone have stolen the car, which was described as a 1940 Ford? And there were no mentions of the sheriff looking into Hennie's whereabouts. Nor were there any stories about a woman's body being found.

How could this be? Either Hennie wasn't in the car, or Governor Cleeland, who would have had the clout and the money, paid someone off. Yes, it was very possible. Grandpa, of whom she had cloudy memories because he died when she was ten, and because he had been such a recluse anyway, would have had no qualms about paying the newspaper, the sheriff, the funeral parlor, whomever he needed to, as much money as it took to shut them all up if he had a reason to. That would explain why his assets decreased so much after the War. It wasn't investments that floundered, but his paying off the town. That might have taken thousands to ensure their silence.

But why? Just family pride? His own vanity? So that his own daughter's memory would not be violated? To protect his only granddaughter? All of the above, or none of the above, or something else?

She became conscious again of her pounding head. Thank goodness she carried pills. She left the archive room for a sip of water to help the two tablets get down. She didn't have time right now, with the festival less than six weeks away, to unscramble this mystery and find out why or how her mother died and why or how she was just now finding out.

An idea struck her. Even if they kept an obituary out of the paper, even if her mother was buried without public recognition, somewhere her mother *was* buried. Nobody in 1947 South Carolina would commit the blasphemous act of not burying a body, and no one in the area had probably ever heard of cremation and urns back then. Somewhere there would be a record of her mother's grave. And if Governor Cleeland had the money and influence to cover up her mother's death, she and Mack had the clout to get the burial records, and maybe find Hennie Cullins' grave.

Chapter 10

November 1929

Zadie graduated from Turling County High School in 1929. Daddy sat on the second row and presented her with a dozen roses as soon as she walked across the platform, received her diploma scroll, and descended the steps. She would receive another dozen roses in a month when she debuted, one of ten young ladies in Abundance from families with enough money and past to consider themselves worthy of producing daughters of debutante status.

Of course, debuting was silly and old-fashioned, and being presented did not silence the question of what she could do with her life. It was 1929! So much was changing. Women could vote and movies could talk now. Not that she'd seen a talkie yet, but she'd heard about them. Girls didn't have to get married and stay home now. They could have careers in offices and live by themselves in big cities like Atlanta. That's why it was important to get out of Abundance, even if Daddy wasn't crazy about the idea. Surely she would get out from under Jessamyn, and then her stepmomma would start acting like a momma to nine-year-old Hennie, who was still, as always, a beautiful child but rotten and mean. Hennie didn't even look bad when she lost her baby teeth, and they came in so straight and fine. Not like Zadie's.

Most of the girls she graduated from high school with, and three of the girls debuting, were already engaged. Eighteen or nineteen and already getting married. Why do that? There was time enough to get tied down to a man and babies. She'd had enough of mommahood already, raising Hennie. Her first choice was to move to Atlanta and find a job as a secretary--she knew typing and shorthand and bookkeeping as well as she knew *Macbeth* and quadratic equations. Maybe at night she'd go to a business college and take some more courses in accounting. Debutantes weren't supposed to work in offices, but she didn't care. Atlanta was the biggest city in the South, bustling and energetic and filled with people who probably never heard of a town named Abundance.

She could go to college, but most girls who went to college did so to be schoolteachers, and she wanted none of that. If she wanted to shed herself of motherhood to her ill-tempered little sister, why would she want to put herself in charge of thirty other little brats? Or girls went to college to find a husband, which seemed silly. No, sirree. Atlanta and an office, maybe an insurance company, yes, that sounded good; that was for her.

But all that *could* wait. Summer would be full of parties, and even if the boys didn't slobber over her because she was six inches taller than most girls, she had lots of friends. There would be swimming parties and picnics and dances and probably some wedding showers. She could move to Atlanta in the fall; it would be cooler then anyway. Right now she was young, she was out of school, and she wanted to have fun.

Summer passed. Then September. She'd been to three showers and one wedding. She'd dated Bill Parton, whose main qualifications were that he was over six feet tall and was taking a year off from the University in Columbia since his daddy had a heart attack and needed help with his peach orchard business. Then October. She began subscribing to the *Atlanta Journal* to scour, well, to peruse, the classifieds for the kind of job she would be good at, or that would be good for her.

Toward the end of October she sent a letter to the 20th Century Insurance Company, which advertised for a typist and stenographer to start on December 1. Also toward the end of October she started hearing people in town talk about a crash of the stock market in New York. She didn't know how a market could crash, and why a market crashing in New York mattered down here.

During the second week of November she received a letter in

reply to her application. An employer was interested! A Miss Phoebe Smith asked if she could come to Atlanta on November 20 to interview for the position. Zadie felt as if her heart would come out of her chest. An interview. In Atlanta. For a real job, with a real paycheck.

"Topie," she ran into the kitchen. "I'm going to Atlanta!" Topie was a junior now at the colored high school. She walked here every afternoon to help her momma with dinner, and then they walked home together. Zadie normally could hear them laughing as they worked in the kitchen, laughing as they left through the back door, crossed the yard to the alley and headed toward the east side of town, over the railroad tracks. Topie and Lula laughed a lot. But today they didn't. The kitchen was dead quiet except for the hiss of water starting to boil in the stockpot.

"What for?" Topie looked up from some potatoes she was peeling.

"To interview for a job." Zadie said, sinking into the chair opposite Topie.

"If you want a job, why don't you find one here?"

"Why should I stick around here? I want to live in Atlanta."

"Whoa, girl. That's a thousand miles away," said Lula, standing at the sink, plucking a chicken.

"No, it's not, Lula. It's maybe 100 miles or so. You can get there by train in less than three hours."

"*You* can get there in three hours. I ain't going anywhere."

"Oh, Lula."

"Your daddy know about this?" Lula turned her whole body around from the sink and looked at Zadie, her eyebrow cocked.

"He will soon. I'm on my way to tell him."

"Yes, Miss Zadie." Zadie recognized that tone in Lula's voice, the one that said, "You may think you know something, but you don't."

Zadie swung through the kitchen door, through the dining room and upstairs to the largest bedroom, the one that served as Daddy's study. Jessamyn had her own bedroom, where she stayed most of the day. Jessamyn liked to embroider, more than anything else, and embroidery didn't require her to come out of the bedroom at the end of the hall, the one farthest from Daddy's room. Zadie was old enough to know what that meant. She had known what it meant for many years.

She knocked on the door and heard Governor say, "Who is it?" Not come in, or enter, but a demand to know who was knocking on the door. Who could it be but one of five women who occupied the house, and why would it matter which one?

"It's Zadie."

"Wait a minute." She heard his chair move and then footsteps. He opened the door. "Well, Zadiah, I was just thinking about you. Come in. I need to talk with you."

It seemed like several years since Zadie had entered Governor's room. How long it had been, she couldn't really remember. It smelled of tobacco and old leather; Daddy needed to open a window even if it was November. The room was disheveled, just like Daddy himself now. He used to be so dapper, in white linen or seersucker suits if he went out in the summer and gray flannel in the fall and winter. He used to keep his hair cut neat, be clean shaven always (at least after beards went out of style before the Great War), and wear a scent. Now he and the room looked tired. Daddy liked to read, thick volumes about the history of the South and the history of Rome and Greece, mostly. Books were everywhere, piled, open, thrown on chairs. How could he read so much? How could he stay up here so much? Because except for this room, the home place on Clive Street was a woman's haven. But now he rarely left the haven, either.

"Sit down," he said. It was an offhand command, not a suggestion or invitation. She had to move a pile of volumes to do so. The one on top was entitled *A History of the Confederacy*.

"Zadie, do you know what's going on in the world?"

"Excuse me, Daddy? What do you mean?"

"All this talk about the stock market crash."

"I've heard tell of it. But I don't know what the stock market is, or how it would crash into something."

"It didn't crash into something. It fell down fast and crashed."

This did not explain anything, so she waited for him to continue. "That means that people who invested in the stock market started selling off their stocks and bonds and investments and no one was buying, so the prices dropped."

"Yes, sir." This did make a little sense. A little.

"We Cleelands had a lot of money tied up in stocks and bonds on the New York stock exchange. Or we did."

"Oh."

"So you see what this means."

She didn't, but she nodded anyway. "Are we broke? Are we poor?"

122

"You don't need to worry about the money, darlin'. We still have lots of land down here. But it's fixin' to be hard on everybody, sooner or later."

"That's all right. I've got a plan for that. I'm moving to Atlanta to get a job. I have an interview with the 20th Century Insurance Company real soon."

"You say you're doing what?"

"I've got a job interview on November 20, in Atlanta. You won't have to support me."

"What are you sayin' about, Zadie? A Cleeland woman can't get a job and work. That's for low-class women, and colored women. You came out. Your job is to get married and set up a home."

"Daddy, I don't want to. Right now nobody in town is knocking my door down to marry me, and getting married doesn't interest me all that much, anyway."

"That doesn't matter, now. You owe your family, first. And there's something else, the real matter I wanted to talk about."

She wanted to say, *You've said enough, Daddy, and you can't make me stay here in Abundance and pretend to be a debutante when you know I look like you and not momma, who was pretty, and I'm plain and big. This is 1929 and women aren't slaves anymore and you can't treat us like coloreds, and from what I hear the colored folks up north don't live like they do down here either. I would think you would want me to move out. It would be one less woman, one less mouth to feed, and maybe you could be proud of me for making my own way.*

But she didn't say all that. After a few moments' silence, she spoke with no emotion, "What is that, Daddy?"

"It's your stepmother. The doctor says she's real sick. He says there's a mass in her, her, female parts." Words for female body parts would never pass the lips of Governor Cleeland. Zadie didn't know if this meant her womb or her breasts. She would find out later. "The doctor says it's cancerous. I'm not sure what that means, except that she will probably die and it will be very painful for her."

Jessamyn had cancer. Jessamyn was fifty now. She had gone through the change two years ago, doing nothing but complain about the being hot part of it. She complained all the time anyway, so at least that didn't take any getting used to. But now Daddy was saying that she was dying.

In ten minutes Zadie had gone from a young woman with possibilities and prospects, who was going to conquer the business world in Atlanta, to a nursemaid for a stepmother, to being sentenced to permanent motherhood of Hennie. On top of that, she finally was privy to the family financial situation, something Daddy thought women's brains were too small to understand, and the news was only bad. Her heart now felt flat and empty, like a popped balloon.

"Daddy," she heard herself saying words she didn't know she had the courage to say. "I don't think this is fair. Lula is here. Lula can take care of Jessamyn. That's her job."

For the first time that Zadie could remember, Daddy looked truly angry, as if he could strike her. He had only spanked her once, and it was for sassing Jessamyn early on in their marriage. "No, Jessamyn is family. It's your job to take care of family. Lula can't be expected to do that."

"Why not? She's a servant. She's your employee."

"Is that how you think of Lula? The woman who raised you, the momma of the girl you played with all your life? You think of her like just another colored woman to be bossed around?"

Why was he saying this? She felt tears coming up. Were they tears of shame for disrespecting Lula, or tears of anger at Daddy for smashing her plans? And why was he defending Lula? He treated Lula better than he treated her sometimes, better, maybe, than he treated his own wife. He certainly treated her better than most white people treated their colored servants. Good heavens, he'd bought her a house when Jessamyn moved in. He paid her more, she knew, than any other colored person in town. Everybody knew that.

"No, Daddy, I care about Lula and Topie. I love them. And I'm sorry for Jessamyn. But I have plans for a life of my own. Why must being a Cleeland mean being stuck in Abundance?"

"Maybe someday you can be the modern career woman. Now, you have to think of family. Your stepmother is going to need care, and with the stock market crash, I can't afford a nurse. And then there's Hennie."

Yes, and then there's Hennie, she thought. If the doctor was right about Jessamyn, Hennie would be in the same place Zadie was in 1918. How could history repeat itself this way?

"Hennie is a *pill*," Zadie said.

"You sound like a child, Zadiah."

"She needs a spanking. Lots of them. She sasses everybody, she steals. She's kicked Topie, me, and Lula in the last week for not getting her way. Jessamyn doesn't correct her when she does pay attention to her. You don't either—"

"That's enough mouth from you, girl," Daddy said.

He sounds like a hillbilly when he talks to me like that, Zadie thought. She was no longer confused about her emotions. She was just plain mad and might as well act like it.

"Jessamyn doesn't do anything. She pawned Hennie off on

Lula and Topie and me. So I get blamed for her being a little brat. Is that what it means to be a Cleeland, Daddy? Or is it just what it means to be a woman in the Cleeland family? If it does, I don't want to be a Cleeland."

She slammed the door behind her on her way out. She knew that, ultimately, her speech would not make any difference. She would stay here until Jessamyn died of the mass or the cancer or whatever it was in the part of her body Daddy was too much of a man to say. She would then stay and raise Hennie until she was out of school, if the little monster would stay in school and graduate from Turling County High. Maybe some man in Abundance would think well enough of Zadie to want to marry her when Hennie got older. And Daddy would never say "thank you" for any of it, would always see it as what a Cleeland woman was both entitled and obligated to do, to serve the family.

Jessamyn died in the summer of 1931. It was a long death. The doctor sent a nurse in to teach Topie and Lula and Zadie how to extract the morphine out of the bottle and inject it into Jessamyn's arm. Hennie was kept out of her mother's room until the last few days. As Zadie watched her stepmother die, she stopped feeling resentful of the woman who had intruded into their house and birthed a child whom she took every opportunity to ignore, and who now was writhing and gritting her teeth and calling out and cursing God in her pain.

Hennie came in and stood by her mother's bed on the last day. Zadie wondered if it was cruel to let Hennie see the skeletal figure with empty, staring eyes. Hennie would have to see her in the casket, too. Zadie never saw her own mother dying or dead.

"Momma," Hennie whispered.

"Speak up a little more, baby," Lula told her.

"Momma, I'm here," Hennie said at her normal volume.

Jessamyn's eyes responded by searching the room. "Hennie?"

"Yes, Momma."

"Hold her hand, honey," Zadie suggested.

Hennie looked like she would rebel with a resounding no, as she often did, but instead reached down and picked up Jessamyn's hand. It wasn't much bigger than Hennie's own, all bone and skin, white, dry. Hennie didn't drop it immediately after feeling its lifelessness, and Zadie was pleased to see that Hennie lifted the hand to her cheek. "Momma. I miss you, Momma."

Zadie felt the tears coming. Up to this point Jessamyn's care had consumed her so much that she hadn't thought about grief. Seeing Hennie display truly sweet emotion revealed something new. Maybe Hennie was more than a brat. Maybe she was capable of more. What would happen to Hennie when Jessamyn was gone? Would Daddy think about sending her to a boarding school? No. He wouldn't want to spend the money; maybe the money wasn't even there. Hennie would stay here, raised by Zadie, tolerated by Lula, ignored by Daddy.

Chapter 11

When Zadie was twenty-five, a new gentleman showed up at St. Michael's Episcopal. Eddie McCann had been sent to Abundance from Raleigh as a supervisor for the WPA. Zadie didn't know she believed in love at first sight until that morning in 1935. Eddie fit every requirement for what she wanted in a husband, and at her age, she had had plenty of time to consider that subject. She introduced herself after the worship service, smiled with lots of teeth, and dropped a hint that he should come to dinner sometime.

Eddie took the bait. Soon he was coming over to the home place three nights a week, sitting with her on the porch. They took in a movie once a week. Having a male friend after six years of what seemed like seclusion made her feel like a teenager. Eddie could tell a funny story. He had gone to college for a while, before the Crash. He had two sisters. His curly brown hair fit her fingers just fine when she wanted to caress his pretty head. He brought home a good salary and attended church. What more could you ask for in a husband?

Eddie and Zadie married in 1936 in a respectably formal but small ceremony at St. Michael's. Daddy gave her away, entering the church for the first time since Hennie's baptism. He wore an old-fashioned suit stiffly and didn't say anything when the priest asked, "Who gives this woman?" Governor just let go of her hand and motioned his head in the direction of Eddie. Hennie, only fifteen, stood with her. She wanted to have Topie as a bridesmaid, but the priest politely insisted that was impossible. Anyway, Topie had already gotten married herself, and for the first time in their lives they found themselves separated and not visiting on a regular basis. Eddie and Zadie found a house to rent over on Franklin Street, four blocks from Daddy, who now had only Hennie and Lula to ignore on a daily basis. Eddie had to travel sometimes for his job, going up to Gaffney or down to Landrum to check on crews that were working on sewer and water lines.

Zadie loved being married. She loved having her own house. She loved lying in bed with her husband. She loved doing his laundry. Men were so interesting. They weren't nasty like some women said. They were strong and hard-bodied and even when moody didn't fuss, just retreated. They made you feel like you were beautiful even when you knew you weren't, because they wanted your body. Well, all this was true of Eddie. Apparently it wasn't true of other men, but she didn't have to live with other men, just Eddie now.

After a year, Eddie asked when they could have a baby. He was thirty, a few years older than she, and he wanted a "passel of kids," he said. She assured him she did, too, and she wasn't doing anything to prevent it. At least, not that she knew of. Another year passed. Every month when the blood appeared and the cramps started, her heart dropped just a little further. In 1941 they had been married five years and had no babies yet. She asked the doctor; he had no answers. Some women were just slow to have babies. "Don't fret," he said. "And love on your husband every chance you get." That wasn't a problem. Loving on Eddie was the easiest thing in the world.

Topie took up with Lawrence Jackson in 1934. Lawrence was a janitor at the colored public school. The Negro students all attended school in the same building, even though there were almost as many of them as white students in the district. Lawrence was an indisputably good-looking man. No self-respecting white woman would say that, but there was no arguing about it. Even if he was a janitor, when he wasn't wearing his work overalls, he cut a fine figure, as they said, walking straight and proud, never hunched, with an assured smile and straight, white, even teeth, an attribute anyone would be thankful for. His clothes hung comfortably on him, never tight or oversized, and one had to wonder how he afforded such fine things on a janitor's salary. His looks weren't lost on women. Topie certainly noticed them. She ignored the talk about him and Fanny Parker, and Dorothy Washington, and Bessie Fickley.

Lawrence had many reasons to like Topie. Topie had a job working in a cotton mill now. It was harder work but much better money than waiting on white people, if you could put up with meanness of some whites who didn't want you making the kind of money they did. Sometimes she got spit at. Most days she got dirty looks and someone managed to call her a name in her hearing, and it wasn't always about her being colored but something much worse. But Mr. Roosevelt was standing up for the coloreds up there in Washington; at least here was a president acting like colored folks actually lived in this country for once.

Lawrence not only liked Topie for her good paycheck. She had her own house, free and clear, that that old crazy white man in the big house, the one with the wild little girl, gave her and her momma. No rent. And it was just right. Indoor water and two bedrooms. And momma didn't have to live there anymore, since the old white man's wife died and Lula went back there to live and take care of him and that hell-raiser of a girl all the time. Hennie, that's what they called her. *Shoot,* he told himself. *They should have named her Rooster.*

Lawrence also liked that Topie was a good looking woman, with green eyes of all things, and unlike Dorothy, and Fanny, and Bessie, didn't weigh more than he did. Those other girls had some meat on them, but that meant they'd have a lot of fat in a few years. Topie knew how to dress, too. And best of all, she worked swing shifts at the cotton mill, and if she was gone of a night, she wouldn't know if he was down at the bar with Bessie or Fanny. It would be easier to keep her in the dark about his other women. Topie didn't hang with the tavern crowd. She got up and went to church whenever she could.

Lula didn't think much of Lawrence. She'd heard things. But that didn't stop Topie from buying herself a lacy white dress and telling her friends to meet her and Lawrence at the church on a Saturday morning in March of 1935. Lawrence moved in to the little cottage that afternoon and they didn't leave until Monday morning when they both needed to be at work. Zadie didn't come to the wedding, even though Topie asked her to. Zadie felt a piece of her was missing now that Topie was married, and she didn't know what to think of Lawrence. She hadn't had many dealings with colored men, except for the ones who came around and did the yard work.

Topie figured having babies was a natural part of being married and living with a husband, so when she came up pregnant in 1936, she told her Momma and said, "Let Zadie know." Eight months later she welcomed Anthony Bryce Jackson. Lula and Granny Samson, the old colored midwife, helped her, and Zadie came the next day with some layette for the cocoa-colored little one with curly hair. "Where did you get that name, girl?" Her mama asked. "Bryce?"

"I saw it on a map one time in school. It's out west somewhere. I'm going to name my children names of far off places so they won't be stuck in Abundance."

"Lord, girl. That's the craziest thing I ever heard of."

"Crazy? You named me Utopia. What kind of a name is that?"

"It means good place. Greek or Latin or something."

"Now where in the world did you learn a name like Utopia? You don't know no Greek or Latin, Momma."

"Never you mind. I heard it one day, and I liked the way it

sounded. Like Eugenia. YOU-TOE-PEE-UH. I asked the Governor what it means. And Felecia means happy. So, girl, your name means good and happy place, and that's what I see when I see you, baby."

Topie smiled at her momma, and then back at the baby. She was in a good, happy place right now herself. Topie liked knowing that about her name, and often remembered it. But soon she learned there would be times when having a name like that didn't mean anything.

Topie took to mommahood of her own baby boy a whole lot more than she ever did to Hennie Cleeland. She sang every song she ever heard to Anthony; she showed him off every chance she could to everybody she could. Lawrence acted like a big man to be a daddy now. "It's about time for him," Lula said. "He needs to settle down."

Lula had to take care of Anthony when Topie worked in the mill. It wore Topie down to work all those hours and have milk to feed Anthony. He seemed to take everything out of her, and never have enough. After two months, Topie grew worried. He didn't seem to be getting any bigger. She took him on the train to see the doctor for coloreds in Davis County, and he weighed Anthony. He was only nine pounds. He'd stopped growing. "Give him canned milk to supplement your own milk," the doctor said. She had to buy nipples and bottles and make sure everything was boiled clean. Doing that took more work, and ate up more of her paycheck. It didn't matter, anyway. He didn't seem to be gaining weight even with the extra milk. She took Anthony back to the doctor. "He isn't thriving," the doctor said. Topie was too embarrassed to ask what that meant.

One day after ten hours on her feet at the mill, she dragged herself into the kitchen of the Cleeland home place to pick Anthony up from Lula. Lula kept him in a cradle in the kitchen so she could be near him most of the day.

"Mr. Anthony Bryce Jackson," Topie called as she approached the cradle. "Mr. Anthony, your momma's here." She picked Anthony up. He was limp. "Momma, Momma, come here!"

Lula had been in the pantry to retrieve some jars of squash for dinner. She hurried when she heard the frenzy in her daughter's voice. "You home, Topie? My, you looking tired—what's wrong?"

"Anthony—Anthony, baby, wake up." Lula dropped the jars and rushed to catch the baby before Topie crumpled to the floor.

Topie took her baby's death hard. Of course she would. She stopped going to work. She lost her job at the mill. She lay in bed. She slept for days. Anthony's embalmed little body stayed at the Matthewson-Petty Funeral Home for a week before Lula and Lawrence and Zadie could convince her to come to a funeral. "Why have a funeral for someone who didn't have a life?" she screamed. But she did go to the quiet service so that her baby could be laid to rest.

Months later, Topie finally laughed in Zadie and Lula's presence about some shenanigan of Hennie's when she was little. That was a good sign. Within a year she was pregnant again. But she woke up in her third month and vomited and grasped her stomach and passed out on the floor. She knew she'd lost the baby. In 1940, it happened again. Then right before the president came on the radio and said the whole country was all going to fight the Japanese, she went through labor for a baby, another little boy, who lived four hours.

Topie wasn't a woman to make decisions. She was a woman who endured what was thrown at her, but losing four babies was enough. So was hearing around town that Bessie Fickley now had a little girl three years old who was looking more and more like

Lawrence's people every day. In 1942 Lawrence came home with that jaunty walk of his one evening from his job at the colored school and found his fine clothes and polished shoes on the dirt road outside their yard. She wanted no more of lazy men and of babies that either didn't come to birth or were taken away from her.

So throughout the late 1930s and up until the war began, Zadie and Topie saw each other mainly when they happened to both be visiting Lula at the same time. Zadie regretted, just a tad, that she had left Lula to contend with her strong-willed little sister, but Zadie also felt that fifteen years of raising Hennie was enough of a service rendered to her Daddy and the memory of her doll-like, distant, aloof stepmother. And as much as Zadie wanted her own babies, she shuddered to think of what was happening to sweet Topie's little ones. Was it worse to never be expecting, or to have the good news of a baby coming and then lose it? Losing a baby had to be worse, and poor Topie had lost two babies she birthed. Zadie didn't have the capacity for that much consolation for her friend. She feared for Topie's mind sometimes, but every time Topie managed to survive and move on.

Hennie graduated from high school in 1940, near the top of her class. Being wild as a monkey didn't stop her from being smart at school, thank goodness. And even if she did like to slip out her window at night and drive off with boys down to a beer joint, or out to the Lake, her strong will also kept her from letting a boy in her pants if she wasn't ready. As far as Zadie could tell, she wasn't ready, because she hadn't come up pregnant. That was the only fate Zadie could see for a girl as loose with her acquaintances as Hennie was.

Hennie took up with Buddy Cullins a year after she graduated from high school. It was 1941. All anybody talked about was the shrimpy little German who pretended to run the world. Germany was nothing; it wasn't even much bigger than South Carolina and Georgia put together, or at least it didn't look like it on the maps.

The United States could squash him like the little bug he was in a couple of weeks, but maybe they wouldn't have to.

Daddy pretended not to notice that Hennie was dating a boy from Union who picked her up by beeping the horn of his 1940 Ford. He also didn't notice that Hennie and Buddy's dating was an on-and-off affair and that they fought furiously whether they were going out together or not.

Hennie loved to make Buddy jealous. She would make sure he saw her at the downtown soda counter with one of what she called the "debutante boys." Hennie refused to "come out into society," herself, but she didn't mind flirting with the boys whose families had money. It wasn't hard. She was beautiful, movie star beautiful. People told her she looked like Vivien Leigh. She did, somewhat—her nose was bigger, but she had the same green eyes and thick, curly dark hair parted in the middle and a smile that could mean half a dozen different things. Being told you looked like Vivien Leigh to a girl in the South after 1939 was the quickest way to ensure a big head and a lot of sass.

Then came December 7. Everything changed that day, above and below the surface. Everyone in Turling County was either going to leave, be left, never come back, or have to make sacrifices for the war effort. There was no turning back. Americans didn't get bombed and turn the other cheek. Japs would be dead because of it; so would Germans. Of course, Americans would be dead, too, but that was what happened when a country went to war.

Hennie played Buddy along for two years, driving him wild. Buddy drove a truck long distance and heard all kinds of stories about who Hennie was seen with when he was on the road. But if you could ever get Hennie to tell you the truth, she would admit that she was as wild for Buddy as he was for her; she just liked to make him crazy with jealousy. One morning early in 1942, Lula noticed Hennie hadn't slept in her bed and started wondering if Buddy had finally convinced her he was thoroughly crazy enough for them to get married. The couple showed up three days later, married by a preacher down in Union. But it wasn't just because they took a notion to marry that night. Buddy was going to be drafted and shipped out in less than a month. Lots of young people were running to justices of the peace and judges and preachers at all hours to get married before the fellows left.

Lawrence Jackson didn't have to get drafted. The army wasn't interested in coloreds right then, and any way, Lawrence couldn't read and had bad feet. Topie didn't care one way or the other. She was done forever with that peckerwood. Let Bessie Fickley worry over him. Topie didn't need a man. What good were they? She had her momma, she had her women friends at church, she had Zadie, and even if she didn't want to admit it, she had that hell-raising Hennie. The pleasure of being with a man, especially one as good at loving as Lawrence Jackson, was not worth the pain they brought. Men broke your heart whatever age they were, even if they were blood kin to you, even if you birthed them or they birthed you.

But for Eddie and Zadie McCann, it was a different matter. Eddie had been working for Mr. Roosevelt since 1933. He believed he was the greatest president, the greatest leader in the country's history, except maybe Washington. As a Southerner, he wasn't quite sure about Lincoln, but he would give old Abraham the benefit of the doubt as maybe fourth or fifth best president. If Mr. Roosevelt needed every single American male to fight Hitler and Hirohito, Eddie would be the first to sign up. He was too old to be drafted, at thirty-six, but no matter about that. And no matter that Zadie pleaded with him to stay home, to keep building public works in the county. "All the money has to go to fight the Nazis and Japs and Italians, Zadie. There won't be any public works projects around here for a while. What good would public works be if we can't defend our country?" Eddie sometimes sounded like a newsreel or an ad for war bonds. She never knew he would be so patriotic.

The four women—Lula, Zadie, Topie, and Hennie—found themselves living without their husbands and forced to depend on each other, despite their differences. In 1942 Hennie found herself pregnant, more or less abandoned by a drafted husband, and forced to choose between living with Lula and Daddy or her half-sister Zadie. She chose Zadie. Zadie was glad for the company.

Pregnancy slowed Hennie down considerably. While Hennie sat around, growing more and more miserable and distended and swollen with baby, Zadie poured herself into the war effort for Eddie's sake and maybe a little for the country. The sisters, eleven years apart, so different in age and temperament and looks, had one thing in common. They lived for letters from their husbands. Eddie and Buddy were both stationed in England, but on separate bases. Buddy drove a truck. Eddie, who wanted to be in combat, convinced the army to let him be a gunner. He had connections, having worked for Mr. Roosevelt for so long, he said. Zadie knew he meant this as one of his jokes, but it wasn't funny. She would rather he be driving a truck like Buddy somewhere in the countryside of England rather than up in a plane, vulnerable but happy and ready to aim at anything with a swastika on it.

Hennie cried out one night in February and Zadie called in Topie, Lula, and eventually the doctor for help. It was not an easy labor. Hennie wore herself out with screaming and cursing, not just Buddy but everybody--Jessamyn, the doctor, Topie, Governor, Lula, Zadie, the baby. Certainly she wasn't hurting any more than most women. She even called Lula and Topie ugly names, as if she had the right to do that. Zadie knew it would be a long time before Lula and Topie forgave Hennie for that show of disrespect, and an eternity before they forgot it. When the squalling little dark-haired girl came out, red but a good chubby size, Hennie screamed one more time and fell fast asleep.

Since Zadie and Topie and Lula had been at Hennie's birth,

they feared the worst—that she would react like her momma did and reject the baby. But once Hennie woke up from her long and deserved nap, she demanded to see her baby and pronounced her name Virginia Mae Cullins, a good, reasonable name. She pulled down her nightgown and let the baby suckle. The three older women breathed a sigh of relief and started in on praising the infant, who probably had had a worse time of the birthing than her mother.

A fifth female added to their circle. Zadie nodded in the chair by Hennie's bed, waking up off and on to watch the baby nurse. She was a noisy eater for such a little thing. Would she be a Cullins, or a Cleeland? The world would treat Virginia better if she took after the Cullinses. They didn't have money, but they worked hard and had big families and probably didn't have strains of, well, eccentricity, yes, that would be the nice word for what a lot of people might call craziness. And Zadie was quite sure Buddy Cullins would be the kind of daddy who perched his pretty little girl—Virginia was bound to be pretty—on his shoulder and showed her off to the town, a little girl made to know she was loved by the most important man in her life. Buddy would never hide himself in a musty library reading books about dead Southern dreams.

The letter came in summer of 1943, when Virginia was four months old. Zadie only had to see the official U.S. government return address to run into her room, slamming her door. She didn't come out until the next day. Eddie was gone. His plane was shot down over France. His body would not be coming home; there was precious little left of the aircraft, much less the pilot and crew. Eventually she would console herself that he died doing what he wanted to do, trying to kill German "goons" as he wrote in his letters, although she wasn't sure what a goon was. Eventually she would tell herself that. For now, she found other war widows and let her grief separate herself from the other women in her family.

Buddy was still alive, safe in northern England, driving a truck and writing Hennie how much he missed her, how much he wanted to hold Virgie Mae, and how boring the service was. Topie, now legally free of that good-for-nothing charmer Lawrence, went back to work at a different cotton mill. Lula rose every day to take care of Governor, now sixty-five and coughing too much. Hennie took to motherhood responsibly, if not enthusiastically. She stayed with Zadie for the duration of the war. Zadie watched the four females whose lives orbited around her. These women, as close as they were, wouldn't understand that she could never love another man again, that no other man could measure up to Eddie McCann, and anyway, she would never let one try.

Chapter 12

April, 1998

Virginia wished now that she had delegated the whole article-writing mess to someone else. She was up to her neck in the festival, and now she knew things she never expected to learn. Yet she really knew nothing. Only, really, that a car registered to her father wrecked and killed someone in it.

She didn't have time for this mystery. She didn't have time to write the articles either. She gave Tom Scanlan a call. He was the editor of the *Turling County Messenger*. She explained her plight in terms of time management, not family secrets.

Tom, too laid back to be a newspaper man, had an easy answer. "Listen, I've got a couple of interns from Methodist College, journalism majors, working for me this semester. They spend most of their time interviewing ball coaches and going out for coffee. Why don't I put them on it? One of these kids—students—grew up here in Abundance, knows your son I think. I'll get them on this."

"Great." What a relief. "I'll come by later this afternoon to give you what I got from my research. They can visit the library for the period after, uh, the end of World War II."

Virginia breathed a "thank you" to God that one more burden was lifted right now. Who knew what crisis concerning the festival might arise? She had to be available to solve it, not hiding away trying to write when all the history of the town just made her wonder more about her father's burned, wrecked Ford. On her way to the newspaper to drop off the research, she'd stop by the courthouse and find out about burial records.

By 4:00 she had handed over the printed microfilm articles, her notes, and some directions on how she thought the stories about the town history should go. She'd have to be satisfied with what the interns produced. Time was limited. By 4:30 she had been allowed into a back room at the county courthouse. She looked through a big three-ring binder full of copies of death certificates, and another one showing the plats of the cemeteries in the county.

Even if Governor had bought the silence of everyone in Abundance, he didn't have enough money to keep the state of South Carolina from issuing a death certificate in 1947.

She found it. It was dated April 26, 1947. Cause of death: automobile accident. Place of burial: Piney Grove Baptist Cemetery. She thought for a minute. Yes, Piney Grove was that little brick church out north of town, almost into Walkerberg County. It was on the historical registry now, having been built in 1840. Its cemetery had the graves of some of the county's oldest residents. A small congregation still worshipped there.

Why a Baptist church? Buddy's people weren't Baptists; they went to the Presbyterian Church, the ones who did. None of the Cleelands were Baptists, either. *Well, Virginia, that's the point. Bury the secret where no one would expect to find it.*

She checked her watch. Mack would not be home until late. He'd driven to Columbia, some business with the legislature on real estate taxes. She wouldn't rest until she saw her mother's grave. Maybe she could wait until after the festival to get the truth out of Zadie and Topie and Daddy, if she could, but she'd waited fifty-one years to see proof that maybe her mother loved her after all and hadn't just disappeared without looking back.

The daylight savings time change had passed last week, so it wouldn't be dark until 7:00. *Is it daylight savings time now, or did it just end?* She wondered. *Does anybody know? It's one of those things we just take for granted. The news people come on and say, "Don't forget to turn your clocks up an hour," and we just do it, not knowing. How much of life is like that? Well, I should know. I have been taking the most important thing in my life for granted for years.*

>   *If I had hired a private detective like Mack and I talked about, would I have saved myself these years of grief? I had no reason to distrust Zadie and Daddy. People aren't supposed to lie to their children once they grow up. What else have they lied about?*

She was getting a headache again. She realized she was hungry, but she needed every minute of daylight and kept driving the country roads until she found Piney Grove Baptist. It certainly was picturesque. It sat 200 feet off the two-lane road, and a rise of land behind it served as the cemetery. No one was buried there anymore; the plots had been depleted. The church, in the old Baptist style with a few steps up to the white double doors, was made of rusty brick. There was no stained glass, and the building couldn't have been more than 3,000 square feet. Her husband was in real estate; she could compute square footage very quickly. Bradford Pears on the property were almost through their blooming season and cherry trees were starting to flower.

She drove up the paved driveway and parked the SUV beside what was probably the office extension. The parking lot was empty since it was after hours. She hoped there wasn't a motion detector that would trigger an alarm in the sheriff's office or something. The church would rightly be wary of vandalism, being so far out of the way. She stepped down from the elevated vehicle seat and surveyed the area behind the church.

The plat book indicated Hennie's grave was in the back, on the east side. She wondered if this was the area for indigents or outsiders or nonmembers. Governor, whom she was having a hard time not thinking of as anything but a snake, probably donated a hefty amount for the quiet, out-of-the-way plot. She started walking. Normally she would have looked at the dates on the graves to try to find the oldest one. Today, no. She just wanted to find one from 1947.

She hiked to the area at the top of the rise. A chain link fence separated the church's land from a pasture vacant of cows. She walked along the fence, counting the plots. She came to one that had a small headstone bearing the words, "Our dear girl, Hennrietta. 1923 -1947." No last name. No month or day of the month.

She knelt on the slight mound. Her khaki slacks would be stained by the fresh spring grass. No matter. At least here, the grave was well cared for. She wanted to weep, but was so overwhelmed that tears wouldn't even come.

Her mother's grave. Her mother was dead. For over fifty years her mother's body had lain not twenty miles from Abundance. Had Zadie, or Governor, ever come to place flowers on it? Had Daddy? Surely they couldn't have been that heartless.

Maybe she loved me after all. She was fifty-five years old and trying to convince herself that her mother loved her. *Maybe Hennie just couldn't drive. Maybe it was raining that night. But why was she out at 2:00 a.m.? And did cars just burst into flames back then when they wrecked?* That seemed so convenient, or staged, like a plot device in a Hollywood movie.

Finding the grave did not answer any questions, nor did it tell her how she would talk to Zadie or Daddy about this revelation. She was too angry and yet anger wasn't all of it. She didn't have a big enough vocabulary for what she was feeling.

Mack got home late. Virginia was still up, sipping her third glass of wine on the sun porch. She'd stayed at the grave until dark and then come home, picking up some Chinese carry out. She had moved the food around on the plate for an hour, bringing little of it to her mouth. The wine was working; she felt warm inside and able to calm herself and bring her mind into some focus without getting sleepy.

Mack was clearly wound up. Virginia wanted to tell him what she'd learned today, how her world had changed. But she didn't have the energy or the words right then. She let him talk because his news was more exciting for him and probably easier to deal with. Anyway, he was having a hard time staying seated to tell it.

"It's worked out. The Kyung Motor Representatives are coming—and guess when?"

Virginia sat up. For a second the gloom lifted. "No!"

"Yes. They are coming in the Wednesday before your festival."

"It's not *my* festival, Mack."

"You know what I mean. It may as well be yours. Anyway, they are staying until Saturday night. You've got your wish. They will be able to come to your festival—the festival—on Saturday afternoon. That might be the right way to end their visit, with something cultural rather than business, you know what I mean? That will probably be the day with the most people there, big crowds, so it will impress them."

"Mack, I'm thrilled." She reached up and kissed him impulsively. "But this just throws a monkey wrench into the whole thing. I've—." She corrected herself when he gave her an "I-told you-so" look, "We've got to rearrange the schedule so they'll hear the better musicians, and we'll have a tent set up just for them, and have the best food, and we've got to keep the weirdoes away from them, you know, there's always those folks who think it's their place to. . ." Her mind was working now.

"Slow down, Gee-Gee. You can figure that all out tomorrow. It's late. What did you do today?"

She paused and tipped up her glass to drink the last of her

wine before she gathered the strength to say it. "I found out where my mother's buried."

"What?"

"I found my mother's grave. It's out by the county line at that pretty old Baptist church and cemetery."

"What are you talking about? You—Zadie, all of you— you've always said your mother abandoned you, ran off or something."

"Yes. That's what I was told. It's not true. I have a copy of her death certificate and found the grave."

She told him how her day started, the long hours of research with the microfilm, how reading the history of the town ended up more like the history of her family, finding the small notice about the car wreck, and how no obituary was even printed in the paper.

"Gee-gee, you've stumbled into some mystery."

"Yeah."

"I'm sorry, honey. This must be very upsetting to you. I'm stunned."

"Upsetting is not the word. It's like I don't know who I am. I mean, I know who I am, just not how much my life would have been different if they had told me she died. Maybe I would have been a better mother."

"Oh, Gee-gee, you're the best mother I know. Don't go there. We've been through this a hundred times."

"But would I have had more children? Would we have started earlier? Would I have been more tolerant of the children, or less tolerant, or less involved, or more involved? Have I hurt them?"

"There's nothing wrong with our kids a little starvation wouldn't help. Or a job in Matthew's case. There's nothing wrong with you, Gee-gee. Please don't beat yourself up over this. I know it's shocked the hell out of you, of course, and it makes me want to take your daddy outside behind the barn for lying to you and hurting you for so long. But maybe in their own strange way he and your aunt had their reasons. I can't imagine what it would be, sounds sick to me, but they did, and after years and years didn't know how to confess the lie." He offered a shrug and then pulled her to him. Then she let herself cry; the wine helped her relax enough to let the tears come.

On Tuesday morning Virginia decided she'd have to put Monday behind her for a while. Every day was another one closer to the festival, and she wasn't sure how they could possibly get it all ready. Because the city council was making the down payment on the festival, she was expected to show up at the council meeting on Tuesday nights to give a report and answer questions about the progress. After the first time, in February, the interrogation went on for thirty minutes. Her second appearance to report, in March, ended up more perfunctory. With the family news bumping around in her head, she hoped—and assumed—April's meeting would be an easy "here's where we are" affair. She wasn't ready to see Maddie Flynn sitting on the front row when she stood up to give her report.

Not that she had ever met Maddie before. She recognized her from the brochure photograph and from a local newscast. Maddie was one of those women who had at one time been stunningly pretty, but who over the years let her love for Krispy Kreme get the better of her. The nicest word for Maddie's figure was stout, but she did keep her hair, nails, and makeup immaculate. It peeved Virginia that a woman devoted to primping preschoolers—and making money off of it—would let her control over her weight go by the wayside. But Virginia pushed those thoughts to the back of her mind to focus on her report and to deliver the big announcement that the Kyung Motors delegation would visit the festival on Saturday.

The audience that night was small, maybe twenty citizens, and Virginia expected questions from only one person. Maddie did not disappoint.

"I'll open it up for any questions, now," Virginia put on her sweetest and most condescending smile, tensing her face muscles and trying to make eye contact only with the back of the room.

"I have a question," Maddie raised her hand and stood. "I have an issue, actually. It seems like to me this festival is about a certain small group of people making decisions that affect a lot of other people."

Bob Smallwood wanted the meeting to be over and jumped in. "Could you be a little more specific about what you're getting at? By the way, what's your name, ma'am?"

"I am Madelyn Flynn. I am a local businesswoman. I have sent a proposal that the children of the Upstate be allowed to participate in the festival, and it was denied, and I really wasn't given a reason."

"Can you explain what this is about, Virginia, I mean, Mrs. Foster?"

"Yes, I can answer both you and Ms. Flynn. Ms. Flynn wants to put on a beauty pageant for little girls aged three to twelve. The planning committee decided that was not the type of venue we want to promote through this festival." She turned her gaze to Maddie, pulling on all her experience as a high school teacher who could stare down a student. "I assume, Ms. Flynn, that you are going to charge those little girls' parents for them to be in the pageant?"

"Well, of course."

"What's the going rate for that kind of thing?"

"$150." A couple of city council members reacted; one laughed, another gasped. Somebody in the audience whistled, apparently impressed by Ms. Flynn's business sense.

"And how is that going to help the festival?"

"I was going to pay the fee, like anybody else, the other vendors, I mean. And I have my own business expenses."

Bob decided it was time to separate the women, at least figuratively. "So, Mrs. Foster, what do you say to that?"

"Like I said," Virginia did not take her eyes off Maddie, "a pageant of little girls dressed up beyond their years and prancing around on a stage is not in line with the spirit and goals of the festival. Anyway, Ms. Flynn wants a Saturday time slot and, to be honest, now that the Kyung Motors delegation is coming, it will be even less appropriate to show off oversexualized children to people from a culture with more traditional values."

"Oversexualized? Are you accusing me of teaching my little girls to be immoral?" Maddie's face was turning red, very quickly. "Mr. Smallwood, I demand an apology."

"Virginia, I really don't think . . ." Bob Smallwood was beginning to think the first catfight in the history of Abundance city council meetings was about to explode.

"This festival is not about making a buck for every person in the region. It is about the future of the city."

"And who gets to decide the future of the city?" Maddie came back. "That is so typical of you."

"Excuse me?" Maddie now had Virginia's full attention.

"You—well, you come by it honest, I guess. Cleeland on one side, and a rich husband to boot. . ."

Bob pounded the gavel. "Ladies, this is not the place. Let's straighten this out, and quickly. Virginia, why can't Ms. Flynn have a different time, like a Friday?"

"My little girls can't miss school to be in a pageant, or—" and here she looked smugly at Virginia—"Sunday School and church. It has to be Saturday."

"Couldn't it be early, early, before the Koreans—I mean, the Kyung Motors people-- show up?" Bob offered.

Virginia could tell that Bob, the man who played Santa Claus, wanted to make everybody happy.

"You're missing the point, Bob. It's not just the timing; it's what the pageant represents." Her voice had become slow and firm.

"I think I'm being insulted," Maddie said.

"There's no thinking about it. You *are* being insulted," a voice from the back called out, as if to egg on the conflict. Chuckles rippled through the room.

"Order, order." Bob gave five resounding hammers with his gavel until the room was perfectly quiet again. But he didn't know what to say. Virginia was ready to land her last punch. She turned to Bob, her back to Maddie.

"Mr. Smallwood, if the council insists on granting Ms. Flynn's request despite the planning committee's objections, I quit."

Several audience members gasped audibly. Maddie Flynn looked dumbfounded.

"You what?" asked Bob.

"You are telling me you don't trust our judgment, after all we've done. What else can I do? It's not like I'm making six figures to do this job. This is a matter of principle, not just impressing the Kyung Motor Corporation, and not just about timing. We are working night and day to make this festival a success and believe it will turn the town to the future. But if the council doesn't trust me, I'm ready to walk."

Virginia just turned her eyes to the ceiling waiting for a response. At first Bob was speechless, only looking at Maddie. He finally managed a "Ms. Flynn?"

"I—" Maddie Flynn could feel the people in the room holding their breath, and then, instantly, that any sentiment in her favor had turned against her. She was no dummy. This was a battle she'd have to fight another day. Maddie Flynn sat down. She knew she'd lost.

"Uh, Ms. Flynn, do you have anything further to say?"

"No, sir, I withdraw my request."

Chapter 13

At the Thursday festival planners meeting, the committee got a full blow-by-blow account of Virginia's victory at the city council meeting. Then the main topic became how to adjust the festival schedule so that they would get maximum public relations advantage from the Koreans' visit and get maximum mileage out of the festival to impress the Kyung Motor execs. Melody would be in charge of the food. They'd serve a special meal of local and typical Southern specialties, including the winning entries of the bakeoff, but stay away from the really bizarre. No pickled pigs' feet or chitterlings. In fact, nothing pork at all—pork was always controversial.

"They are Korean, Melody, not Jewish," Ted Sneed said. *Is he trying not to roll his eyes?* Virginia thought.

"I know they aren't Jewish, Ted," Melody clarified with a testy voice. "But some other cultures don't like pig meat. Fried chicken is safe. Nobody could find fault with that."

"The chickens, maybe."

"Thank you, Ted, for that observation," Virginia interjected. "Lots of vegetable dishes, Melody. Asians like vegetables. They like spicy, too."

"OK. I got it covered," Melody said, writing notes to herself.

"Now, let's talk about bands that will be playing while they are here," Virginia moved on. The discussion turned into a debate that almost turned into an argument about music and whether they could get some sort of children's dance group to perform something Korean. Audrey said she'd look into it, but also warned that trying to copy another culture might come across tacky or even create an international incident. "The whole point is to get them well disposed to putting the plant here. We have to look smart, not like a bunch of hayseeds."

"Fair enough, we'll just see if the dancing studios have any ideas. We can always have them spend more time in the arts and crafts area and be sure to give them some samples of the best work, as gifts."

Audrey also had great news about the bakeoff and the Double-Dutch Flour Company. Instead of having to rent and haul in ovens and find some way to wire them up, the Abundance Square Bakery had agreed to let the town use its ovens as its big donation to the festival. In one stroke the bakery had solved two problems.

And Ted was not to be one-upped. He had arranged for full-page ads to appear the next weekend in the Sunday edition of every major paper in Georgia, South Carolina, and North Carolina. Anyone who wanted information could call a 1-800-number that Frank Templeton had established and staffed with volunteers from 8:00 a.m to 9:00 p.m. every day and with a recording for after hours.

"Folks, I think we may actually pull this thing off," Virginia smiled at her committee. She couldn't deny the five others had exceeded all expectations. After three hours they came to a resolution on how they could honor the Koreans, win the argument that Upstate South Carolina deserved an auto plant, and yet accommodate all the other visitors who might not give a rip about the foreigners coming here. It was a tiring but satisfying meeting, and she celebrated by having lunch with Tally and Leah, this time at the Bungalow, a local tearoom that actually fit the description.

"You look tired, Virginia," Tally said, not one to mince words if she wanted to make a point. "This stupid festival is wearing you out. You've got to let up."

"I will let up in six weeks. I'll sleep until noon every day after the festival weekend. I'll have Mack take me out of town for a week after that. But now we're in the thick of it."

"I hope you think it's worth it," Leah warned. "In all fairness, Tally, I do hear a lot of good buzz in town about it. Some of the biggest dead-heads are talking about it. And the shops downtown—I saw one actually getting a paint job."

"Exactly. The business owners are trying to spruce up their places," Virginia assured them. "And by the way, Tally, it's not a stupid festival. The festival might be instrumental in getting the Kyung Company to build a plant here."

"And what will that do?"

"Tally, I can't believe you are so backward. JOBS. People stay in places where there are jobs. People come to places where there are jobs. People spend money and pay taxes that improve roads and build schools where there are jobs."

"OK, OK," Tally waved her hands. "Stop the public service announcement. I get it. When there's a big ugly polluting factory outside of town, I'll blame you."

"Pooh. Modern factories don't pollute. They aren't allowed to."

"Well, Mack's set to make a million off this deal," Tally reminded her. "Lots of land will pass hands, with a 6% commission. Not bad."

"Maybe. Probably. But he also has civic spirit."

"Good for him. Here's to civic spirit," Leah raised her glass. "May it not send our friend Virgie Mae to an early grave, or the mental hospital."

Virginia wanted to laugh at Leah's innocent wisecrack, but couldn't.

Despite the festival, Virginia faithfully kept up her weekly visits to Zadie and Topie. She planned them so she could stay two or three hours. She figured a fifteen-minute visit would only insult them. How she was going to get through three hours with Zadie and not tell her what she knew would be impossible. Maybe Zadie would say something that could help Virginia bring it up.

She wrestled with this thought as she drove out to St. Ambrose on Thursday afternoon. She came at different times in the week. She liked the element of surprise for the staff, just in case. And as for Zadie, she would see where the conversation headed. If Zadie was in a reminiscent mood, she'd prod a bit. If Zadie was low or complaining, having a bad day, she'd let it rest. Even if Zadie had colluded in a type of family fraud, she was still Aunt Zadie who would have only done such a thing out of misplaced love.

This time she went to Topie's room first. Topie was in bed, not asleep, but not really awake either. Virginia stuck her head out of the room and caught a staff member walking by. "Could I ask you a question? How is Miss Utopia doing?"

The girl, red-haired, a little chubby, wearing scrubs and looking younger than Bethany, frowned. "Not so good. No really bad days, but we have to help her get up a lot now. Occasionally she'll get herself to the bathroom, but you know, she soils herself some. Um, I think," the girl looked side to side as if she were going to say something that would get her in trouble, "the head staff is thinking about having her moved to the nursing home facility."

"Is she that bad?" Virginia's eyes widened as she asked. *Have I been so blind to how she's going downhill?*

"Yes, ma'am. I'm sorry, though. Mrs. Jackson is a real sweet lady."

"Thank you," Virginia said absently. The young woman

moved on down the hall and Virginia slipped back into Topie's room.

She sat down and reached for Topie's hand. If Topie had to be moved to a different building, how would Zadie react? She'd be lost, or at least very lonesome. Virginia rubbed Topie's hand. It was dry, with protruding blue lines across the bones, and her ring finger was bent outward with arthritis. Now, after years of hard work, grief, and living, it was indistinguishable from the hand of a white woman.

Poor Topie. Sweet, funny, laughing, moving, humming Topie. How had her parents come up with the name of Utopia? That was definitely original; Virginia had never met or even heard of another Utopia. Once when Virginia was little, maybe five or six, she'd asked Topie where her daddy was. "He works on a train, up in Charlotte," Topie said. "Or he did. I really don't know what he does now. He gave me his last name. That's about it, baby. That's about all I'd say about Lawrence Jackson, too." Topie didn't believe in putting frosting on the truth.

Neither Topie nor Zadie had ever remarried. It was from grief, no doubt. For Zadie, the loss of Eddie. Zadie didn't get to see her own momma buried because of the epidemic, and she didn't get to see her husband buried because of the war. How things have changed in fifty years. Back then, people took disappointments, deaths, and tragedy as requirements of living. Virginia's generation, and her children's, always seemed so surprised by death and disasters and war, as if the passage of the twentieth century was supposed to make such events extinct. For Topie, her choice not to marry again was probably both disappointment in love and the desire to never face the possibility of losing a child again. She'd had more grief than her share. Virginia sighed, wiped away a tear, and patted Topie's hand.

"Who is it?" Topie questioned, startling Virginia.

"It's me, Virgie Mae, Miss Topie."

"Oh. I thought it was one of those silly girls that work here. Could you get me a glass of water, honey?"

"Sure." Virginia found one of the plastic mugs with a flexible straw and filled it with ice. Each room had a chest the staff stocked with ice every morning, a nice touch, and they left bottles of water.

"Let's sit up, Topie," Virginia assisted her and handed her the mug. Topie sipped a bit. "That's good. I get so dry. I think it's all these old medicines. How is a body to know what they have you taking?"

Virginia did know all of Topie's medications: blood thinner, high blood pressure medicine, something for cholesterol (which seemed silly at her age), and a new drug that was supposed to slow down the dementia. Keeping track of the side effects was another matter. One of them, perhaps the dementia medication, made her nod off quite easily and probably contributed to dry mouth.

"Have you seen Zadie today?"

"No, honey. Well, yes, I'm sorry, I did, at lunch."

"Of course. You want to sit in your chair?"

"Yeah, honey, help me up."

Virginia settled her into the rocker. "I'm going to go see what Zadie's up to. We'll be back here after while."

"That's good, Virgie Mae."

Virginia slipped out, knocked on Zadie's door, and entered. "Zadie, what you up to?"

"I was getting ready to go over there and bother Topie for a bit."

"Well, let's go." Soon the three were sitting and visiting. Virginia told them all the news of the festival, all about the Korean car company that might come to Abundance, about the bakeoff and the bands. Zadie wanted to talk about the food and whether there would be a carnival. She loved a carnival when she was young.

"No. The committee decided against that for this first year. We had our reasons. Maybe in the future."

"Carnivals bring in the riff-raff and hillbillies, but I still used to enjoy 'em," Zadie said.

"Are you having prizes for pickles and jellies?" Topie asked. She once won a blue ribbon for her pickles.

"No, that's what they do at the county fair in the fall."

"Well, then, what's the difference between a festival and a county fair anyway?"

"The county fair is about farms and agriculture. The festival is about biscuits, and really, it's about making the town look good."

"Did you hear that, Topie? Virgie Mae is gonna make the town look good."

"Humm," Topie murmured. She wasn't really hearing them now. "Oh, I would love to have me some good chicken and dumplins right now. And black-eyed peas. And fried cabbage."

"That does sound good," Virginia agreed. "What for dessert?"

Topie didn't answer this time. "I know what I'd want," Zadie said. "Pound cake."

"Yum."

"Your momma made a good pound cake."

What an odd thing for Zadie to bring up. "Why do you say that, Zadie?"

"Because it's true, Virgie. Your mother was the best cook I knew back then."

"Hennie? A good cook?"

"Yes, girl. Didn't you know that?"

For once, Virginia wanted to tear into her aunt and say, "How would I know anything about my mother, anything true that is? The picture of my mother you gave me was a cheap, wild, unsettled mess. Daddy didn't give me any picture. As far as he was concerned, I was found under a cabbage leaf. How can you ask me if I knew she was a great cook?" Instead she said, "No, Zadie. I didn't know." The time was right. Topie was already asleep now; this wasn't really her concern anyway.

"Zadie, have you ever been out County Road 376, to that old Baptist church, Piney Grove?"

They were all turned toward the window, taking in the view of the gardens the Community meticulously cared for. Sometimes Virginia thought they should spend less money on the gardens and more on the nutrition, but gardens made for pretty pictures and impressed visitors. At the mention of Piney Grove, Zadie slid her eyes toward her niece. "What do you know about Piney Grove Baptist church? You and Mack are Methodists."

"I went out there Monday. It's a very nice drive. Beautiful cemetery."

"Yes, I know." Zadie looked down, and sighed. "How did you find out?"

"So you know why I was there."

"Did you find your momma's grave?"

"Yes. With no help from you, I might add. It was pretty well hidden in plain sight."

Now Virginia didn't try to hide her anger. Zadie might be 87, but her mind was plenty sharp and she knew exactly what this conversation was about.

But Zadie wasn't speaking. Virginia had upset her, but for once she didn't care.

"How did you all keep it out of the papers? How did you keep it from me? What does Daddy know?"

"Don't blame your daddy. We outvoted him."

"Why would you need to outvote him? My mother died in a car wreck. What is so shameful about that? How could you tell a child her mother abandoned her when the momma had no choice in the matter?"

"You don't know what you think you do, Virgie. You couldn't know it."

Chapter 14

April 1947

By late 1945, men were starting to come home from Europe and the Pacific. With every boy and young man and husband Zadie saw around town, a hand seemed to squeeze her heart and wring it dry. Eddie will be home soon—no, Eddie will never be here again. She was glad for the safe return of the males who would start to energize the town again. The whole town had become too feminine a place, like the Cleeland household.

Buddy got home in early 1946 and promptly moved Hennie and Virgie into the best place he could find, an old farm cottage a mile outside town. It was hard to tell which one he was happier to see. After kissing Hennie in public in a way that you only saw in the movies, he snatched up Virgie, pronounced her the most beautiful baby ever born, and insisted on taking her to see his own momma out in the country that very day.

Things were good between Buddy and Hennie for about six months. He returned to his truck driving job, transporting cotton bolts between the Upstate mills to Ohio clothing makers. Hennie didn't like being home by herself, but Buddy didn't want her moving back in with her sister and daddy. She was married now, and 24. It was time to be a momma and wife and stop letting Zadie take care of her. Anyway, Buddy didn't trust those Cleelands. One reason he loved Hennie was that she wasn't like those snobby kin of hers who thought they owned the town and had lots of people convinced they did, when he knew the truth. Sure, they had money, but not the millions they would have, or could have, if Hennie's daddy wasn't such a nut.

For months after coming home Buddy wanted to do nothing but make love to Hennie, tease Virgie and show her off, and eat Hennie's cooking. One thing Zadie had done, or maybe it was their colored maid, was to teach that girl to cook. After three years of army food, he wanted a home-cooked meal twice a day when he was home on Fridays and Saturdays from his runs up north. All he could get up there was sandwiches.

But Hennie made everything she touched ooze with flavors. She could do spicy if he had a hankering for it. She could fry chicken right to the point where the outside was crisp but the inside was still juicy, something his momma never got right. And she let her cube steak cook for hours until it collapsed when the fork touched it. Her beans and black-eyed peas found the right balance of fat meat flavor and vegetable. Her pound cake melted as soon as it touched your tongue. The funny thing was, she wasn't one to fill up her own plate, no matter how good it tasted. She ate like a bird, which was all right with him, because he didn't want her getting fat unless it was to birth him a son.

"You ought to open up a restaurant, darlin'," he said one day.

"I don't have time for that. This house and those chickens you want me to raise and that young'un are enough."

"One young'un isn't enough for anybody. When are you going to have a boy? The way we've been going at it, you should be expectin' by now."

"Buddy, you weren't here when I had Virgie. Ask Zadie how I carried on. I don't like having babies."

"Don't like having babies? Or don't like raising 'em? You sure don't have any trouble trying to make 'em."

She had to smile. Buddy and she never did have a problem in that department. "No, I'm talking about the labor, the bringing of the baby. I screamed bloody murder."

"Shoot, girl, your family is so backwards. You had it in that old house with the colored women and your sister there. Women don't have babies in houses anymore. They go to hospitals, and get a shot or something and don't feel any pain. Good Lord. Get into the twentieth century."

"Humm. They don't feel the pain?"

"From what I hear, maybe a little at the beginning, but they let the doctor take care of all that."

Hennie wasn't convinced that a woman could have a baby without feeling like a knife was cutting through her, but it didn't matter anyway. It wasn't just the birthing she didn't like. Virgie was a beautiful baby, no doubt about it, and she loved her daddy, this man who had showed up one day and treated her like a princess. And Hennie loved her baby. What kind of a woman wouldn't love her baby? She'd definitely never say such a thing around Zadie, who never got to have one, and poor Topie, who should have had four little black children running around her house by now. But she wasn't *in love* with Virgie like Buddy was; she wasn't in love with raising babies and giving herself up to their every need. One baby was plenty. She'd found a way to keep Buddy from getting another one, and she hoped he didn't find out, because as the time went on he was going to be talking about getting a son, or two or three.

Anyway, she was feeling restless. Staying home didn't suit her. She wanted to go out at night, be with other people, drink a little beer and dance to a juke box or a real band. Buddy didn't do that. He said his granddaddy was a drunkard, and one time in the army Buddy got almost dead drunk, got in a fight, got his lip smashed up, and woke up the next day swearing never to touch a drop. No matter that he was in the service and drinking was what everybody did, he wouldn't end up like his granddaddy. She wasn't sure she believed that, but so far he was staying true to his word. He also couldn't dance, and wasn't about to make a fool of himself trying, he claimed. When he came home from those long truck drives he only wanted to eat, love on her, and play with Virgie. He was a simple man, easy to get along with but without much ambition.

The restlessness started to eat at her. Every day she plotted how she could get out to the roadhouse that night, but her nerve, which used to be fearless, would waiver. She could leave Virgie with Zadie, who had moved back in with Daddy in that monster of a house on Clive Street, but Zadie would get suspicious real fast. Maybe she could hire a colored woman to come in and stay with Virgie some nights. That might work.

Plotting a way to what she considered a rightful social life only made her want it more. Why had she married Buddy before the war? Because that was what everybody was doing and because she was afraid she was expecting. She wasn't on her wedding day, but was late and got scared that he'd leave her to run off to England and her without a wedding ring. If she'd have known for sure she wasn't pregnant, would she have married him? Would she be stuck in this farmhouse, a mile out of town, without even a phone or a car to drive, because Buddy left it at the mill when he left on his truck runs? She hadn't learned to drive a car, anyway. At least they had good electricity out here, and an indoor toilet.

Is this what was wrong with her momma? Momma didn't seem restless, just unhappy, all those years. Momma didn't want her. Momma let Zadie and Topie treat her like a doll, a plaything, and when she pitched a fit nobody knew what to do with her. "I don't know what to do with me," she thought. "What did Momma want? Why did she marry Governor in the first place? Did she think he'd take care of her, since he had money and land and a big house and a servant to do all the housework? Did she give up on life and then eventually life gave up on her?

"I am restless, and I'm unhappy," she told herself. Then, "I hate Buddy for making me live out here when we could live in town." Later, "I'm being pushed off just like Momma and Daddy did."

Eventually: "It's Virgie Mae's fault."

These thoughts did not come in logical progression. Over six months, nine months, they looped and looped around her brain, in and out. Like gophers in a yard, they would pop their heads out, then in, and then appear elsewhere or at another time out of nowhere. They started with unsettledness and moved toward suspicion and blame and even paranoia. Hennie knew, at times, that they were awful thoughts. Other times, they seemed true and right.

She hired an old colored woman, Bitty Franks, to come over at 5:00 when she finished her cleaning for a white family in town. Bitty could feed Virgie supper and put her to bed. Hennie could walk to the roadhouse-- it was only a mile or so--and be around people. She could dance with the men, a lot of ex-soldiers, who were looking for dates. She wouldn't be unfaithful to Buddy. She just needed out. Once a week.

Within a month she was out three times a week. She had taken up with Tommy Biggles. He'd served in the Navy and had been a grade ahead of her in school. Buddy didn't ever like Tommy, who'd been a football player and popular. Buddy was never popular; the Cullinses never did anything that would make them stand out, anyway. Tommy was handsome enough. Tommy was . . . there, and he liked to dance and have some beers.

Tommy took her out in his car to the Lake and they sat for a while, but he wanted more, even if she was married and had a child at home. She let him, once or twice. It wasn't good like it was with Buddy. Tommy would drive her home and leave her at the road at midnight, and she walked up the dirt path to the house, tired and dizzy. Bitty didn't like getting home so late, so she quit. Hennie woke up those mornings only when Virgie was pulling on her hand and asking for some grits and butter.

Virgie was . . . was trouble. She always wanted something to eat, and was asking when Daddy was going to get home, and if she could have a doggie or a kitty to play with, or a little brother or sister. She wanted too much. Maybe Hennie could send her away, to Zadie. Zadie needed a baby. No, she couldn't do that. Buddy would never let Zadie raise Virgie in that big house with Daddy getting so old and cranky. "Buddy loves Virgie more than me," Hennie convinced herself. "I don't love either one of them. I don't love Tommy Biggles either, but I've got his baby in me."

She used to just feel restless. That gave way to discontent, and then desperation.

Word got to Buddy that his wife was seen out at the lake, and other places, with other men, especially Biggles. "Nah, you've got the wrong woman," he said the first three times, getting looks that said, "If you want to be a fool, go right ahead, but your wife is a woman people notice."

Buddy came home the last Friday night in April. A lot of rain up in Kentucky had caused a mudslide across the U.S. Highway he travelled and the state patrol had detoured traffic over 100 miles out of the way, so he was four hours later than usual, and exhausted. He hoped Hennie had made one of his favorites because he was starved, but the way she'd been acting, she might throw the cold plate at him when he came in the door, not bothering to ask how his day or his week had been or why he was late.

What had happened to her in the year since he'd been back? He knew those men at the mill weren't lying. She was stepping out on him. Well, she could leave any time she wanted, but no matter what the law said, she wasn't getting Virgie Mae. No judge would let a mother like her keep a baby. He and Momma would have to find a way to raise Virgie out there in Union; those crazy Cleelands weren't going to get a hold of her.

"Virgie! Hennie!" He called, throwing his jacket down on the ladder-back chair by the front door. He should have come in the back door like he always did. All the lights in the house were on, even though it was well past midnight. There was no answer. He walked through the house, which didn't take long in the two-bedroom cottage. He found Hennie in Virgie's room. Her back was to him. She sat in a rocking chair they kept in Virgie's room. Virgie liked to be read little story books in that chair. Hennie had the chair turned so she could look out the window, across the field in the direction of the Lake and the taverns that lined its shore. Virgie lay in her baby bed, but her eyes were open. "Hennie, shouldn't Virgie be asleep? Turn off the light and come on out here."

"Daddy!" Virgie called, but she looked at her mother with scared eyes, as if she was afraid to move without Hennie's permission.

"Shut up, Virgie!"

"Don't talk to her like that! Come on out of there, Hennie."

"Daddy!" This time it was a desperate, terrified cry instead of a surprised call.

"Shut up, I said." Hennie turned around. A pistol hung from her left hand. For the first time Buddy noticed the bottle of Jack Daniels, almost empty, on the floor by the rocker.

"What the hell is going on here?" The gun was his. When and how did she find it? She knew he had one, but he thought he had hidden it well enough. *How stupid of me to leave it in the house.*

"Hennie, come on out, let's talk. Give me the gun."

"No!" She swung it up to point the gun under her chin, but the whiskey had weakened her muscles and when she pulled the trigger the force pushed the barrel away from her face. The shot hit the ceiling above and behind her. Dust, wood splinters, plaster, and asbestos exploded and rained down on them. Virgie screamed, hysterical. He rushed Hennie, his only thought to get the gun away from her and throw it somewhere, in the toilet, out the window, anywhere she couldn't get it.

He tried to grab the hot barrel of the pistol but her fingers tightened on the handle as she slipped out of his reach. She ran and was out the door and in his car while he tried to soothe Virgie. He picked Virgie up and rubbed her back as he heard the car squeal away.

"She can't drive. She'll run into the lake or something." Maybe that would be best, he thought. Crazy woman. She'd never see Virgie again. They'll put her in the asylum in Columbia and maybe in ten years they'll let her out. Fine with him.

The sheriff showed up at 3:00 a.m. Buddy was sleeping on the sofa with Virgie on his chest. Maybe she would think this a bad dream. Maybe he could tell her in the future it never happened. Maybe. He heard the knock at the door and went to it after putting Virgie back in her bed.

Ham Lillard, the sheriff, was standing outside with a young boy who also wore a uniform but didn't look old enough to drive, much less be a deputy. Ham squinted into the dimly lit living room. "Buddy? Is that you?"

"Yeah, Ham, come on in."

"Well, I hate to tell you this, but somebody stole your car and crashed it and burned it pretty much to cinders out on route 7 a little while ago."

"I know."

"You know? Uh, is your wife here, Buddy?"

167

"No. I reckon she's dead, right?"

"If she was the one in the car, she is. I'm real sorry. What was she doing driving around at 2:00 in the morning?"

"She went crazy tonight. No, she's been going crazy for a while. She had a gun on the baby. She was drinking and ran off in the car. Doesn't even—didn't even—have a license."

"That's too bad. But it's not all. She went to Lumby's Tavern looking for Tommy Biggles. Then to Finn's. He was there. She pulled the gun on him, said she was having his baby. She shot at him but managed to miss, and then was gone before anybody could catch her. He was lucky, I guess."

"Yeah, lucky bastard. She might have killed somebody else, like she almost killed—" He paused. "Maybe she was just trying to scare the hell out of him. I guess I'm supposed to be the one to want to knock his head in but I know it was all Hennie's idea, them being together."

"It would have been awful bad if she'd a hit him." Ham stopped talking for a while and the two men sat on the delicate furniture of the small living room, uncomfortable. Finally Ham decided it was time to say something, to be the official one. "Can I do anything for you? You want me to have one of the deputies go get your momma and bring her up here? You're going to have to come down to the site and then to town."

"Yeah, why don't you do that? If Momma can't come, my sister can. She lives near Momma."

"Will do. Billy, radio the other car and have them go get Mrs. Cullins—what's her address, Buddy?"

Buddy told him, then sank back into the sofa, worn out, numb. What had got into Hennie? How could she think to hurt

Virgie? Maybe she wasn't going to hurt Virgie. Maybe she was going to kill herself. Maybe she sat there trying to down enough whiskey to get the courage, but she might have missed and hit Virgie at any moment. At the thought that he might have lost Virgie, that a bullet, intentional or not, could have pierced her body and that she would have lain there bloody and dead in her baby bed with her favorite blanket wrapped around her, was too much. He started to heave with the reality of what could have been, and threw up, not getting to the bathroom in time. He felt the tears on his face as he leaned over the commode. *Oh, God. What if I'd been later? What if I'd been earlier?*

He remembered then that his baby was alive and his wife was dead. To assure himself he checked her room again, even though it had only been five minutes since Ham knocked at the door. Ham. He better go back in and talk to the sheriff.

Ham, a patient man, and concerned for his friend, offered to make him some coffee. "The baby is all right, ain't she?"

"Yeah, she cried herself to sleep though. Scared to death. I didn't think you could see that kind of fear in a little child's eyes." His head, everything, was starting to hurt. He hadn't had any dinner. He had hoped Hennie would have something for him in the Frigidaire when he got home, some stew he could heat up. All he had wanted to do was get a meal, kiss his wife, stroke his baby's cheek, and go to sleep. Instead he saved his baby's life and lost his wife, who had reached the end of whatever it was that was driving her out at night after other men.

"Do you think we need to tell her sister in town?" Ham asked, bringing in a mug of black coffee. Ham didn't know how to make it right, not like a woman would, but Buddy appreciated the effort and sipped it anyway.

"Not now. Not til later. No telling how that clan will react."

They sat quietly. Yeah, no telling. And this would be all over the town by 9:00 in the morning. People would say he was a bad husband. Maybe. But people knew what kind of girl Hennie was. He didn't care so much about himself, what the town hags and gossips said, but it would eventually matter to Virgie. Maybe he would take her and move away. Maybe he could get a job in Ohio. He liked it there, well enough. Truck drivers made better wages. He'd have to join a union, but he didn't care. Lots of G.I.s from the south were moving up to Detroit and Cleveland and Pittsburgh now. Well, he couldn't make that decision yet. They'd have to bury whatever of Hennie was left.

Any love he had left for Hennie disappeared when that gun went off. It was dwindling anyway, knowing that she was cheating on him and not even keeping it secret. He'd married her because she was fun and pretty and a good cook and ready for anything back when he was wild himself before the War, and because she thought she was expecting. He wasn't the kind of man to treat a woman like garbage, use her and leave her. He was older now, and he'd seen what war could do. If he ever thought to get married again, it would be with a settled woman.

His momma came in the deputy's car about an hour later, blubbering and worried. He calmed her down and left with the sheriff to see the site. "Yes, that's my car," letting himself think for a minute where he was going to get a new one by the time he had to go back to work. The body had been moved to the funeral home, so that was the next stop. The body was unrecognizable, but Hennie always wore a necklace with a small ruby pendant of her momma's, and he identified it.

Like he figured, by 9:00 the word that his car, more than likely driven by his crazy, two-timing wife, had crashed and burned. That afternoon Zadie McCann showed up at his doorstep. He let her in. She took a seat without being invited, removing her white gloves and straw hat, two items as necessary to her formal nature as a dress and shoes.

"Buddy, I heard what happened from the funeral home director. What went on here last night?"

"Why was that old cheat calling you? I'm her husband."

"You know we're old residents of this town. Once you identified the body found in the car as Hennie, that was all he needed to know."

"Well, then you know."

"No, I don't. What happened?"

"I came home to find your sister with a gun nursing a bottle of whiskey by Virgie's bed. I figure she was trying to work up the nerve to shoot herself, but maybe she was going to kill Virgie first. The gun went off, she ran away, and you know she can't drive. She was about pretty lit up anyway."

"You sound so cold about it, Buddy."

"What do you expect me to sound like? I'm still shaking to think that she could have shot Virgie, or that it would be me laying in the funeral home now, or both of us, or all three. Maybe she wanted to be dead, Zadie."

"What a thing to say."

"That's the least of my worries. I got to pay for a funeral now, a new car, and fix the hole in the ceiling and roof before the landlord finds out. That's just the money stuff. I've got to hope andpray that I can convince Virgie this all never happened, that it was a bad dream or something, that her momma didn't try to kill her with a .45 in a drunken fit. And I'll have to find a woman to live in and take care of her, or move her down to my momma's. Momma is too old to start raising young'uns again."

"That's why I am here. We'll take care of all the expenses."

"Oh, yeah, the rich Cleelands will clean up their mess."

"Maybe. But you don't have the money. We do."

"Yeah?"

"We are prepared to give you $25,000. That ought to take care of everything."

$25,000 was a figure that caught his attention. "That's a lot more than I'm gonna need. You must want something."

"We want Virgie to stay with us when you're gone. You can see her when you're home on the weekends."

"Living with you and your daddy and Jessamyn and those colored women didn't do much for Hennie's mind, if you ask me. I don't think you Cleelands know much about raising children. Why do you think I'd let you all have her?"

"Because . . . I don't have an answer to that. Make it $30,000. You can buy your own truck and be your own boss that way."

"I'm thinking about moving to Ohio."

"And take Virgie away from us? She belongs here."

"She's my baby. Hennie wasn't overly concerned about her." He paused. "I got to bury my wife, what's left of her. I don't want to talk about this now."

"There's another thing. Daddy doesn't want this story to get out."

"The way people talk around here? Are you kidding?"

"The funeral home and the newspaper have agreed to keep everything private. No death announcements in the paper. The sheriff's office won't let it out that she was in the car, but that it was stolen by some vagrant and you left the keys in it by mistake."

"How are you going to explain where Hennie is?"

"Hennie has gone on a vacation for a while, for her health."

"How much is this going to cost you, to buy the silence? And where are you planning to bury her?"

"For a donation of $5,000 to renovate their sanctuary, Piney Grove Baptist is willing to provide a grave in a discreet location for a nonmember." Zadie sometimes used words like that, Buddy thought, to let people know she was better than them, or could be if she wanted to.

He sat for a while. How much did it cost to cover up a suicide, a scandal? It was costing her $35,000 so far, and there was a lot more to tally. How much would the city want? The newspaper and funeral home? What a way to waste their money, but the old man was never good with it anyway. He hadn't given them a dime for a wedding present, but now he was willing to spend fifty grand or more to keep his name out of the papers. Hypocritical snobs. Did they want the town to stay ignorant that some kind of insanity ran in the family, a kind that made women reject their babies and turn away from life? Or did they just want to stay out of the public notice, trying to pull puppet strings from behind the scenes?

Buddy was tired now. He'd slept only an hour after getting Virgie to bed, and he hadn't eaten since noon the day before. "We'll talk about this later, Zadie. Go pay your money to the fools in this town. And yeah, I'll take your thirty grand. But keep your hands off Virgie."

It all went as Zadie planned. It took a while, but Buddy finally came around to the facts. His momma, with congestive heart failure, was not up to dealing with a four-year-old. His sister already had five of her own kids. He wasn't a businessman, and being an independent trucker was more headaches and paperwork than any man would want. Virgie came to live with Zadie during the week and got picked up by her daddy on Friday nights. She was a Cullins on the weekend and a Cleeland during the week. This arrangement worked fine when she started to first grade, since the grammar school was located two blocks from the home place.

Buddy made sure Virgie leaned toward the Cullins side, watching for any sign of the potential craziness that inflicted Hennie. So did Zadie, but they were pleasantly disappointed to find no signs of Hennie's personality in Virgie. She was a little girl who generally complied, worked hard in school, and respected her elders, although she was afraid of Governor, an old man who sometimes forgot to bathe, smelled of tobacco and whiskey, and coughed in long outbursts.

Virgie finally asked where her mother was when she was five. "Your momma went away," Zadie said. She wasn't sure that a five-year-old would understand death, so "went away," would have to work for now. Zadie rationalized that telling her Hennie was dead would lead to, "How did she die?" and "Where's her grave?" and "Did I go to the funeral? I don't remember." From time to time she would ask again, and be told the same thing, until that was what she told her friends and what she believed. Hennie went away. Hennie disappeared. Hennie vanished without a trace. Hennie was somewhere else.

Chapter 15

April 1998

"So how much did Governor pay by the time it was all over?" Virgie wanted to know. She spoke in a low voice through slightly clenched teeth, not wanting to wake Topie, who had drowsed through the whole long story. Zadie had told what she knew of it, the bits and pieces Buddy had allowed her to know through the years. Despite Buddy's initial refusals, in the long run he colluded with Zadie in it all. Daddy would answer for this, or at least explain himself, someday. Today was Zadie's turn.

"About $100,000 dollars. We ended up selling some land. That land where Bosley's peach orchard sits used to belong to us."

That was an astounding sum in 1998, and probably worth five times as much after the war. One hundred thousand dollars--for what result? Certainly to enrich the town, and her daddy, and the Baptist church. She was always told Governor lost the money in bad investments and the stock market crash. It was really in 1947, to cover his shame, to hide the fact that he was a worthless husband and father, that the family had insanity coursing through its genes, or at least had married with other families that did.

"I'm glad I'm a Cullins, Zadie." That superficially innocent remark was meant to hurt Zadie. "At least I have some hope I won't turn into a mean, crazy, old woman."

Zadie didn't turn her head to look at Virgie. "You are more Cleeland than you want to admit. You look like your momma. And you benefitted from the Cleeland money."

"Money isn't everything."

"Only people who don't have to worry about money say that. Topie would laugh to hear you say it. Our money made your life

175

good. It paid for your education. It put you in a place where you could marry well. Do you really think you would have had the life you did if we let your daddy raise you?"

"But it wasn't a normal upbringing. I lived with old people. I didn't have any brothers or sisters."

"Blame that on your daddy, not me. He didn't want to remarry when you were young. And maybe being raised differently made you see people and the world differently."

Zadie was right on that point. For one thing, Virginia was spared seeing much of the typical white superiority about African-Americans. Zadie treated Topie and Lula like best friends, never like servants or employees, and that cemented respect for minorities in Virgie.

"I did the best I could, Virgie. The best I knew how. Did you ever think you weren't loved?"

No, Virginia answered herself. Zadie and Topie adored her. Daddy, for all his faults, thought she walked on water. "No, Zadie, I had lots of love. It was secure. But any child whose mother goes away is going to think it was her fault, and that has haunted me for years. Maybe my momma was a freak or insane. Maybe she really just wanted to commit suicide and couldn't bring herself to do it. Maybe she was a tramp. Maybe she wasn't. I know a little more now, but I'll never know *her*."

Zadie thought for a minute. "You could know her through her cooking."

"How would that be?"

"In that box, those recipes cards. Have you ever really looked at them?"

"No, Zadie. I'm sorry. I don't mean disrespect, but I don't cook."

"Take them down and look at them sometime."

Zadie grew quiet. "I think I'll have you walk me back to my room, Virgie Mae. Then come back and help Topie get into bed, will you?"

She knew Zadie was tired, but Virginia needed to mention one other thing to her. The staffer's comments about Topie's decline—were they reliable?. As she held Zadie's hand and helped her through the door of room 207, she said, "You know, about Topie, I, I don't think she's doing too well. Has anyone said anything to you about her?"

"No. You are the one with the legal say over us. They'll only talk to you. I tried to ask. They politely told me it was none of my business."

"I'm just wondering. . ."

"I can tell you she's not getting any better. She's only getting worse. She knows me, most of the time, but she talks about Anthony, the only baby she ever really knew much. Bless her heart, she talks like he's coming to see her."

"How sad." Virginia helped settle Zadie into bed. She made a mental note to call the administrator of the facility in a few days.

"I'm going to lie here for a while," said Zadie. "They'll come taking us to dinner in a bit, I think."

"You want the light off?"

"No, no." Zadie paused. "I'm Topie's memory now. She depends on me, just like I always depended on her."

"Yes, ma'am. Bye, bye, Aunt Zadie." She slipped out.

After Virgie Mae left, sweet Virgie, who had got herself all wrapped up in this county fair thing she called a festival, Zadie lay in her bed, unable to nap. She was tired, but that was her normal state; it wasn't the same as sleepy. The pulled, heavy drapes made the room as dark as possible at midday in spring. The air conditioning was working already; it seemed early in the year for it. It kicked in. Every sound, every machinery hum, every clock tick, hit her ears. She couldn't sleep.

So many years had passed since Hennie's death. At first, when Virgie was a young woman, no older than Hennie before she died, Zadie could see Hennie's face in Virgie's. Virgie was a taller woman than her mother, owing to Cleeland and Cullins blood, and her eyes were brown instead of Hennie's green—also from the Cullins. Virgie inherited some of Hennie's fire and determination, but she almost always turned it to the good, not to destruction. And she loved her children.

If Virgie had known more about her mother growing up, it would have come to no good. Now, at her age, a middle-aged woman, she can understand that something grabs hold of women, or anybody, and won't let go and makes them do evil and crazy actions. *It wouldn't have done for a child to know what Hennie did. Virgie is mad now, and thinks she has the right to be. One day she'll get over it. She thinks we did wrong by her, but if she had been there, had had to make the same choices, she would have chosen the same.*

Zadie had told herself these words many times before, but never in the face of Virgie's knowing the truth. Deep in her heart, she had believed for years that she would make it to her grave without having to tell Virgie everything. She believed the same about Topie, too, that what she knew could remain known only by her. Today's conversation told her that wasn't going to happen, that it shouldn't happen.

After lying there for half an hour, Zadie decided that

pretending to sleep made no sense. She struggled to sit up, found the switch on the lamp, and put on her glasses. She could see around the room. She slid her feet back into her slippers, found her walker, and padded slowly over to Topie's room.

Topie was lying in bed, but her eyes were open. "Topie, it's Zadie."

"Zadie."

"Yes, darlin'. Move over."

Zadie sat beside Topie, then leaned forward and brought her feet up until she could recline on the edge of the bed.

"Zadie." The fact that Topie knew her name satisfied Zadie.

"Virgie knows all about Hennie."

"Hennie?"

"Yes, Virgie's mother."

"Hennie died. She tried to shoot that man. She was in a crash."

"Yes, Topie, she did. Virgie found out."

"Virgie?" This time it was a question.

"Yes, Topie, you know Virgie. The little girl who lives with us. We take care of her."

"Oh. Virgie. Virgie Mae."

"Yes, honey."

They were quiet for a while, but Topie's eyes stayed open, staring straight ahead. *At least she hasn't gotten mean, and hurting other people. Or wandering away yet. They say that's what happens with Alzheimer's,*

Zadie thought. *What is in her head now? A million things, but maybe they swarm like bees and never settle. Maybe there is very little in her head, like her memories have gone somewhere.*

Zadie pondered for a while. Memories were not her problem. She had too many. They were still too vivid, even after the stroke. They played like TV shows in her head sometimes. She wished she could turn them off, but she couldn't. They weren't always shows she wanted to watch.

Maybe if she was Topie's memory, she had extra to give. She had waited too long. Why had she waited too long to tell Topie the most important thing of all, and now Topie wouldn't understand? Maybe she would. Maybe Topie would surprise her. Maybe knowing would give Topie more time, would change something.

Zadie knew that was not true. That was like praying for something you knew was impossible. But she didn't want to make the same mistake she had with Virgie.

"Topie."

"Hummm?"

"I need to tell you something."

"Hunh? What're you sayin'?"

"I need to tell you something. Maybe it's too late. It's something I should have told you a long time ago. . . . "

Being told to get the recipes down and look at them just meant one more thing on Virginia's to-do list. She would, some day. She'd had enough rummaging through her past in the last few days. She needed the distraction of the festival. It started five weeks from today, she realized as she drove home. The down payment on the spacious Cape Cod style house on an acre lot had come from her inheritance from Governor, the last of the old fortune.

The five weeks until the festival promised to be as busy as the eighteen months she had spent after Zadie's stroke. Every minute seemed consumed with meetings, conference calls, decisions, wrangles with some city official, merchant, or church or civic group, more decisions, and schedule conflicts. The program for the festival had to be finalized and approved by the first of May in order to get it to the printer in time. That single task—arranging for everyone who wanted a piece of the action to have a space, time, and place on the program—ended up the single biggest challenge.

The festival would take place around the town square on the eight streets that bisected or ran parallel to the square for a block or two. Abundance's founders—among them several Cleelands—had asked an architect from Savannah to plan the downtown, and he hadn't looked far for inspiration. Three stages would be provided for entertainment. One would be in the small park in the middle of the town square. Severson Park, named after a Confederate hero, comprised only about an acre, but it would do. The best acts—the ones from out of town, the ones the festival had to pay for—would perform there. Enough seating for about 500 people, folding chairs donated from churches and lodges, would be available.

An additional stage would be on the street to the west of the square, and one other to the east. The proximity of the stages demanded that a loud bluegrass band could not be playing at the same time as the high school jazz group. Children's programs, a comedian, a storyteller, and a magician could be performing at the same time as the country swing band. A very delicate balance had to be maintained, not just acoustically and artistically, but politically. It wouldn't do to anger any faction during the first festival. The dustup with Maddie Flynn had expended all her credibility. Maybe after five years certain people would understand the festival was about attracting outsiders, not about showing off for family. But not now. Not yet.

It also wouldn't do to have medical emergencies, car break-ins, pickpockets, or lost children. Remedies for those potential problems were being arranged: six water stations; a first aid tent; shady areas for seating; lots of volunteers floating around looking for disconnected children; volunteers from Public Security Systems, Inc., wearing their uniforms, as well as a few sheriff's deputies.

Vendors would be spread out to the north and crafters to the south of the square. "Vendors" was loosely defined. Churches could set up for proselytizing if they kept it low key. So could Boy Scouts, Girl Scouts, the YMCA, the 4-H clubs, lodges, and other nonprofits. If the group truly had nonprofit status, they were given free space. The bakeoff would be held at Abundance Square Bakery, conveniently located on the square.

Across from the main stage, Biscuit Central would be set up. The three town bakeries were going to sell, at fifty cents a piece, three-inch-wide biscuits. Stonefield Dairy, a local organic producer, was going to donate butter at cost; and jellies and jams--peach of course-- were coming from the Bosley Orchards, which actually made more money from their specialty preserves and pie fillings than from fresh peaches. Virginia and her committee would have preferred that all the bakeries use Double-Dutch flour. "No can do," they said. Their suppliers sold them another brand, one stored in warehouses more local to South Carolina, and Double-Dutch was just too expensive for commercial bakers. Double-Dutch would be the flour of the bake-off and logos only. Maybe in the future Biscuit Central would add ham, sausage, eggs, and chicken filets to its menu, but this year, for the sake of branding and the sake of Double-Dutch's support, biscuits alone would be the center dish of the festival.

The question kept coming up, from skeptics and a few

nervous city council members, "How will the festival make any money?" Virginia and her loyal festival planners insisted that first, making a profit the first year was not a reasonable goal. If at least half of the $50,000 budgeted for the festival was more or less still in the coffers when all the bills were paid, the festival would be a success. But as for income, parking within the large designated lots cost $5.00 a car. That way, if 1000 cars showed up in the parking lot, $5,000 would be collected. That would suffice as an entrance fee. If people wanted to walk, they could get in free, but few would. For-profit vendors paid a flat fee agreed upon when they signed their contracts; crafters would pay a percentage of their sales. Nonprofit organizations that wanted a table had to make a case for their contribution to the festival. Double-Dutch was kicking in $10,000 for the P.R. the festival would bring. The musical acts constituted the biggest expense, but there was no way around that.

The general schedule for the festival involved a start on Thursday night with a concert and block party for the locals and volunteers. Folks were encouraged to bring their own—food or beer—to tailgate, potluck, whatever, and enjoy live music. Friday's schedule included Round One of the baking contest and activities for seniors and retirees and anyone who wanted to avoid the crowds on Saturday. Friday night boasted a beach music concert and dancing, including what South Carolinians called "shagging." Saturday the festival would start early. By 9:00 things should be roaring. Round Two of the bakeoff. Live programs on all the stages, on the hour. Food and drink flowing. Town shops open for business. Down past the food vendors, an antique car show, antique defined broadly, and on the other side of the crafters, a petting zoo. Saturday night another concert, this time country-western, with line dancing available. Some folks wanted fireworks on Saturday night; after looking into the prices and the insurance, Daryl argued convincingly that it would be a lot of buck for a little bang.

Sunday would start with an ecumenical service for those who

felt disloyalty to their own churches could be forgiven for one week; more music; a dog strut; more food; a sports and muscle car show (with entrance fees); awards announced for the bakeoff. The festival would wind down at dark on Sunday with something they hoped would keep people coming. A photographer would circulate and shoot pictures all weekend and create a slide show Sunday afternoon. At sundown, the pictures would be projected on the largest screen available, placed behind the main stage. The planners hoped that the promise of photos of cute kids, performers, and smiling guests would motivate a significant number to stick around and keep spending money.

The most satisfying accomplishment of the whole endeavor, to Virginia, Audrey, Melody, Daryl, Frank, and Ted, who were now considered the festival extraordinaire team, was the amassing of over 500 volunteers. Everyone, from young teenage boys who would haul chairs from the Masonic Lodge and back, to church ladies in their seventies and eighties who would make sure plenty of butter and preserves were set out for the hungry crowds at Biscuit Central. This meant one thing: buy in. The townspeople had been persuaded a festival was worth it.

Four weeks out, Virginia was amazed that the only blip of contention had really been Maddie Flynn. As she drove to the city conference center for Thursday's planning meeting, she was feeling confident that everyone was on board. But when she walked into the meeting and saw two faces she didn't know, her buoyant mood immediately turned wary.

The two newcomers were seated away from the table around which sat Ted, Daryl, Frank, and Audrey. Melody hadn't arrived.

"Hey, guys," she greeted them, trying to remain upbeat. "Uh, can I help you?" she asked the two visitors. One was a woman, middle aged, perhaps; her long dark brown hair with hints of gray was pulled back into a braid. She was wearing a skirt and white blouse and the kind of shoes called sensible. Her companion, a thin, graying, and stern man wearing an out-of-date suit, looked about her age. While the woman smiled when Virginia spoke to them, the man merely nodded in acknowledgement and maintained an expression that was half frown, half judgment.

Audrey spoke up, "This is Mr. and Mrs. Powell. Uh, actually, Pastor Luke Powell and his wife, Deena. They have come to talk about the, uhm, festival."

Virginia didn't want to say the wrong thing, and she didn't want another Maddie Flynn incident. These folks didn't look like anyone who would want to hold a baby beauty contest at the festival. They probably wanted their church or ministry to host a table or booth. "Oh, really. Well, um, that's fine, we're always glad to have members of the community come see how they can help us with the festival." She flashed a smile that she hoped wasn't too fake, and settled herself into a seat at the table opposite the side of the room where the Powells sat. She unpacked her folders from her carryall, and then thought for a second. She'd put these people on the agenda first, in front of the other business. There was no need for them to stick around, and actually she didn't want them to. Some matters got discussed in these planning meetings that were best kept confidential.

"Has everybody been introduced so far?" Virginia asked, hoping to stall for a minute, and then looked at her watch. "I'm Virginia Foster, by the way."

Melody made her entrance; she was wearing workout clothes. "Hey, you all. Sorry for the yoga outfit; I just changed my day at the studio to Thursday." The outfit was loud and formfitting. Ted noticed her, obviously, but Frank looked up from his cell phone long enough to nod a greeting and Daryl kept reading the newspaper.

"I've always wanted to try yoga," Audrey said, making conversation while Melody seated herself and got comfortable.

"Oh, you should try it. It's just wonderful. Have you ever done it, Virginia?"

"No, 'fraid not. Just a little too, I don't know, California, for me. I hear it helps stress, so maybe after the festival is over!"

"It's based on a pagan religion," Mr. Powell said. "It's worship of false gods."

"Excuse me?" Melody's eyebrows jumped an inch higher. "We don't worship false gods at the studio."

"Um, this is Pastor Powell and Mrs. Powell," Virginia said, eager to change the subject. "Well, good morning, everybody," Virginia started. "Since we're all here, and we have visitors, let's get the meeting started. I thought we'd let the Powells go first. Uh, before we get started, Pastor Powell, what church do you represent?"

"I'm the pastor at Evangel Community Church of the Living Faith."

"Oh, I don't know that congregation. Where is it?"

"It's over in Reeceville, you know, about ten miles from here."

Reeceville was a village of less than two hundred people, a wide place in the road as some called it, that used to have a railroad depot.

"Yes, I know where you're speaking of." She paused. The church was technically in Turling County, so they at least were eligible for a table if that's what these people wanted. "So, what can we do for you?"

"I've been hearing a lot about this festival you all is planning, Mrs. Foster. We want to know if it is something that's gonna honor God or something that's gonna serve Satan."

Virginia had been taught to be mannerly and had practiced old-fashioned Southern politeness all her life, so she had learned early in life not to let the first words out of her mouth express how incredulous she felt at this moment. But the best she could come up with was, "Mr. Powell, I have no idea what you are talking about."

"We been hearing a lot of things about this festival, and we have to take a stand against it if it's not going to honor the Lord."

"I don't believe there is a person in this room, or any of our volunteers, who would seek to dishonor God. Have you heard something that would make you think otherwise?"

"You tell me. Are you going to have gamblin'?"

"It depends on what you mean by gambling, Reverend Powell." Frank had decided to speak, either to help Virgie or to avoid being bullied.

"I don't go by Reverend. That's putting a name on a man that only God should have."

"OK, then, Pastor, what do you mean by gambling? We're not having roulette wheels or craps or poker. But there will be raffles run by some of the nonprofit groups."

"A raffle is gamblin'. Then what about music? And dancin'? And drinkin'?"

Now Virginia's politeness began to wear thin. Audrey felt the tension in the room and jumped in. "We are not having anything during the day at the festival that you wouldn't see on the streets of any town. It will be perfectly family friendly."

Melody, finally able to compose herself after the condemnation of her yoga studio, spoke up. "But what people do at night is their own business, and yes, we are going to have bands and country music and if people get thirsty and want to drink a beer, that will be available."

Virginia, who already knew the Powells wouldn't support the festival and were just trying to make a point, didn't want Melody to antagonize them.

"So you're going to bring gamblin' and wild dancin' and drinkin' in and make it sound like it's a good thing for the town and the county. Are you going to have fortune tellin'? And women dressed immodestly to put on a show for men?"

"You make it sound like we are planning some sort of orgy," Virginia finally spoke. "This is a festival, not Mardi Gras. And many churches are supporting the festival and helping out with chairs and tents and tables. We are even having a worship service on Sunday morning to start the day's activities."

"People ought to be in the house of God of a Sunday morning. You're trying to get everyone to worship together no matter what they believe. We come out from among them and are separate at our church."

I bet you are, all six of thse committee members thought at the same time. But Ted said it. To balance out Ted's lack of diplomacy, Daryl stepped in. "Pastor Powell, if you don't feel like your church can participate, you are free not to. We aren't forcing this down people' throats. But the numbers speak for themselves—we've got over 500 people going to volunteer, and a bunch of civic groups and church and charities, and the schools."

Virginia noticed that Mrs. Powell remained silent through all this, although her earlier smile had flattened to something expressionless. "Poor woman," she thought. "She'd probably want be anywhere else than here. On the other hand, she made her choice. Maybe she is in total agreement with her husband."

"So, we're sorry if you feel like this is not something you can support, Mr. and Mrs. Powell. But the festival will go on. We hope you'll change your minds."

"No, that ain't likely to happen. There's already too much sin in this community for us to be behind bringing more in. We are trying to fight sin and what it does to people, not make it more available. We'll be praying that the blessing of God will be withheld from this festival as you call it and from this town for having it until it repents."

"And we'll pray the opposite, and see what happens," Daryl finally said, having heard all he could take. "I think we're done here. You better leave now, Mr. Powell."

Melody, Virginia, and Audrey felt relieved that Daryl, the former bank official who could deal with unruly customers, put an end to the conversation, but at the same time they wondered if he thought he was rescuing them. For Pastor Powell's part, being thrown out of the meeting was a common occurrence and perhaps a badge of honor. "Just like I thought, you all, the comfortable and wealthy people of this town, you don't want to hear anything but what would tickle your ears. You don't want to know that the sin you bring into the town will hurt the poor momma and her children, or will encourage the young people to turn from God. You've got your way. But God will have his one day."

"That's enough, man. Get on out of here," Ted commanded. Pastor Powell exited, letting his wife through the door first and then slamming it.

"OK, tell me that didn't just happen," Audrey commented, with a puzzled look on her face.

"I'm afraid it did. He might cause trouble, but I don't think it's anything we can't handle," Daryl said. "I've seen this type before. They think getting a little church gives them a right to something."

"What do you think he would do?" Virginia asked. She wasn't worried, except that he might create a scene when the Kyung Motors delegation visited. However, very few, other than the festival planners, knew they were coming.

"Oh, he might print some flyers, post something up on some bulletin boards or shop windows, get a bunch of church members to picket the entrance, that kind of thing," Daryl conjectured. "We can tell the security to be on the lookout. Believe it or not, they are harmless when all is said and done. They only have control over a few people."

"Let's hope so," Virginia said. Her heart, racing a few minutes ago, was slowing down. Standing up to Maddie Flynn and her beauty pageant was one thing; religious conflict was another. "OK, now let's get down to what we're really here for, which is working on the final draft of the official program so we can get it to the printer."

Chapter 16

Virginia was scheduled to be interviewed Monday morning by a network affiliate out of Charlotte and on Tuesday by local radio stations in Greenville, Spartanburg, Columbia, and Gaffney. On Wednesday a reporter from Atlanta was coming up for a short piece that may or may not get air, they were told, depending on how slow the news days were up until the festival. She'd have to get her hair done Saturday to be ready for all this attention. Ted, the veteran media celebrity, was doing plenty of his own talking on the airwaves.

The only missing pieces were a parade, the fireworks, and a carnival, she told Mack one night.

"What, no hot air balloons? No side shows? No circus elephants?"

"No, and no dancing girls or baby beauty contests, either."

"Too bad." It was Friday night, two weeks before the festival. They had gone out to dinner to celebrate their thirty-second anniversary, a down payment on the vacation they were planning to New York City after the festival. They were getting ready for bed, or Virginia was; Mack had the TV on, flipping channels between a Braves game and the news, long enough to say a few choice words about Bill Clinton. Mack detested Clinton, and the talk of his messing around with an intern only made Mack's words about him choicer. He turned off the television in disgust.

"As long as Kyung Motors gets treated like royalty, I'll be happy. So will the governor and every other politician north of Columbia."

Above all, the challenge of welcoming the Kyung Motors Company delegation without offending the masses loomed large in the planners' minds. The Korean guests would be treated to a sumptuous meal catered by the best restaurant in town, the Village

Gate, in a special air-conditioned tent in case the temperature soared to the 90s, which it sometimes did in May. They would eat a variety of Southern dishes served on china, sprinkled with salt and pepper from real crystal shakers, using real silverware and drinking from glass tumblers, while the rest of the crowd would be eating food on a stick or barbecue on Styrofoam plates with plastic forks and drinking tea from paper cups.

"Royalty, I don't know. No polo ponies or crowns. But we've got it covered, I think."

"Now once you prove the town can pull this thing off, are you going to retire?" Mack asked. "You're wearing me out, and you're going to end up in the hospital."

"Oh, pooh. If one more person tells me that! I'm in my element. Anyway, it keeps my mind off of other things."

"Like what?"

She wanted to say "Like Matthew," but didn't. "My past. I haven't told you this, because we have had so little time together, but I found out some disturbing news about my mother. Zadie told me the long, sad story a couple of weeks ago. Momma, well, Daddy came home one night from one of his truck trips. She was drinking. She had a gun, shot it into the ceiling, and ran off in his car. She wrecked the car and died. It may have been an accident, but I think she killed herself on purpose."

"Gee-gee, why didn't you tell me this before? You've been walking around with this all bottled up? You *are* going to end up in the hospital."

"It's not something you bring up in dinner conversation, Mack. A part of me doesn't even want to believe it or talk about it. Zadie lied to me all those years, why would she be telling the truth now?"

"Maybe she feels like she's coming to the end of her life and she better make things right."

"I'm not sure she did. She did say something interesting. She said she was Topie's memory now. Topie's not doing well. The administrators want to move her to the Alzheimer's unit, but I'm trying to hold them off a little longer. I can't oversee a move for her right now. Anyway, I don't think Zadie is just Topie's memory. She was the memory for a lot of people, me included, and she has to pass the job on."

"I'm sorry about your momma, Gee-gee." He pulled her close after getting under the covers. "But like I told you before, you're a great momma and wife and person. Whether your mother left you or died in an accident or really did kill herself, it doesn't change who you are. Don't be so hard on yourself."

She reached over and turned off the lights. Mack was wrong. It did change, something. A lot.

Mack went to sleep quickly, and he was a sound sleeper. Too sound, sometimes. She tried to drop off for an hour, but she was tense. She could get up and take a pill; but something else weighed on her. It was the box of recipes in the back of her closet, the ones she prized from Zadie but only because Zadie gave them to her, not because recipes fit her life. Zadie had made a point to tell her to look at them. She never had, not even to open the box. Perhaps it was time.

She had placed the box in her bedroom closet three years ago when Zadie and Topie moved into St. Ambrose. Virginia's closet was not just a place to store her clothes. It was her sanctuary. When she had to hide, and while rare it did happen, the closet provided her privacy and a sense of security she didn't understand but appreciated. The large walk-in closet, nine feet deep, had racks of clothes on both sides: winter to the left, summer to the right. Nine feet of pole and hangers, then three feet of shoeboxes. Above the hanging clothes were shelves for accessories, mementos, luggage, and photo albums. Zadie's box was over the summer clothes. She lay there in bed, thinking through the layout of the closet and location of the box before she slipped out of bed and crept into the closet, closing the French doors before turning on the light.

Zadie, a practical woman, had used a box that once held canning jars. Inside, Virginia found six small metal boxes used for 4 x 6 index cards. Virginia had expected to find a cookbook, maybe one of those old ones with the red checkerboard cover you often saw in antique stores or on kitchen shelves. No, just the metal boxes, looking very new and shiny to be over fifty years old. Virginia opened the first one.

Virginia opened the first one, anticipating that she would find recipes in Zadie's scrawl. This was someone else's hand, very delicate, very precise. Some of the recipes spread over cards, which were paper clipped together. Those had rusted over the years, some quite a bit. *This must be my mother's handwriting,* Virginia realized. She pulled out the first bundle of cards, three together. It was a recipe for Salisbury steak.

No, this was not a recipe. Virginia knew enough about cooking to know recipes started with ingredients, then a paragraph or two of directions, using words like blend, fold, broil, sauté, simmer, boil, separate, blanch, glaze, or coddle. Even if she didn't cook and adamantly considered it old fashioned and maybe even demeaning that women were expected to be mavens of the kitchen, she knew what those words meant--vaguely. Coddle had to do with eggs. So did separate, usually, unless it referred to meat drippings for gravy. Sauté referred to cooking onions and peppers in oil without letting them get black. Zadie and Topie had tried to teach her cooking, but she considered it like changing oil in her car. Better to pay someone else.

What she held in her hands was not a typical recipe, but a set of detailed, annotated directions for making Salisbury steak, as if the writer had experimented with creating the best dish and wanted a record of her find. She made comments about the best place to buy the meat. How the peppers should smell. What brand of canned tomatoes would work best. Unlike Topie's cooking, which involved dashes and pinches and what Topie called "throws" of salt and sugar and spices, this writer was precise. Ingredients were measured out in half and quarter teaspoons, in ounces, even drops.

She settled herself onto the stool she kept in the closet. This was not a collection of recipes; it was a journal. Her mother, at least she assumed it was Hennie's work she held in her hand, noted when she had made her discoveries and what the family, especially Daddy, thought about it. She made warnings of what absolutely not to do when preparing this or that dish. Normally Virginia would have flipped through recipes causally, disinterestedly, but not tonight. She couldn't sleep, and this was not about cooking.

She grew uncomfortable on the stool and decided to slip out of the closet, the bedroom, and down to the sunroom. Mack would not wake up. She envied his ability to conk out. As she reached the bottom of the stairs, her footsteps woke up BoJo, who rushed in with her high-pitched bark. "Shoosh, baby. It's just me." The dog followed her as she poured herself a glass of ginger ale and then threw a treat into BoJo's ready mouth. The ginger ale would help her uneasy stomach, and she'd had enough wine already tonight. She nestled onto the loveseat and started to read. BoJo jumped up beside her, settled next to her hip, and went back to sleep within a few minutes.

She read recipes for fried chicken. Pies. Casseroles. Sweet potato soufflé. Stew. Even for some things that she thought women just knew how to make without written instructions, such as mashed potatoes. She found the recipe that had settled into her memory and was the one thing she associated with Hennie: chicken and dumplings. From what she could tell, it was unique, not like what she was used to eating in country-style restaurants. Hennie had put a note in it that it was a Yankee version of chicken and dumplings. If I had the nerve, I would submit this to the bake-off, she grinned to herself. Now, *that* would be a disaster.

Hennie also included recipes for baby food, how long to cook the sweet potatoes, how much salt to put in the carrots, the best way to mash the chicken. Virginia caught her breath when she saw the first note: "Virgie likes it." Then, "Virgie will not eat it if . . ." This was the first time in her life that she had encountered any evidence her mother cared for her. She stopped and wiped away tears for a while. She knew she was getting tired now, and should stop. But she couldn't. Maybe there would be more notes about herself. Maybe there would be some secret knowledge uncovered through these detailed discussions of canned goods and chicken parts and beef stock about what her mother really wanted, and why she died.

Zadie had said something about pound cake. Virginia found it. Hennie did not categorize her recipes by deserts, main dishes, and vegetables. Her filing system may have been chronological, or based on what she or Daddy liked to eat in the same meal. No telling right now. So the pound cake recipe wasn't anywhere near the seven-layer cake recipe, but behind the fried okra one.

Virginia read.

> Take out five eggs from the refrigerator and let them
> sit three or four hours. Or just don't put them in the
> refrigerator after you pick them out from under the
> hen. Like with everything else, the fresher the
> ingredients, the better. Do not make this recipe if you
> use cold eggs. It will fall flat and gooey in the middle
> even if it's black on the outside.

If you have a good electric mixer, that is best. You'll
wear your arm out beating, but lots and lots of
beating is the only way to get the texture that I like
and Buddy goes on and on about.

When your eggs are warm, turn the oven on to 325
degrees. Get out two sticks of butter, ½ cup of lard
(the Crisco will do even better if you can find it in the
store), If they aren't soft, put the butter and Crisco in
the warming oven in a good metal or glass bowl until
they are soft, but not melted. Only a couple minutes
on that. Then pour in three cups of sugar and mix
that real good. Pour a cup of milk and measure out
about four cups of flour, maybe 3 and ¾ if you can.
Under no circumstances should you use that crummy
Abundance Mills Flour. I don't care if they think they
own the town, it just doesn't make a good cake. It's
ok for gravy thickening, but that's about it, or for
making something to give the chickens to peck on.

Virginia stopped. So her mother had a sense of humor, sort
of. Or maybe it was just a cynical and unhappy view of life and
surroundings.

Pour a fourth of the flour, about a cup, into the
sugar and fat mix. Beat until all is combined. Then
pour in a third of the milk. Same, then back and
forth until that's all done. At some point throw in
what Topie would call a dash of salt but I call 1/8
teaspoon. Right now also put in 2 teaspoons of
really good vanilla, the kind from Mexico, not
extract but the real thing, and you may have to
send off for it because Piggly Wiggly doesn't sell it.

Now, the part that makes all the difference. Take a bowl and crack an egg into it. Beat the egg with a fork or whisk for a minute, then pour it into the batter and beat for a minute. Keep doing that until all five of the eggs are gone.

I put the batter all in one big tube pan, but some people like putting it in two loaf pans. Bake it for an hour but don't open the door to look at it. If it's not done after an hour, bake it a little longer, but be very careful.

I got this recipe from Myrtle Bowles down at the Episcopal church at a potluck. Mine is better than hers, though, because I modified it and came up with the way to do the eggs. It's real good with fresh fruit on it. It's too sweet for ice cream as a topping.

Virginia read through the over one hundred detailed recipes. They all read like technical manuals, and she noticed one thing. As the dates progressed—all of them were marked with when Hennie wrote them down—they became more and more detailed, more and more critical of others who couldn't cook as well as she, and even more negative toward her husband. The last recipe was dated January 1947. Three months before she left. It was a recipe for crepes, of all things.

Virginia looked at the kitchen clock she could see from the sun porch. It was 4:30. Good grief, she had a hair appointment at 9:00. She would end up in the hospital if she didn't get some sleep. Her body was exhausted and her eyes dry and red from the reading, but her brain was churning.

The recipes fascinated her but didn't provide any answers. Why did Hennie decide to devote so much time to cooking?

Boredom being at home with a baby all day, first her husband gone to war and then back but traveling all week? Maybe because it was her special gift and she was just plain good at it? By all accounts she was; Zadie said Buddy wanted her to open a restaurant and share it with the public. Maybe one day Zadie and Topie told her she was too young or wild or something to put a meal together, and their criticism worked as a catalyst on Hennie to show them wrong. In other words, because she was told her she couldn't. Yes, that could be it.

But one thing was clear. It wasn't enough. Whatever drove Hennie to spend hours perfecting recipes and then writing the specifics down in a clean, small, precise hand hadn't worked. It didn't keep her from wanting more, more attention from men, more fun, more drinking, any more than having a baby and a husband did.

Mack found her asleep on the loveseat at 7:00. "Gee-gee, what are you doing down here?"

She looked up at him, and squinted from the sunshine. "I couldn't sleep, got to reading something. What time is it?"

"About seven. Go on back to bed. You look like you need the rest. I'm meeting some other realtors for breakfast this morning. We are declaring a truce in light of the Kyung Motors Plant."

"Getting the plant here is not a done deal."

"That's no way to talk. We have to move forward as if Abundance is the front runner."

"OK, have a good breakfast." She'd sleep for another hour and would still have time to get to the hair appointment. Or she could call them and get a later appointment.

For the first time in months, she let herself think about life with or without Kyung Motors. She'd read the prospectus, well, parts of it. It would be a godsend economically, for everyone from the North Carolina border to the Georgia line. No doubt about it. The departure of the mills over the last decade or more was hurting a lot of people. She doubted NAFTA would turn out the great advancement it was touted to be. She wasn't an economist, like Bethany, so she didn't understand it all. On the other hand, the farms and fields around Abundance, so lovely in spring and fall, the rolling hills with such a variety of trees and flowers, what would happen to them if a huge chunk of land was invaded by a factory? What would happen to the people of her county?

"I'm just tired," she thought. "Virginia, you're getting melancholy with looking at the recipes of a woman you barely remember, who, by the way, thought it better to kill herself, or possibly you, than stick around and raise you." Yet she couldn't make herself hate Hennie. She never had been able to, not even now. Hennie was to be pitied. She was mentally ill, back in a time when such things were hushed up and shoved in the back cabinets of family life. Hennie obsessed over the smallest details of recipes recorded for—who? Zadie? Maybe, at least Zadie had kept them. Whether she followed them, Virgie didn't know. For Topie? Topie was a woman who would scoff at such precision about preparing food, an act that should be as natural and carefree, essential and artless as sex. For Virgie herself? Probably, in some way, at least early on. So what could have been an act of compulsiveness could have started as an act of love, somehow.

Virginia had always maintained she was at heart a Cullins, from a big, rowdy, somewhat redneck family who knew their ancestors showed up in the Carolinas sometime in the 1800sbut didn't much care about the particulars. That was her name, theone she held on to even after marrying Mack. So often in her teen years, especially after Governor died, she didn't want any part of being a Cleeland even if she did live part of the week in the big Victorian and even if it paid for her to be a sorority sister at the most esteemed university in the Upstate. Identifying with the Cullins would never change for her, even if she was so mad at Daddy right now that she could spit sometimes.

But in her fatigue this morning, in her state of wanting to hunker down on the love seat and drowse the rest of the day rather than rush to another meeting or appointment or interview, she found herself questioning. Questioning the value of Kyung Motors. If Abundance really needed to change all that much. If she was all that different from Hennie.

Chapter 17

T minus three days and counting: Monday of Festival week, the proverbial quiet before the storm. There simply was nothing left to do. Over the weekend, even new shrubs had been planted along the side streets. Everything was in place, and unless an entire band came down with the flu, or the weather turned really nasty, or a salmonella outbreak hit the area, Virginia and the other planners felt confident that the festival would meet expectations, if not exceed them.

Matthew moved back home from Charleston for the summer. She roped him, in his words, into volunteering the whole weekend. He would drive the truck that would carry folding chairs from the funeral homes, churches, and lodges, wearing an official First Annual South Carolina Biscuit Festival hat and bright green vest, like the 500 plus other volunteers. Bethany promised that she and Roger would arrive Friday night.

Mack wanted to be supportive, but he had informed her early on that escorting, courting, pleasing and generally kowtowing to the Kyung Motors reps would be his priority from Wednesday to Saturday, as it would be for several other Chamber of Commerce leaders and city council members. She couldn't expect him to park cars or drive around in a golf cart trouble-shooting. He promised to be there on Saturday night during the concert intermission, when the leaders and volunteers for the festival would be recognized. She knew he would make sure he was beside her to hand her a dozen roses and would whisper in her ear how she wowed everybody, of course.

That Monday morning in May dawned cool but cloudless; the air was just brisk and dry enough to be comfortable, and Virginia breathed a silent prayer that the humidity would stay down for the next seven days. No matter what one planned for, weather could make all the difference. As she sipped her coffee that morning, she felt waves of contentment between slight, nagging whispers that said, "When will the other shoe drop? When will something go wrong?"

She opened the paper to browse and see if the *Turling County Messenger*, not known for exacting editorial quality, had gotten all the information and advertisements right. And then the phone rang.

"Hello, Foster residence."

"Is this Virginia Foster?" a strange, urgent voice asked.

She didn't want to admit to it; could this be the fulfillment of those whispered prophecies? Or just a telemarketer calling way too early? "Yes, this is she."

"Mrs. Foster, this is Tom Rylings at the *Turling County Messenger*. I wanted to get your statement on the editorial printed in the paper this morning about the festival."

"There's an editorial about the festival?" she asked. "Who wrote it? About what?"

"It was written by Reverend Powell, the pastor of the Evangel Community Church of the Living Faith."

Virginia caught her breath to keep from saying something she didn't want to be quoted. "Yes, I am familiar with Mr. Powell."

There was a pause on the other end of the line, as if Rylings, whom Virginia didn't know, expected Virginia's opinion. When nothing came, he went on. "Mr. Powell says that the festival is bringing evil into the town and is supporting pornography."

"What?" Virginia said. She stopped herself. Even though the *Turling County Messenger* had been supportive of the festival, she also knew it wasn't above stirring up a ruckus. Didn't they print that unnecessary story about the minister out in Stansboro who was caught with another man at a rest area, and then the poor man committed suicide? No, she was not going to give them any fodder.

"I do not know why Mr. Powell would make a statement like that, or why the paper would publish it and give him a forum. If you don't mind, I will read the editorial right now—the paper is on my breakfast table—and look into it. But under no terms am I going to give a statement to the press before I have the facts. So thank you. Good-bye." And she tried not to slam the receiver down.

In less than five seconds she had turned to the back page of the front section of the local paper and found the editorial. No, it wasn't an editorial. It was part screed, part sermon.

The city of Abundance and the people of Turling County have agreed to participate in the so-called festival in honor of the city's past as the home of a flour mill. There is nothing wrong with honoring the hard work of the town's former citizens, now long gone.

So glad he approves, Virginia thought. *Now get to the point.*

Abundance is a beautiful community with thousands of God-fearing people. As the pastor of a congregation on the outskirts of town, I know many of them. However, the town has been duped into sponsoring a big party that will supposedly bring money and jobs and fame and fortune to this part of the Upstate. Money has been poured into this event that could have been spent on better things, such as schools and helping the poor.

Oh, please.

There is no guarantee that the economy will benefit from this party in honor of a biscuit. On top of that, people are being discouraged from attending their own churches on Sunday morning.

However, the biggest concern of this writer is that this so-called festival will encourage young people to drink and gamble. That was, until I went to purchase some products as the Healthy Loaf Bakery on Culver Street. This establishment is the only one that sells gluten-free bread, the only kind my wife can eat. So I stopped by last Friday and was stunned to see a painting of a naked woman hanging on the wall to the left of the counter. When I asked the owner why he had such filth hanging in a public place, he said, "This is one of the entries in the festival's art competition. We've had a really good response, and I agreed to show some of them." And he pointed me in the direction of the wall behind me, where another naked person was hanging, along with two landscapes.

Oh, no.

Since when does pornography have anything to do with honoring the history of this town, or with biscuits? Why does this festival bring vulgar art into our environs? If the city of Abundance wants to go through with this festival, it is the duty of Christian people to boycott it and take a stand for morality and righteousness.

All right, Virginia. Keep calm. This is a public relations nightmare— no, no, it's just a blip. We'll get over it. First things first. I need to go look at this so-called pornography.

As much as she didn't like to leave the house half put together, she managed to walk through the doors of Healthy Loaf Bakery, which was two doors down from the TownSquare Gallery, in about forty minutes. And there it was. A four-by-six oil in an Impressionistic mode of a fully nude, dark-haired woman, seated on a red velvet couch in a relaxed pose. Her breasts were normal but audacious, as was her expression.

205

Thanks to the morning editorial, Healthy Loaf Bakery was doing a good business, or so it seemed. Customers, if they were really there to buy bread or pastries, were not staring or leering at the painting, but they were definitely not ignoring it, and from gestures she was trying to ignore, Virginia could tell they were discussing the art work, which seemed as much out of place in the bakery as it did in Abundance.

"Hello, Virginia." She heard a voice behind her and turned. It was Audrey. "Did you get a call from the paper, too?"

"Yes." Virginia sighed. "What do you think?"

"I'm no art critic. I don't think it will win first place in the competition. But I think it will be the one most remembered."

Virginia turned around, remembering that Powell's editorial had mentioned two nudes. "Oh, heavens." This one was even more provocative. She couldn't see from where she stood if the same artist had signed them both, but this one was in a different style. The figure was less realistic, more elongated—a nude male, thankfully from behind. To the sides of it hung two safe and none-too-impressive landscapes of the same lake and dock, one in fall, one in spring.

Before they knew it, they were both suppressing laughter. "Well, I'm trying to figure out," Audrey finally managed to say, between giggles, "if this will bring in more people or fewer?"

"Unfortunately, probably more, now. However, we are going to have to do something about this. Damage control. I mean, seriously, what was Daniel thinking? He could have hung those in his gallery, or in some place where typical people aren't likely to go."

"They would like it down at the truck stop," they heard the voice of Ted behind them. "At least Miss Red Couch over there."

"Hi, Ted. Guess you read the editorial, too," Virginia said.

"No, ladies, actually I come in here for the muffins. Of course, I read it. And it looks like half the town did and decided to judge for themselves if it's pornography. What's your verdict?"

"It's not porn, but it doesn't belong here," said Virginia. "We're going to have to talk to Daniel."

"He's two doors down. Let's go," suggested Audrey. "The sooner we deal with this, the better."

"But what are you going to say?"

"Uh, I don't know. We'll think of something on the way."

"Think fast," cautioned Ted. "Because I think this is him."

Daniel had just entered the bakery. "Oh, hey, Mrs. Foster. Hi," he greeted Audrey and Ted, clearly not remembering their names. "How do you like the art? Todd has been great to put these up. He's really wanting to support what the artistic community is doing around here."

"Um, yeah, Daniel, we wanted to talk to you about that. Could we go back to your shop?"

"Sure, let me get my breakfast. Go on down and I'll be there in a few minutes."

The three committee members obeyed, thankful for the time to confer. Daniel obviously didn't see anything wrong with full frontal nudity hanging in his friend's bakery, nor did his friend.

In ten minutes the four of them were seated in Daniel's pottery studio at the back of TownSquare Gallery. "So, what's up?"

"Well, first, uh," Virginia tried to start. "Uh, how is the art competition going?"

"Oh, super. We ended up with 50 entries—let me see, twenty-five oils, twelve watercolors, and thirteen other media, so that's half the prize money. And the town's been great. We have some up in the library, the high school, businesses, banks. All over. So far, no complaints and no damage. I'd say it's been a success. It's helping my business, too, because I'm selling some of them on consignment and we've had several offers."

"Your art's not in the contest, is it?" Audrey said.

"Oh, no, that wouldn't be right. I'm not even one of the judges. And the winner's already been picked, you know. We'll announce it at the festival on Sunday."

"Could you tell us who the winner is?" Ted asked.

"Oh, yeah, if you can keep a secret. It's the acrylic in Todd's bakery, the one on the wall opposite the counter."

"The, uh, male, nude?" guessed Virginia.

"Yeah, I guess so. Guy who did that really understands light and texture. Neat technique."

"I see." Virginia looked at the others and then at Daniel.

"Is something wrong about that?" he asked.

"Well, you see, Daniel, there was an editorial in the paper this morning, a certain person, a sort of minister in the county, who was protesting that the Bakery had two nudes hanging in it and those were part of the festival."

"You're kidding me."

"Ah, no." Virginia paused again,

"Hey, listen. It's Todd's shop. It's not like I put them up at the elementary school. Todd can hang what he wants in his business, can't he? And I'll admit, the female nude is not that great, but that's not the point. Freedom of expression is."

"That's true, but . . . "

"You're not going to let one ranting guy in a newspaper column tell you what to do with your festival, are you?" Daniel asked.

"That's just it, Daniel, it's not *my* festival."

"No, I don't mean it that way, it's the town's festival, and the town is okay with it. Has anybody complained about the paintings other than this guy? They've been up two weeks already, and you didn't even know about it."

"He's right," said Ted. "If people in the town had a big issue with it, we would have heard by now."

"We might not have heard about it at all if Powell's wife didn't have a wheat allergy," Audrey added.

"You've got that right," Virginia said. "But I don't know, Daniel. With all the people coming into town for the festival, especially coming downtown into shops, you just don't know who's going to be seeing things. I can't believe I am saying this."

"I can't believe I'm hearing it," said Daniel, clearly mystified by the disapproval of the paintings and on guard about what he expected her to say.

"No, I'm not saying don't show the paintings. Especially if one of them is the winner. But, perhaps, could you hang them in your gallery and put something else up in Todd's bakery, for the rest of the week?" She felt herself cringing as she made the suggestion. "If nothing else, it will give his customers a look at the other art in the competition."

Daniel looked down; she couldn't tell if he was showing disappointment, disgust for small-minded people, or a desire not to spend his time switching out paintings. "OK. But you know this is saying you are giving in to a crackpot."

For a second Virginia felt like she was being scolded by someone young enough to be her child, and that was something she didn't allow. But she paused. "It may seem that way, but I prefer to think of it as a compromise."

"Sure. I'll take care of it."

"We appreciate it, Daniel." She thought about complimenting him on the fine work he had done in arranging the competition, but decided not to; it would sound patronizing, considering the circumstances.

"Yes, we do," agreed Audrey.

"Thanks for everything," said Ted, ever the conciliator, shaking Daniel's hand. The three of them left and entered the street. They stopped for a few moments to view the preparations taking place in the square.

"Did we dodge that bullet?" Ted asked.

"No, but it only inflicted a flesh wound," Audrey answered.

"Maybe," said Virginia.

"Are you going to talk to the paper?" asked Audrey.

"No. Daniel said he would take care of it, and he'll take care of it. I am not going to dignify Powell's remarks, and shame on the paper for printing them. They just wanted to stir something up. It's unforgivable, especially right now on the verge of this whole thing being such a success. I mean, look at this square. It hasn't looked this good in ages."

"That's for sure," Ted agreed.

"No, Powell's done all the damage he's going to. I guess a few people will stay home because they believe him, or think they are going to be exposed to some kind of sin city down here for three days. What nonsense."

"I still think it will probably do more good than harm, although I'm not sure how it will go over, that painting being the winner. It struck me as a tad on the, you know . . ."

"Don't say it, Audrey. I know what you're thinking. We should have thought about this when we agreed to the art competition. What were we expecting? Grandma's watercolors of flowers and rabbits in the garden? That's not exactly what Daniel shows in his gallery."

"Yeah, I'm with Virginia. And let's face it--95% of the people who are going to come out of the hills to attend this festival are a whole lot more interested in getting a fried turkey leg than viewing an art competition."

"I hate to say it, but you're right, Ted. Thank goodness for the other five percent," Audrey said.

Virginia decided to stay in town and view the work that was going on to construct platforms, string wires, and plant some last-minute landscape plants. She strolled around the town, making small talk, giving an opinion here and there, trying to praise a lot more, lending a hand when she could. She didn't want to come out of this experience with the same reputation as the well-off descendant of one of the town founders, someone who thought she could supervise but not contribute to real work.

On Wednesday, Mack disappeared early to meet the Kyung Motor Company delegation at the Greenville-Spartanburg airport at 8:00. They were flying in from Chicago, their corporate American headquarters. She was up with him, sharing a cup of coffee and wishing him luck. Today she literally had nothing to do; any more tweaking would ruin the delicate balance. This would be a good day to visit Zadie and Topie. She hadn't seen them in over a week, and she regretted her oversight. But she'd take them both on an outing if she could, at least Zadie, after the festival. Zadie liked the Biltmore in Ashville. She could ride a wheelchair if she couldn't walk the mansion and estate, which would be lively with spring now.

She decided to see them early; she usually visited in the afternoon, and it wouldn't hurt for the staff to see her at a different time. The element of surprise had its perks. Anyway, she wanted to talk to the administrator. They had been playing phone tag, and on her last message Virginia, a bit frustrated, had promised to drop in soon.

Virginia felt upbeat. Her melancholy about Hennie and its tendrils touching Abundance, the children, and herself had lifted in the flurry of the festival. The day would be beautiful, and the loveliness would continue until Monday. The weather promised to be sunny, but of course hot. The WSPA weathergirl said something about a high of 91, but low humidity, and no rain in the forecast. Perfect. Well, no, perfect would be seventy-eight degrees, but at least a fairly cloudless sky was all she could see from horizon to horizon.

And just to make sure, she had swung by Healthy Loaf Bakery. She could see from the street that Miss Red Couch had been replaced with a sunset in a simple frame, so she assumed the prize winner was also now occupying a wall in Daniel's gallery. If Powell thought he had won, he hadn't. The festival would go on and people would love it. Maybe like Ebenezer Scrooge, he would be visited by three happy spirits on Sunday night telling him how much they loved the festival.

She reached St. Ambrose Community and walked through the doors. The residents ate breakfast about from 8:30 to 9:00, and the staff could be heard clearing plates and vacuuming the dining room now at 10:00. The door to the administrator's office stood open, so she decided this was the best time to fulfill her promise that might have sounded more like a threat after five missed calls.

The door bore the sign, "Dianne Foster, St. Ambrose Patient Care Coordinator." Even thought their surnames were the same, Mack and Dianne were not related. Ms. Foster had moved here from Birmingham, willingly transferred after a divorce, and she hadn't bothered to change her name yet. Virginia knew all this because she had asked when Zadie and Topie came to live at St. Ambrose, and as a true Southerner she had to make sure no long-lost relatives were in the room.

Virginia knocked, and heard a "come in." Dianne was a plain woman who could have helped herself a little bit by cutting and frosting her mousey hair and wearing contacts. "Oh, good morning, Mrs. Foster," Dianne stood up to shake hands.

"Please call me Virginia." She didn't want to hear a conversation with her last name repeated over and over again. "You well this morning?"

"Oh, yes, and I hear great things about the festival. I plan to come Saturday."

"I'm glad to hear that. I think you'll be pleased, and everyone else. Something for everybody, you know how that is."

"Sounds great. What can I do for you?"

"One of the staff members—I can't remember who, she's a red-headed young woman who works on the second floor—I stopped her one day to ask about Mrs. Jackson and she told me that she is not doing well. The young woman sort of hinted that Mrs. Jackson would need to be moved soon."

"Ah. Yes. Well, we're not quite there yet, but yes, she probably will very soon. Her dementia is just getting to that stage where she can't be left unsupervised for any time. She can still get out of bed to use the bathroom, and come down here for meals with some guidance, but how much longer that will be true, well, it's pretty iffy."

"I understand. I don't see her as much as I used to, at least not for the last couple of months, and you all see her every day. Where will she go?"

"To the Alzheimer's facility. It's a separate building, to the west side of this one. She would still have her own room—we can't let them share a room like in a regular nursing home but as you know this is not a regular nursing home.

"That's for sure," Virginia thought. She spoke, "That will be hard on my aunt. She is very, very attached to Mrs. Jackson. I'd say they were sisters if I didn't know any better."

"Yes, they truly are devoted to one another. But Mrs. McCann's mind is very sharp, and it's likely that when she goes—which I assure you is probably not going to be for years—it will be from heart failure and not from Alzheimer's."

Virginia remembered that Dianne Foster's credentials included training as a nurse practitioner and a graduate degree in gerontology, so she wasn't offended by the diagnosis. Her opinion could be trusted. "So Aunt Zadie will be by herself? I hate that, but it can't be helped."

"Yes, it's unfortunate, but I think she's resilient. She'll make friends with other residents."

Virginia wasn't sure about this. Zadie had a stubborn streak, and eighty some years as a member of a faded but once illustrious and wealthy family had made her just a bit of a snob, something not likely to change now. "Maybe. I suppose it's one of those life passages. One of them is bound to die before the other."

"I'm afraid so."

"Well, I'll be going. I'm going to visit them this morning."

"Excellent. You do a much better job of that than most family members, even children."

"Oh, I thought you knew. Mrs. McCann raised me, from the time I was four. She is my mother, really, as far as most things are concerned. And Topie is the next best thing."

"I didn't know," Dianne remarked, with a quizzical expression that Virginia was not about to satisfy today or ever.

Virginia left and took the stairs to 207. She'd see Zadie first. She dreaded the day when she would walk into Topie's room and get a blank stare of non-recognition, or even worse, that Virginia's sudden presence would send the fearful old woman into a frenzy and a staff member would have to be called. That day would not just be a sorry one for Topie; it would break Virginia's heart. Perhaps it would be safer to enter Topie's room in Zadie's presence.

"Aunt Zadie, you in?" she called as she entered.

Zadie was up, watching some talk show on TV, something like a doctor call-in program. Virginia didn't watch much television, despite the fact that they paid for one hundred cable channels.

"Yes, Virgie Mae, come on in."

"How you feeling?"

"Pretty good. We had prunes for breakfast. That's old folks' food, but it did the trick."

Virginia laughed. They chatted a while. Zadie could make

funny observations, and then change the subject quickly to catch you off guard.

"Did you talk to that other Foster woman about Topie?"

"Yes, ma'am, I did. She said, sooner rather than later, Topie'd have to go to the Alzheimer's building."

"Lord. I was afraid of that." Zadie sat quiet for a while. "Did she give you a date?"

"No, but after I rest up from the festival, I'll probably pursue it and get the paperwork done, Aunt Zadie. I'm sorry, but I'd rather be in charge of what happens to her than be pushed around."

Zadie mulled this over. *She's probably thinking that's just how I am, trying to control matters,* Virginia thought. She'd heard it before from Zadie, but Zadie only noticed because she herself was so controlling, even pushy, or had been before the stroke.

But Zadie, as if the time left in the conversation was short, changed the subject again abruptly. "Did you look at those recipes of your momma's?"

"Yes, I did," Virginia smiled, and took Zadie's hand. "I thought they were your recipes."

"No, those were Hennie's doing, all of them. Even when her dishes weren't any better than mine, she worked ten times harder on them and writing them down."

"Her recipes were—almost like masterpieces. Works of art. Or short stories. Lots of details. It almost made me want to . . ."

"Meet her?"

"No, well, not just meet her. Cook with her."

Chapte18

Virginia arrived at Biscuit Central by 7:30 Thursday morning. The square bustled with the volunteers who represented the retired and homemaker segments of the population, with city and county maintenance employees, and with some workers who had been sent over from generous businesses to clean the streets, finish the platforms, and set up chairs. The weather was as beautiful and dry as yesterday.

The festival was scheduled to start at exactly 12:00 noon on Thursday. Virginia knew the first day would be slow and the crowds too sparse to be called true crowds. The committee had debated long and hard about waiting until Friday to start, and maybe they would revisit that topic for next year's festival, but she hoped to attract the "RV" crowd by starting before the weekend.

Vendors were pulling in their vans and hooking up water and power. The square was achieving its final transformation from a sleepy, grassy area surrounded by parking spaces and skirted by shops and small businesses into a full-fledged tourist draw. All the banners and signage were up. Abundance, South Carolina, for the first time in Virginia's memory, looked prosperous and alive.

Did she have regrets at this point? Sure. She should have had a larger planning team, although the six of them had done amazing jobs. Melody surprised her—the woman Virginia expected to try to steal the show only seemed interested in stealing a date with Ted Sneed, who was still a good-looking man and knew how to show a woman a good time. The other regret—they just should have started earlier. Four months was not long enough, despite all her assurances to the festival planners, City Council, Chamber, and volunteers. Assuming this festival turned out a success—and they had set the bar for success kind of low—preparations for 1999's event would have to start when she and Mack returned from their planned New York trip. Any other regrets were minor, niggling little matters that could easily be remedied next time around, such as which brand of paper towel to buy for the portable toilets.

Matthew drove by in a club car. He stopped with a screech. "Hey, Mom." She hadn't seen him much in the week he'd been home from college. Was he avoiding her?

"How's it going, darling?" He needed a haircut, but he was a good-looking boy with all those thick blond curls and that nose—yes, that Cleeland nose.

"Great. I got the best volunteer job here."

"You've got connections."

"Don't tell anybody."

"I think they know. Hey, when this is all over, let's go out to breakfast and have a long talk." Yes, that was the other regret— she'd allowed the festival to distract her from Matthew's life. She didn't want to be one of those hovering mommas, but colleges didn't send home report card to parents, no matter how much they were paying.

"Uh, sure." He sounded wary. "Well, got to go." His walky-talky squawked at him, and he pulled off, driving a bit too casually for Virginia's taste.

She walked around the square, then down the side streets to survey the transformed downtown. Even though she greeted most of the people she saw by name, and they her, she felt a little anonymous, *in cognito*. She wasn't needed today. *If I left town until Saturday night, would they even notice?* That was the sign of good organization. She liked, for once, not pulling her cell phone out of her purse every minute to answer or make a call. The town was buzzing because of the last four months of her labor, and now she could sit back and relax. But then she remembered she was expected to help escort the Kyung Motors personnel.

By Friday evening, Virginia was starting to wonder if she should write the textbook on how to run a town festival. Already, by estimates based on parked cars (figuring two to three persons per car), 5,000 people had attended, and certainly more would show up Saturday. She had asked the parking attendants to keep track of license plates. So far South Carolina was leading the pack, followed by Georgia, North Carolina (of course), Tennessee, Virginia, Florida (naturally), then points west—Alabama, Kentucky, and West Virginia. Four from Mississippi had been spotted, five from Ohio, two from Indiana (all RVs), two from Arkansas (Double-Dutch employees) and even one from Missouri. That meant, already, visitors from fourteen states! And who knew what Saturday would bring, along with guests from the farthest distance, Korea.

All the minor disasters were averted or solved quickly, such as banners falling. One person, from out-of-state, did pass out from the heat and was taken to the hospital for observation. A couple of wandering, screaming toddlers had to be returned to parents who weren't paying attention. Considering what could happen, these were nothing. Oh, and the incident with the congregants from Evangel Community Church of the Living Faith.

A small group—Virginia counted six at one point, and then five at another, with different faces—set up camp at the entrance to the parking lot on Friday. They carried colorful homemade signs that read "This festival does not glorify God," "God doesn't want you at this festival," "This festival supports pornography," and "Go to the house of God this Sunday—not this 'festival'."

Since the parking lot was public space, and since the protesters weren't breaking any laws, Virginia chose not to make a scene by asking security or the police to deal with them. Maybe they would go away, she reasoned. They might persuade some folks not to attend the festival, but Virginia doubted it.

But as much as she needed to keep walking through the crowds, surveying, and trouble-shooting, she couldn't help but watch the little group that wanted to convince the crowds that the festival was Satan's business. Most people would think the same things she did—that their protest was weird and sad, pointless and pitiful. *Yet I have a choice, like we always do: to stand back and scoff, or be kind.* She found a water station, scooped up six bottles of cold water from the ice-filled vats, and walked over to the entrance to the parking lot.

"Howdy, folks," she greeted them. "You look hot, and you're not in the shade. Here's some water."

The three women and three men, all over forty, all overdressed, and all sweating, took the water bottles and acknowledged thanks in some way--a nod, a phrase, or a smile—but did not speak. "Well, have a nice day," she finished, and walked away. *I've done the right thing, if nothing else.* The groups stayed there into the afternoon on Friday, and then went away as quickly and quietly as they appeared. If this protest was the worst thing that happened during the festival, Virginia decided she could feel satisfied. Sometime in the future, when she could sort out all her feelings, when Topie was settled into the Alzheimer's ward, after she could deal with Matthew, she would make peace with Mr. Powell, would extend an olive branch. But not now. And they would keep a tighter leash on Daniel next year, if he still wanted to help them. Maybe he wouldn't after being called a pornographer. Today, she would let Pastor Powell think he had won some kind of victory, if that was what he wanted.

Throughout Friday, she strolled. If she saw something awry, she made a call. Mostly, she greeted and smiled until her face hurt and her feet, despite the comfortable walking shoes, were pinched and aching. About 3:00 the crowds were thinning a bit due to the heat; thank goodness they had decided on May! She was beginning to feel very pleased, with herself and with the community. As she turned the corner to walk down a side street off of the square, she was stopped abruptly by a stout woman in an oversized lavender top, owl-eye sunglasses, and denim Capri pants.

"I guess you're pretty satisfied, aren't you?"

Virginia kept herself from speaking before she had time to size up this woman and situation. Did she know this person? Was she from out of town? Then Virginia noticed the unnaturally blonde hair and the ball cap emblazoned with a logo of a little girl in silhouette and the words "Pageant Babies."

"Oh, hello, Ms., um, Flynn, isn't it?" Virginia turned on all the charm she had available in the 90-degree sun.

"Yes, it is." Maddie Flynn took off her sunglasses to stare eye-to-eye with Virginia, but she said nothing. Virginia kept her sunglasses on, and began to search through the mental file cabinets she had created for the festival and pulled up the incident at the town council meeting in February, the first and last time she had met Maddie Flynn. The woman in front of her looked as if she had dropped thirty pounds since that encounter, but she didn't look any less angry. Virginia decided to let Ms. Flynn do the talking.

"So, my little girls were too *sexualized* for you, but you let those adult nudes be shown in public places."

"I didn't *let* the nudes be shown, Ms. Flynn. I don't *let* anybody do anything. Someone else was in charge of the art competition. They were moved from the bakery to a more appropriate location when the committee knew about it."

"The committee. Likely story."

"It's the truth, whether you believe it or not."

"Well, anyway, you missed out. There would be a whole lot more people here if you'd have let me hold a mini-pageant here, like I requested, fair and square. You think you know so much, but you have no clue how many people come to pageants."

Maddie Flynn's voice was getting louder, and Virginia was conscious that some passersby were looking at these two middle-aged women on the sidewalk. The fact that Virginia was trying to keep calm and smiling was probably lost on the ones who were wondering if a cat fight was about to break out.

"That may be true, but we've got a good enough crowd here, even for a Friday. I don't know how much more the town could handle right now."

"Humph. Who died and made you the one to decide what Abundance and Turling County could handle?"

"I wasn't making a decision—just an observation." Virginia paused. She really wanted to say something that would cut deeply enough that Maddie Flynn would never bother her again. But since only insults came to mind, she held back and let Maddie land the next blow. Turning the other cheek would at least keep Virginia in the right.

"Right. This festival was your baby from the beginning, and it's all about a way for your husband to make more money. You called the shots from day one. It's okay to have naked pictures in the bakery, but no, we're not going to let some little girls dress up and have a good time because Mrs. Virginia Foster of the Cleeland family, the old money, says we can't do that."

Maddie needed a good slap across her mouth for bringing up the Cleelands, but Virginia grasped her own right hand with her left to keep it in place. "My mother's family has absolutely nothing to do with this festival, Ms. Flynn. That will be all. Good afternoon. I hope you enjoy the festival."

Virginia started to walk away. She had taken four steps by

the time Maddie Flynn started in again. "Your mother's family. Everybody knows about your mother's family. You think the town doesn't know what went on in that house all those years ago, and what happened to--"

Virginia turned abruptly. She removed her sunglasses in a swift motion and was two inches from Maddie Flynn's nose before Maddie could finish her sentence. But she took care to keep her volume low and intense.

"You will *never* speak of my mother or her family in my presence again. It's time for you to shut your fat mouth and get on down the street. Go run a pageant in some hick town and leave the festival and the people trying to have a good time alone."

"You don't scare me, Virginia Foster."

"I don't care if I scare you. But you don't scare me, and no whiny display you make is going to make me regret the decision we made to keep you and your sickening spectacles away from this town square. Good day. Don't bother me ever again."

Virginia turned and left at a definite but calm pace, trying not to draw attention to herself. Ordinarily, such a confrontation would have sent her heart racing, but this one was too gratifying and too long coming, even if Maddie did have the nerve to bring up ghosts of the past. Virginia smiled a little to herself. Maddie was the kind to try to file a lawsuit, but the festival was using the city's lawyer and Virginia had already checked on whether the festival was liable for not allowing particular vendors to participate.

After walking a block, she noticed that she was in front of Biscuit Central. She stood for a moment, smelling the strong odors of leaven, butter, and peaches. Those turned her attention away from Maddie Flynn and the sad protesters, and she decided to indulge in something hot, flaky, and warm. The elderly lady who was passing out biscuits at that moment recognized her and handed her one for free, with a wink. The first bite of the hot baked dough with real butter and peach preserves with just the right amount of crispness and sugar satisfied her craving. Biscuits might not be the most nourishing and healthy food in the world, but there was nothing like what she held in her mouth and hand right now.

Virginia chatted with the elderly woman who had provided this morsel for a while, finding out she was Flora Johnson from Jasper Springs Baptist Church and that she liked the festival but was glad she wasn't the one standing over a stove making all these biscuits.

"Thank you, Miss Flora. I needed to hear somebody say something sweet."

"It's the truth, honey. But I don't think I'll want to eat a biscuit for a while after seein' so many."

A hot buttered biscuit dripping sweet peaches in one hand, a bottle of water in the other, Virginia continued her stroll. Well, what had she expected? You can't do something and make everybody happy. There would always be the Maddie Flynns and the Preacher Powells. But there were enough of the Flora Johnsons to make the festival work. She was thankful for all the people like Flora who didn't have to be here but decided that the town was more important than their comfort and convenience for a few hours one day in May, and who weren't interested in making a name for themselves or a buck.

Saturday of the festival dawned as pleasantly as the two previous days. The festival workers braced themselves for the onslaught. They were not disappointed by the crowds, which started filling the streets by 9:00. On Friday 3,575 biscuits changed hands in the town square; that was a lot of flour, shortening, butter, and jelly. Today it would be a challenge to keep fresh, hot, biscuits coming and to keep the lines down. Perhaps by lunch time the taste for biscuits would be slaked and visitors would move on to corn dogs, funnel cakes, barbecue, fried turkey legs, and onion rings.

The Kyung Motors delegation was scheduled to arrive at 11:00. Its first stop would be the main stage, where the visitors would, even though Virginia insisted it was the corniest thing in the world, be presented with a key to the city and "hopefully, the key to a wonderful relationship in the future." These words from Bob Smallwood, Mr. Santa Claus, almost made Virginia roll her eyes. Then they would listen to a concert of bluegrass music (for twenty minutes, only three songs), and then be escorted around the festival area. At noon they would enter the air-conditioned tent for the "authentic" meal of local cuisine.

Virginia foresaw only a couple of potential problems in the arrangements, although she wasn't in charge of the Kyung Motors' visit and could only complain, not change anything. First, the locals had constantly referred to the group as "the Koreans"—she'd done it herself. Only two of the visitors, out of seven, were truly Korean in origin and spoke no English. She'd read everything biographical she could find about the delegation. Jeffrey Kim may have a Korean name, but he was reared in California. The translator's mother was Korean but her father was military, and she grew up in the Midwest. Three others were assistant vice presidents for marketing, distribution, and sales, and they hailed from New England, Pennsylvania, and Kansas, respectively. So she hoped no one slipped and referred to them carelessly as "the Koreans" instead of the representatives or delegates from Kyung Motors. That would be insensitive and probably a deal-breaker.

Second, she wasn't quite sure what fell into the category of local cuisine. Peaches, but they weren't in season. Okra, not in season either. Tomatoes, green or otherwise, also too early. So if those were on the menu, they would either be shipped in and therefore not local, or frozen, an unappetizing prospect. Barbecue was a Carolina specialty, but it would have to be chicken versions. Seafood was a South Carolina mainstay, but not here. A Lowcountry boil could be nice, but again, Abundance wasn't in the Lowcountry and a boil included sausage. Maybe they had been hasty about the matter of the pork. Asians did eat it, didn't they? Well, the Chinese did, but God forbid anybody confuse Koreans with Chinese! Desserts would not be a problem, but Asians did not prefer heavy sweets, or so she had heard. Then she reminded herself that she was thinking in stereotypes and only two of the group could be considered "Asians" anyway.

If Virginia had remained calm and collected through Friday, nerves set in at 11:00 Saturday when the delegation arrived and she came to realize the enormity of the festival's hosting the Kyung Motors delegation. She was supposed to accompany the delegation in case any of them had questions about the festival, but keep a low profile otherwise. A special assistant to the governor would lead the group. She was thankful the governor wasn't coming. The Kyung Motors folks had probably seen enough of him, and he would just consider this a campaign stop anyway, since he was up for re-election in November.

At 2:00 she could breathe in relief. The delegates had graciously asked to hear some more music after the luncheon, and in a few minutes, miraculously, a canopy was set up and they listened to the high school's string quartet. Better that than Miss Debbie's Dancing Toddlers. And the meal went splendidly. The Village Gate set up lazy Susans for the round tables that seated six guests each, filled with fried chicken, barbecued chicken, potato salad, fried okra (imported from Central America of all places), pinto beans, cornbread (strangely, no biscuits at the biscuit festival; she'd have to find out who made that blooper), and coconut cake. The restaurant wisely did not sweeten the iced tea and kept the fried food to a minimum. The guests loved the Chow-Chow, and the translator explained that the Koreans had a similar relish dish, but much stronger.

She sat with the two Korean gentlemen and their interpreter, engaging in pleasant but superficial conversation about food, climate, children, and American sports customs. The utter graciousness of her guests charmed her, though. They smiled a great deal, even if they seemed to find it difficult to look her in the eyes. Cordiality reigned. She hoped no one talked car plant at the other tables.

When the delegation was packed into cars—the highest end automobile that Kyung made, of course, the Solana—and were driven away, she wanted to collapse. She needed and wanted a nap, badly. The festival still had twenty-nine hours to go, and she wanted to sleep for thirty. The heavy meal and the heat didn't help. Would any one notice if she slipped away and came back for the concert? It was worth a try. By 2:30 she was stretched across her bed with the alarm clock set for 6:00.

Chapter 19

Country-western music was not Virginia's cup of tea, but from the beginning of the festival preparation she made a commitment not to design it around her own preferences, except in the case of Maddie Flynn's pageant plans. Virginia would have liked oldies, or jazz, or big band. She showed up at Severson Park just as the crowd was starting to dance. She sat down to enjoy people watching until the intermission. Before her nap she had turned off her cell phone, which she wore in the pocket of her khaki slacks, and forgotten about it. She wondered where Mack was. He was supposed to accompany the Kyung Motors group to the airport and be back by 5:00.

The band played for about an hour, a lot of more recent tunes she didn't know. A few struck her as unoriginal, one as rather profound and touching, and most as something good to dance to. This band, from Raleigh, had produced one CD, about two years ago, and most of the crowd knew the songs and sang along in spurts. A line dancing group had started on one of the side streets. After 7:00 beer sales were permitted, not on the square but off in the food vendors' area; nothing crazy had happened Friday night with the beer flowing, but there were twice as many people dancing and milling around tonight. The crowd was loud, but she didn't hear any profanity and they seemed well behaved, just folks having fun in the cooler air and waning sunlight.

The band thanked the "great crowd" and said they were going to take a break for half an hour while the festival gurus—that was the word they used—would take over. A few of the younger folks booed, but the crowd in general applauded enthusiastically as the five band members set down their instruments and dismounted the stage. Bob Smallwood, the man of the day, beardless and looking like he had dropped thirty pounds since Christmas at his doctor's advice, took over the microphone. His speech was punctuated with responses, catcalls, applause, and "yeahs" from the audience.

"Hello! Good evening! Y'all having a good time?" Mr. Santa Claus knew the business of friendliness. "I know I am. How many biscuits y'all eat today? My doc told me to lay off 'em, but I didn't listen. They were awwwesome!" *He's a little too old for "awesome,"* Virginia thought, but her mind was really on preparing herself to go up on the stage in a bit for the obligatory recognition.

"We have a lot, a lot of people to thank for this festival. We had over 500 volunteers. Let's hear it for the volunteers!" He led the applause. "Now, I want to say that there are volunteers, and then there are volunteers. I am up here to give recognition to the people who really were the brains behind this great festival. I want the festival planning committee to come on up here!"

From various parts of the square, Audrey, Melody, Ted, Daryl, Frank, and Virginia gathered on the stage behind Bob, looking a little embarrassed and very tired. "These folks have worked night and day since the city council agreed to this little shindig." *Where does he get these cornball words,* Virginia mused. "They are all long-time members of our community who were willing to give of their time and theirselves to help Abundance think about what it could be with a little muscle work and a lot of team work. Let me call their names. First, Mrs. Audrey Pike." Audrey waved to the applause. "Mr. Ted Sneed, y'all know Ted, Mr. Golden Voice." Ted waved, too, but with much more crowd-pleasing confidence. "Miss Melody Hamblin." *Were those wolf-whistles in the back of the crowd?* "Mr. Daryl Washburn. Daryl, I have paid off my mortgage, thank you," Daryl pointed his finger at Bob as if it were a pretend gun. "Mr. Frank Templeton." Frank, who looked like the quintessential computer nerd, gave a little wave and smiled in what could only be called a sheepish manner.

Bob, having taken the microphone off the stand, now walked over to Virginia, and put his hand on her shoulder. "We owe a lot to these people, but I think they'd agree with me that the one person who we owe the most to for this festival is this last little lady. I remember back in January when she stood up and presented the idea for a biscuit festival. My first thought was, I got to be honest, 'A festival about biscuits?' But she made the case for it, had done her homework, and she'd been working like a house afire for this community for the last four months. I don't know where she gets her energy. Mrs. Virginia Mae Foster, take a bow."

Virginia was not about to take one, but she flashed a smile and waved broadly to an audience, who hooted, hollered, and clapped. Those who were seated stood up. In a couple of seconds, Mack was standing by her side, with a dozen roses and a concerned, almost frantic look on his face. He bent over to whisper in her ear.

"Gee-gee, where have you been?"

"I went home to take a nap after the Kyung Motors people left. I could barely move I was so tired."

"You turned your cell phone off. I've been trying to reach you. St. Ambrose has, too."

"What's wrong?"

In the back of her mind Virginia was conscious that they were carrying on a conversation in front of the crowd, one that couldn't be heard but that was going on too long.

"It's Topie. They found her unconscious. She had a massive heart attack. It's bad."

"Oh, my heavens!"

As the applause died down, she pushed the roses back into Mack's hands and rushed off the stage.

"Damn!" She thought. This was the moment for swearing. "I turn my cell phone off one time in five months, and this happens."

She was running, now, to the parking lot and her SUV. She put her hand in her pocket and pulled out the phone. She switched it on, heard the series of tones, and then dialed Matthew. "Pick up, pick up" she breathed. She heard his voice.

"Hey, mom. Where'd you go? You ran off the stage."

"I have to get to the hospital. They took Topie there. She's bad off. She's had a heart attack."

"Oh, man."

"I need you to go get Zadie from St. Ambrose and bring her there. If Topie's not going to make it, she'll want to be with her."

"Mom, I can't do that."

"Why not?" she snapped.

"Don't you remember? I don't have permission. Whatever they call it. Only you and Dad and Bethany can take her out of there."

"Oh, that's right. Shoot. OK, call Bethany; tell her to go do it. I shouldn't be talking when I'm upset and driving."

She hung up without saying good-bye. She could get to the hospital in less than ten minutes, normally, from the part of town where her vehicle was parked. But with the streets roped off and all the traffic, she'd have to do the best she could.

Just a few days ago I was talking to Dianne about Topie dying from Alzheimer's. Now this. If she makes it, she'll be in rehab and then the nursing home. . . No prospect looked good. Zadie would have to adjust, either way. The decision had been taken out of her hands.

Twenty minutes later she pulled into the hospital parking lot. Abundance Medical Center, a 50-bed hospital, did not have a trauma unit and the likelihood that Topie would get the care she really needed was small. *She should be at a hospital in Greenville, and maybe I can have her moved* . . . Virginia was trying to arrange the future. It had become the habit of her life.

The doors opened for her but not as quickly as she liked. She rushed into the fluorescently bright facility, stopped at the directory, breathing hard, and turned to the right, pushing hard at the doors she encountered.

"I need to see Mrs. Utopia Jackson, please." She spoke to a nurse in the Emergency Room. The woman looked at her with unasked questions, such as why a well-dressed middle-aged white woman was close to panting from hurrying down the hall and asking about an old black lady. But the nurse did her job.

"Yes, ma'am, they brought her in from St. Ambrose Community. She's been taken to ICU, room 4."

"Can I go there?"

"Are you family?"

"Sort of. I have her power of attorney. She has been connected to my family for a long time."

The nurse looked doubtful, but she waved her on. "Go on down this hallway and talk to the nurse outside ICU. She might be able to help you, but it's past visiting hours."

Virginia had little familiarity with hospital vigils, and soon saw a sign that indicated ICU visiting hours went from 8:00-8:30, evening and morning, 10:00-10:30 a.m., and 3:00-3:30 p.m. She'd just missed it, but maybe that wouldn't matter now.

"Hello. I'm Virginia Foster. I need to see Mrs. Jackson. She was just brought in from St. Ambrose." This nurse looked older, and seemed to have no preconceptions about who should or shouldn't visit Topie, She was also very ready to please this evening.

"Yes, ma'am, we've been trying to reach you."

"I'm so sorry. I forgot to turn my cell back on."

"We're glad you're here. We'll let you go on back anyway."

Buttons were pushed, double-doors opened, and Virginia entered the hexagonal ICU. Only three rooms were occupied. She slid the door to Room 4 and walked toward Topie's form on the bed.

If she had thought to do it, she would have counted seven separate wires, tubes, or appliances connected to Topie. The apparatus was more prominent than Topie was. *How tiny she has gotten,* Virginia thought. She remembered Topie as a slender bundle of energy. *How pitiful. I don't know what all these machines are doing, but it looks like she'd be dead in two seconds without them.*

A nurse, a young bearded man, entered. "Hi, I'm Ben. I'm taking care of Mrs. Jackson tonight."

"Thank you, Ben. What can you tell me? I just rushed over here from the festival and haven't had a chance to talk to a doctor or anyone."

"She's had a major cardiac arrest—heart attack. Everything's blocked, to be honest. She's got lung problems, too, not able to breathe on her own. How old is she?"

"85."

"Wow." He opened Topie's eyelids and looked at them with a penlight. Virginia noticed how green they were. *How odd for a black woman to have green eyes,* she thought, wondering why she had never noticed that before. Then Ben spoke, "Can I ask, how you know her? You're the first fam—uh, visitor here."

"Her mother worked for my family for years and years. She and my aunt are best friends. She helped raise me, really. I can't remember not knowing her. When she got older, my Aunt Zadie and Mrs. Jackson gave me their power of attorney, you know, medically and all that, so I have to be here if, something, you know, has to be . . .done."

"Yes, ma'am. I see. Well, you're welcome to stay. She might pull through this, but she's pretty low, really."

Virginia realized that she was being allowed to stay only because Topie would probably not live much longer. *If only Bethany can get Zadie here.* She settled into a padded chair by Topie's bed, wishing for a cup of coffee or anything, when Bethany appeared at the doorway, helping Zadie enter. Virginia jumped up.

"Thank goodness! Thank you, Bethany."

"No problem, Mom. What's going on?"

Zadie was ignoring them. She hobbled over to Topie's bed on her own power, bent over, and whispered something they couldn't hear into Topie's ear. Zadie brushed the back of her hand over Topie's forehead, as if she were checking a child for a fever.

"Here, Aunt Zadie, sit down."

"Let me get you a chair, Aunt Zadie," Bethany offered, now the mature young woman instead of the self-absorbed college graduate with the tattooed boyfriend. *She's a lovely girl, really*, Virginia thought. *I'm too hard on my children. No wonder they stay away.*

Bethany slid a hospital chair under Zadie and helped her sit.

"What happened, Zadie? Do you know?"

Zadie sighed, not taking her eyes off Topie. "I went into her room after dinner. She wouldn't wake up. I called the staff girl.

Before I knew it there were buzzers going off and ambulance people there. They wouldn't let me come 'til Bethany showed up."

"Was she having any signs of a heart attack or stroke today?"

"No. She wouldn't have been able to tell me if she did. This morning, she couldn't call my name. She just looked at me, like a child. Then she said, 'What's your name?' Can you imagine? My own sister didn't know me."

Bethany and Virginia exchanged glances. Was Zadie starting to show signs of dementia too? "What did you say, Aunt Zadie?"

"I never thought I would see the day when my sweet sister would not know me. We've been together so long."

"Zadie, why are you calling Topie your sister?"

"Because she is."

"No, Aunt Zadie, it's late, and I think you're confused. Topie is *like* a sister to you. Your only sister was my mother, Hennie, and she's been gone for fifty years. Topie is not your sister. She's your friend."

"You don't think I know my own sister?"

Bethany's eyes were wide. Virginia took a deep breath. "Zadie, think. Are you telling me that Topie is your flesh-and-blood half-sister?"

"Yes. Why do you think we made you legally responsible for her and all that? You're family, Virgie. She's your aunt."

"That means Grandpa—Governor—was her real daddy?"

"Yes, ma'am."

Chapter 20

April 1947

When Zadie won the battle of Virgie Mae's upbringing, or at least when she and Buddy Cullins came to a truce about it, she had to rearrange her life. Lula, now fifty-seven and almost crippled with arthritis, was not much use around the house, but Zadie couldn't fire her. Only a cruel, worthless person would do something like that to a colored servant of almost forty years. Topie, working at the mill, still lived with her mother in the house that Governor had bought them. Zadie planned to redecorate a room for Virgie, put her in a private kindergarten at the parish school, start private piano lessons soon, and prove to Buddy that Virgie belonged here, at least part-time. She would make up for the mistakes they all made with Hennie, if truly mistakes were made. Even if Hennie was just born that way, predestined to cause trouble and pain, Virgie would be protected from it. The Bible was clear on it, "Raise up a child in the way he should go, and he will not depart from it." She must have, since she was young, done something wrong in the raising of Hennie. Not again, not with Virgie.

So Virgie's life on Clive Street started in early May of 1947, at four years old. Except for a snatch of a recollection of a fragrant kitchen on a spring day, probably not long before Hennie's death, her memories started there. With an old man called Grandpa the Governor who came down for meals, occasional walks around the neighborhood, and who rubbed his rough hand on her head after dinner. With Lula, a patient woman with dark skin and gray, wiry hair. With Zadie, the biggest lady she knew. With a Sunday School teacher, Mrs. Logan, and the priest, Father Bragg, at the Piscerble building the grownups called a church. With two little girls in the neighborhood, Leah and Talicia.

And with Topie, Miss Lula's little girl who wasn't little, but not as big as Zadie, who came by sometimes and ate dinner in the kitchen with her momma instead of in the dining room with Grandpa the Governor. Zadie acted one way in the kitchen with Lula and Topie, and another stiff, sort of mean way with the old man in the dining room or other parts of the house. It was almost like magic how her face and voice changed once she came through those swinging doors, as if she was happy in the kitchen and sad outside.

Although Virginia was too young to remember how or why, they had a funeral for Grandpa the Governor when she was ten. There were a lot of people coming and going for about a week before it happened. Dr. Meese, a funny name, she thought, came three times and talked softly to Zadie. Grandpa was very sick. Old people must get sick easy. He was 75, Aunt Zadie said. The funeral was long and quiet, and not as many people were in the church as there was on Sunday. Somebody told her she was "the air" of the family. She wasn't sure what that meant, but Zadie said that when everybody else was dead she'd get the house and what money was left.

After Grandpa, whose momma and daddy named him Governor and who never was a real Governor of South Carolina, not even a mayor of Abundance, after he died, something else really bad happened, something that was even more upsetting to Zadie and especially Topie. Miss Lula was sleeping in her bed at night and something went wrong with the wiring and the house burned down. She died because she couldn't get out of bed fast enough because of her artheritus. Topie was working at the cotton mill at the time, and now she didn't have a house. She moved in with them. Lula always slept in a little room downstairs by the kitchen, but Topie moved into an upstairs room like she was white.

"Why is Topie living upstairs with us?" Virgie asked.

"What kind of a question is that?"

"She's colored."

"I ought to slap your mouth, Virgie Mae. What difference does that make? What kind of a host would I be to invite someone to live in that bedroom behind the kitchen?"

"But Lula used to. You told me."

"I don't care what Lula used to do when I was little. That was a long time before you were born. Lula liked it down there. Topie's going to stay upstairs here." She paused. "And let this be alesson to you, Virgie Mae. Things are changing in this country, even in South Carolina. Someday colored people—Negro people is what we should call them—won't be treated so bad. There's people up north, and even down here, who are starting to change things. And I'm all for it."

Virgie didn't understand, but that little speech stuck with her. When Dr. King started speaking and leading protests and sit-ins, she had reason to be proud of her aunt, who could have been just as closed-minded and prejudiced as anyone else of her generation. She might be living in a big old house that was getting more and more rundown, but at least their attitudes were up with the times.

Zadie's concern for her daddy was building in 1953. His cough was raspy. His skin was as gray as his mane of once dark brown hair. He wouldn't give up the cigars. One day she saw him cough at the table, and blood stained his napkin.

"Daddy, what's wrong? You're coughing blood."

"I do that sometimes, girl. None of your business."

"It is so my business. You might have some contagious disease, and I would just as soon the rest of us not get it. But it's more likely you're really bad sick with a lung disease."

"Ah, a little bleeding won't hurt me. Anyway, the doctor will come in here and tell me to give up cigars or tobacco or go to the hospital and get poked and prodded, and I'm not doing that."

She called the doctor anyway. Dr. Meese came and said he couldn't diagnose Governor fully unless he came to the hospital, but if he had to make one here, he'd say he either had advanced tuberculosis or lung cancer. But his temperature was normal, so it was probably the cancer. And it probably wouldn't take long.

He was right. Once the old man heard the word "cancer," what killed his beloved but strange Jessamyn, he gave up, stopped eating, worried Zadie to death, and deteriorated quickly. One night, very weak, he called Zadie to his side.

She expected him to talk about money, and what she should do with the house, how she should invest the family portfolio, what she shouldn't donate money to for the town. But he didn't.

"I think you need to get the priest, that Father Bragg. I want to talk to him about my funeral."

"Daddy, you shouldn't talk that way."

"Hush, Zadiah. I'm going to die soon. I'm not a fool. I'm 75, that's long enough. You're the one who quotes the Bible around here, doesn't it say a man's supposed to live to 70."

"It says three score and ten, and maybe up to 80."

"Then I'll split the difference. I'm worthless anyway. Have been for a long time, some people would say. Never did get around to writing that book about the Cleelands in the Confederacy. Never could get to the end of reading all the background material."

She didn't even know that's what he'd been doing in his study all those years.

"You're not worthless, Daddy. What will I do without you?"

"Plenty. But there's something I have to tell you. This is gonna be hard for you, but if I'm going to meet God, I better tell you the truth."

Her concern for his health now turned to fear for her own future. Was he going to tell her the money was all gone? That she'd be out of a home within the month? What would happen to Virgie? Virgie would go back with Buddy, and Zadie couldn't bear that.

"Zadiah, I've been married, in God's eyes, three times."

She breathed a sigh of relief, and almost laughed. "No, you haven't, Daddy. You were married to my mother, Bonita, a long time ago. She died in the Spanish flu epidemic. And then you married Jessamyn when I was, what, eleven or twelve or so. She died too. That's only two." Was he losing his mind now?

"No, Zadiah, I said in God's eyes, not the state of South Carolina's."

"Well, who was this mystery woman?"

"When your momma had you, she got to where she didn't want to be around me. I think you know what I mean by that. Oh, she could be the perfect hostess, sit in church with me, walk the street with me, spend my money and take my name, but she wouldn't enter my bedroom. She said she didn't want any more babies, you were enough, and unless something happened to you, she didn't feel responsible to give me another heir, boy or girl. She'd done her duty as a wife, she said."

Zadie did not remember her mother well, but this description did not surprise her.

"Well, I am sorry to have to tell you this, but I was young, and a man gets lonely. I was visiting a business associate and he had a young colored woman working for him. Dark, almost black skin.

240

Small and lithe. Beautiful eyes with curled lashes, and a smile . . . she grabbed my heart when I saw her. I'm not saying it was right, but when I could I kept company with her, which of course was mighty hard to do."

Zadie saw it all clearly now. He didn't have to tell her the rest of it, but in his last days she would be the obedient daughter and listen to a story that resounded of slaves and plantations and ugly masters. *I thought we were past that,* she thought. *We weren't when I was a little girl, and in some people's minds, we probably aren't now.*

"She lived with her big old family, a mess of kids, you know how those people can be, and I told her she could come be our servant. By then she was expecting. She married another colored man, name of Powders, who worked on the railroad line, but when he realized she wasn't a pure woman and was with a baby, he left her pretty soon.

"She had the baby. I think you know who it is."

Lula. Topie. All these years, under her own roof. Not in the slave quarters, but in the room off the kitchen, and then in their own little house, hidden in the Negro part of town. Daddy may have thought he had answered her questions with the confession, but he only seeded more in her mind. Did he really "keep company" with her, or was it something she didn't want to name, something violent and mean? And did he sleep with her after Momma died, even when Jessamyn came, and after Jessamyn died?

I don't want to know, but of course he did, she thought. Of course he did. She remembered that day before he married Jessamyn, when she found Lula pitching piecrust dough out the kitchen window and cursing men, or a man, under her breath. Maybe Lula had come to care for this white man who used her but in his own pitiful, medieval way, tried to do right by her. Maybe Governor truly loved Lula, but couldn't make it public and right. Of course he couldn't. He was eccentric and reclusive, but he was a formal, affluent, respected Southern gentleman who had to keep up appearances, who still believed that keeping up appearances was all that really mattered.

She had to ask, "Does Topie know this? Does Topie know you are her daddy?"

"I don't know. If she does, if Lula told her, she never came to me about it."

Perhaps Topie didn't know. She thought back to when they were children, when she would tease Topie about having green eyes, because colored people didn't have green eyes. When she asked Topie about her real daddy, and would insinuate she wasn't loved, had been abandoned by the man Topie proudly said worked on the railroad between Charlotte and Greenville. Topie may still think Mr. Powders, the man in that deceitful wedding picture with Lula, was her real daddy. How cruel of Zadie to belittle Topie that way, even as a child. How cruel of Daddy. But in his own way, Daddy probably loved Topie, as much as he did Zadie, and probably more than Hennie.

"I want you to promise me something, Zadiah." Her father's breathing was labored, and he spoke now in a harsh whisper.

She didn't want to promise him anything. She didn't even want to be in the room with him. She wanted to close the door on him and let him die, at that moment. He would probably ask her to always keep his secret, or some other selfish request.

"What?"

"Take care of Lula and Topie. I didn't put them in the will, but I trust you to make sure they have plenty, never want for anything."

She said nothing. For him to ask her to take care of Lula and Topie, her two best friends, showed how much he didn't know her.

She didn't need to be asked. She might be so mad at him now that she wanted to spit, but this was at least a request she would fulfill gladly.

"All right," was all she could say. She sat down by the bed, confused and tired, while he drifted off to sleep.

Governor died three days later. Zadie stumbled through the funeral, through the reading of the will, through the sessions with the lawyer to know how much she really inherited from Governor, after Hennie's death, after the Depression, after his lack of diligence.

"Enough," the lawyer said. "Enough for you to live on from the interests of the investments that still exist," although he added, "you're still a young woman. You could marry, or get a career."

Marriage was out of the question. She wasn't bringing another man into this house. She was through with men. She'd had the only good one. She might think about getting a job, now that Virgie was at school all day and didn't need her so much, and Lula still came to take care of the house. She applied for an assistant librarian position at one of the branches of the Turling County Library System and was hired, maybe in deference to her family connections, maybe because she was willing to work for the minimal pay. But working there served the community like Cleelands were supposed to, she liked to be around books, and she didn't need a college degree to do the job.

What wasn't so easy for Zadie McCann was what to do about Lula and Topie. Her grief and confusion and mixed emotions over her father's death seemed minimal compared to the knowledge that Lula and Daddy had relations, probably many times and over many years, despite his marital status and despite his position in the community. Topie's green eyes were no longer a genetic mystery;

they were the same green eyes she, and Hennie, and Daddy had.

At the funeral, Lula and Topie sat two pews behind the family. They wore their best clothes—somber colors, but not black, with stylish but tasteful hats. A couple of Uncle Lyons' and Aunt Margaret's sons, her cousins, came to represent that branch of the family; neighbors, and a few other parishioners of St. Michael's for Zadie's sake, but probably fewer than twenty people were there, and fewer than five who were "family." But Topie and Lula *were* family, as much as Zadie and Virgie Mae were, and much, much closer than her cousins, who barely knew Governor.

After the funeral, the small group moved to the homeplace for a potluck meal brought in by the church ladies of St. Michael's and Lula's Zion AME church and by the neighbors. Zadie received all the attention, and tried to be gracious to her fellow mourners, despite the distraction of trying to make sense of this new universe in which her father had loved a Negro woman and had protected her for dozens of years, and in which Zadie's childhood wish for Topie to be her sister had come true. Lula had been the lady of the house,really, for many years. And in her quiet way, she remained so today, smiling, making sure all the guests were fed, the glasses were filled, the windows were open and the fans were running to cool down the room filled with bodies.

Despite her age—she was now well past sixty and afflicted with arthritis—Lula was still beautiful, still very dark and small. No wonder a man loved her. She could have married again, she could have found a man, yet she stayed with a cranky, eccentric old white man who broke her heart and could never and would never give her his name. And more than that, Lula had mothered Zadie since those days back after the epidemic, those days of World War I. Lula had loved her as much as any woman had, without ever saying the words. And Topie—her sister. When Hennie died, she felt so alone, not because she and Hennie were close, but because now she believed herself to be the only child again, as she had been for the twelve years before Jessamyn came and bore Hennie. All that time, a real sister had been in her house.

It didn't make sense. Was she, Zadie, the only person other than Lula who knew this secret? Could she, should she, go to Lula and . . . and, what? Say, "I know Governor took advantage of you, and spent years trying to make it right in some unbelievably awkward way?" But was Lula really a victim? She had agreed to stay all these years, even when Jessamyn came into their circle. There was no etiquette book for dealing with this, for making it right. She could not talk to the priest for advice. How did she pray for the words to approach Lula? If Lula had told Topie, perhaps one day Topie would demand her rights as a daughter. If Lula had not told Topie, and never planned to, perhaps one day Zadie would have the words to speak to both of them.

Zadie found it an action best put off for later. After all, procrastination was not always a moral fault. Wisdom might grow in her and give her the courage and eloquence and sensitivity she needed for this, the most delicate of subjects.

But in this case, procrastination made full disclosure impossible. Three months after Governor died, after he was in the ground and the will was read, after Zadie tried to settle into a life alone in the big house with Virgie, with Lula coming to help, eventhough it was hard for her—those three months when Zadie began a hundred times to say, "I know, Lula. I know. Daddy told me. Not everything, but the most important part. I know. And I don't know what to do or say about it." Zadie heard, late at night, a far off siren of a fire truck, and she wondered whose house was burning. In the morning Topie was at her door, devastated, barely able to walk after the shock of the fire and her mother's death and working third shift, almost speechless, and now homeless.

Through the sobs, the choking, the halted breathing, Topie

got out words. "Momma—the house—she couldn't get up out of bed. The fire trucks--didn't get there til the roof fell in. Oh, Momma. Dying like that. Oh, my God! My momma, my poor sweet momma. I hope to God she died before the flames got to her."

Zadie could do nothing but enfold her sister and let her cry for as long as it took. Topie would grieve, and would have to grieve, for a long time. To her thinking, her whole family was gone. She and Lula had been so close, so inseparable, so protective of each other for so long, for more than forty years. No words would comfort, so Zadie didn't say them. Over and over she wanted to say, "I am family, I am your sister," but it didn't seem right. How could her saying that help the pain of losing Lula in any way? No, not now. Later.

The firemen were able to find Lula's burned body in the wreckage, but Zadie persuaded Topie not to identify the body—who else would it be, anyway—or have an open casket. That just made everything harder. It took little persuasion for Topie to stay with Zadie; Topie could barely put one foot in front of the other for days after the fire. All Topie's clothes and belongings were gone, devoured in the fire; she was starting over in life, without her mother, without possessions. Zadie bought her clothes for the funeral, and then ordered lots of items in Topie's size from the Sears Roebuck catalog, dresses and skirts and blouses that she knew Topie would like. Topie didn't protest. She was dependent on Zadie now, at least for a while. If Zadie couldn't tell her the truth, not yet, at least she could offer her what a sister should.

They raised Virgie, who graduated from high school in 1962, the fourth best student in her high school class, and who then left for Clemson three months later. Now Zadie and Topie would grow old together. Both had seen enough of life, of death. As the years passed, Zadie tried a few times to tell Topie, but always managed to argue herself out of it at that moment. Besides, Zadie felt some strangle loyalty to her father, although she couldn't explain its origins. Daddy didn't deserve a good reputation, but Zadie would prefer he, or at least the family, have one, all things considered. It would not serve Virgie Mae well to have it known that Governor fathered a child out of wedlock with his black servant. Zadie was not proud of her reluctance; she knew it partially came from the sin of pride. She lived with a deep current of ambivalence, of being torn between an old way of thinking and the new way, between loyalty to her father and loyalty to her closest friend, to her sister, between the unspoken truth and lies.

Zadie knew something now that might break Topie's heart, or that might unleash an anger that would never heal. What would be the point of telling secrets? Keep them locked up. Virgie didn't need to know her momma went crazy. Topie didn't need to know her real father was an old white man who seduced her poor, uneducated, hungry momma even though he had a wife and child at home. If you couldn't forget, you could at least not make others remember.

Virgie loved Clemson. She loved the classes. She loved pledging for a sorority and getting accepted. She loved the fact that Tally and Leah were there. She loved meeting boys from all over the state and the South, and even farther, and a lot of them loved meeting her. She loved being away from home, since it really wasn't that far. She loved the football games as the weather got cooler. She loved living where people didn't know about Cleelands and wouldn't much care if they did.

She wanted to major in business, but as she entered her junior year decided attaching a minor in teaching may not be a bad idea. She also decided that going out with John MacEntire Foster, whom everyone called Mack, might not be a bad idea, either. His name sounded like a literary figure or tycoon of industry. He might be one of those one day, but right now he was the son of mill workers from Walkerburg County. He didn't come to Clemson with much money, but he did come with more ambition and drive than any other fellow she met. He was tall, a plus; he looked like he'd keep his hair for a long time, another plus, and he was well groomed but not prissy. As far as appearance went, those were her requirements, and Mack Foster fit them nicely. But she wasn't that shallow. Mack tried to get her to go out with him all through sophomore year, and persistence was a trait she admired. She gave in, found out after three dates she was as crazy about him as he was about her, and that pretty much sealed the deal.

They married in June after graduation in 1966. Mack had a job at the First Carolina Bank in Abundance. He didn't want to stay in banking, but he had to get started somewhere and it wasn't a mill. He planned to go into real estate after he earned some banking credentials. Mack studied trends, and the trend, he said, was southward. People wanted to live in warmer climates, especially now that air conditioning was available and building the interstates was underway. He wanted a houseful of children as soon as Gee-gee was ready.

But Gee-gee, as he loved to call her, was not ready. In fact, once she set up housekeeping and began living day to day with her husband, who showed every sign of devotion, hard work, and good sense, three valuable assets in a husband, she realized that the serious thought of children scared her to death. First, she never had siblings. Second, she'd never been around babies or small children any longer than at a church picnic or potluck. In fact, she'd never even held a newborn. Third, she came from a line of women who didn't do motherhood well. Bonita—not really a grandmother but part of her legacy. Jessamyn. And Hennie, the worst of the lot. One rejected her husband, one rejected her child emotionally, and the last rejected her child in every way possible.

Thank goodness for Zadie and Topie, grounded women who, denied their own children, aimed their skills at her and did an admirable job, in Virginia's opinion. And of course, she had no cause for concern from the Cullins side, people who truly believed children came straight from heaven and should be treated as such. The Cullins were as normal as dirt. But, still, fear is fear. It couldn't be reasoned away. For the first time in her life, she began to realize that losing Hennie might have reached more deeply into her psyche then she ever realized, that she might need professional help, and that if her mother was out there somewhere, she should be found.

Virginia struggled throughout her late twenties. Should she hire a detective, using what was left of her inheritance, not telling Mack? It would feel like such a betrayal; Mack tried so hard to fill the void with his own love and goodness. Should she just go ahead and get pregnant, trust in God and modern medicine, despite the fear that what caused Hennie's and Jessamyn's disturbances would recur?

Despite how much he loved Virginia, Mack grew impatient. They were approaching thirty. She was waiting too long. The time for having children was dwindling. But one day she realized she had overlooked refilling her prescription for birth control pills, and the matter was out of her hands. Nine months later Bethany was born. She was a Foster, through and through. Not actually a pretty baby, but Virginia was blind to that. She didn't know she could love this much.

Why had she waited? Why had she denied herself this—bliss, this passion for something? Yet, would something snap, a few months into motherhood, and turn her heart away from Bethany? She could either throw herself into this new role, or sit back and be consumed by introspective worry. She decided to risk it all. A year passed, and her elation with Bethany only grew, surpassing even Mack's, who had to be the world's most doting father.

Eventually she accepted that whatever afflicted Jessamyn and

Hennie, had bypassed her, or had been exorcised. She found herself uninterested in any scheme of finding Hennie, if she still lived. Such total rejection only deserved the same. She knew she was supposed to forgive. It was easy for other church people to say forgive, and she would when she got good and ready. Maybe. But she would forgive her mother from afar, long distance. She did not want to meet her.

But that did not remove Hennie from her consciousness. When Bethany was four Virginia achieved pregnancy the second time—she was getting older, almost thirty-five now, and she read in a magazine that fertility diminished with age. Matthew entered the world in 1978. She fell in love again, and the differences in their ages hindered the sibling rivalry. Bethany excelled in school; when Matthew got to the end of first grade year, his teacher advised a repeat, putting him behind a year. They decided to invest in private school and never regretted it. Both of the children flourished.

Throughout the '80s and into the '90s they lived the American dream. Growing business, growing children, growing prospects, and growing cadres of friends. They moved into a new home. They took the obligatory trips to Disney World and then spent two weeks in Europe when Bethany graduated from high school. Virginia continued to teach high school business courses for the children's tuition and to pay the domestic help. Time passed. The little girl sent to live with her aunt and grandpa and their black servants was no more. No one needed to know about Hennie Cleeland. Neither did she.

Until she committed herself to delivering the economic shot in the arm their town needed. The town that had nurtured her needed nurturing itself, she believed. Life was good in Abundance, but it could be better. And in the process, she quite by accident opened doors that opened her eyes to her past.

Chapter 21

June 29, 1931

For a second time in Lula's memory, this house was a house of death. Unlike the first time, when the influenza came in the door like a robber and took Miss Bonita Cleeland's life, this time death stayed and paced over the dying until she was weak and crazy and tortured with pain. Now two mommas had died, wives of the same man.

This cancer thing took everything out of a body dying of it, and it took a lot out of the people who waited on the dying. Zadie looked ten years older from caring for her stepmomma, and she was just a young woman, a girl, who shouldn't have been forced to be a nursemaid at her age.

But burying Miss Jessamyn didn't mean anything would go back to the way it was before she came. She'd left that young'un Hennie, who raised Cain about everything. And Governor marrying that woman in the first place was just about the last straw. She was pretty, and liked to talk and act high class, but she was the do-nothingest thing, even for a white woman, Lula had ever known. He did get some of her money, well, her husband's money, when they married, but that didn't seem like a fair deal, not to Lula, considering how much he put up with from Jessamyn.

And the worst of it, he'd be trying to get in Lula's bed, or get Lula into his, before long. Not this time. Never again. He cooked his goose when he brought that Jessamyn home.

Her family made fun of her for working for that same white man all these years. "You cook like a dream, girl, you can go work for another white family." She'd heard that over and over again. And her momma said, "Get yourself a husband who can take care of you, give you his name."

But Momma thought there was decent Negro men out there,

and there wasn't. As far as Lula was concerned, all the good ones, all the ones with any gumption, had moved up north for decent jobs. That didn't leave much here. And why should she be dependent on a man anyway? She'd married that Sylvester Powders, and he left her in the first month, claiming he didn't know she was with a baby, which was a lie. So marriage didn't solve anything, in her mind.

She'd taken up with a few other men, gone dancing with them, even sat with one in church for about a month. She would have plenty of men interested in her, if she let them. But she liked being alone. A husband would be expecting more than she wanted to give. Governor let her come and go, even though something bound her to him.

Her family could make fun, could boss her, but none of them lived in a house as nice as she did with a room for her and one for Topie. And since this thing they called a Depression, which was a word she didn't understand, all she heard was that people was out of work and couldn't find it. She had a job, and she made twice the money working for Mr. Governor than she would working for any other white family. That meant she could have nice furniture in that little house and order clothes from the mail order catalog, where nobody knew if you was white or colored. She couldn't go in the best stores in Abundance, but J.C. Penney didn't care what color you was as long as your money was green. She could get a job at a mill, like Topie was doing, but she wasn't strong like Topie. Her hands were already knobby and sore, and she knew what that would mean in ten years.

Topie. Yes, Topie was strong and smart. Topie was her main reason, all these years, to stay in the big house on Clive Street, even when Governor brought home that Jessamyn. Imagine, one day, he is asking me into his room to clean it, then saying pretty words to me and wanted to kiss and take my clothes off, and the next day he shows up and introduces Zadie to her new stepmomma, with no warning for any of us.

He knew she was mad. She slapped platters and bowls of food on the table for the next week. She burned his beans and served him chewy, half-cooked pot roast until the wedding. She slammed doors. He had the nerve to call her into his room to ask if there was something wrong. She pretended to be shocked.

"Wrong? What could you mean, Mr. Governor?"

"You been slamming doors and making noise for four days."

"Oh, yes sir, I have. I am doing it because I am just so happy that you are getting married and bringing another woman into this house when you been saying you love me."

"I do love you, Lula."

"You are a *liar*."

"What would you have me do? Marry you?"

"If you loved me—"

"Good God, woman. I'd be in jail so fast my head would spin. Whites can't marry coloreds. It's against the law in South Carolina, and a lot of other places."

"So you just up and marry some pasty woman from up north, after all these years with me."

"Yes, Jessamyn and I will be married, and there's nothing you can do about it. My family says it's unseemly for a man to go on without being married after his wife has died, and I need a proper stepmother for Zadie."

"Fine. I don't have to stay and watch it."

"I need you Lula. You can't leave us."

"Yes I can. I can take Topie and you won't see her again."

"Now, now, Lula. You don't want to do that, especially when you find out what I did for you."

This stopped her. "What did you do?"

"I bought you and Topie a house. Over on Thomas Street."

"A house? Why?"

"So you don't have to live here anymore. You can come to work every day like other colored women do, but have your own place."

She felt the tears coming. "Why did you do that?"

"I told you I love you, Lula."

"Do you love Jessamyn?"

"You shouldn't ought to ask me that, Lula. She pleases me, and she's a pretty little thing, and she needs a husband. She is no good with money. It fits for us to get married."

"But you don't love her?"

"It's not like it is with you, Lula."

She sighed. "It ain't right. People that's in love, it shouldn't matter about their color."

"You are dreaming, girl. But that's a nice dream."

The Governor and Jessamyn had a wedding a few days later and pretended to be married. They must not have pretended all the time, because Jessamyn eventually ended up with a baby, even though she was past forty and this was her first one. That is too late to start making babies, Lula said, shaking her head, over and over. And it didn't set well with her, so Lula and Topie and Zadie got a new project on their hands, raising that tiny thing her momma called Hennrietta. What handful she was.

Governor might have been unfaithful to his first wife when he was a young man, but he was not going to make that mistake again. Neither was Lula. She wasn't going to take another woman's man again, no matter who he was or what their history. Besides, by the time Hennie was born, Governor was going onto forty and not so interested in loving as he used to be. And Lula wasn't in the house all the time. So anything they felt for each other was now in the past, at least as far as showing it.

Yes, she loved him. She did. She knew she shouldn't. Back when she was seventeen and working for Mr. Butler Drayton and his wife Mary, Mr. Governor came to visit and before the night was up he offered her a job working for him and his wife. It wasn't long after she moved over to their big house that he started making eyes with her, and touching her hand when nobody was looking. Then one day she went to clean his studying room, and he was in there, but he wasn't supposed to be. Yes, back then, she was a fool, yes, she let him love her, and it was the first time, and she lost her head.

She started loving him before she knew him. She was so young. Maybe so stupid, so green, so foolish. He seemed to love her in spite of what she was and because of what he was. He wasn't any better that way than the other whites. Somehow he saw her, and Topie, as something other than colored. She could hate him sometimes when she heard him talking to other people in town about her people, her kin, her kind, making jokes, even calling them by hurtful words. Maybe she had just wanted to know what it felt like, to be held, to feel white skin on her face and body. Maybe she was flattered because he thought, because he said, she was beautiful, and no one else had done that before. Now, so many years later, she didn't know why she had let him touch her. She had tried to stop over the years. It was wrong. And then another time, and another. Until she knew Topie was inside her.

Governor said she wasn't his, at first. He said he couldn't father a colored child. "Yes, you did," she told him.

"We need to get you married off to a colored man."

"I don't know any I want to marry."

"We'll find one."

Governor had a friend who oversaw the Negro workers on the railroad, the porters and janitors and cooks and waiters. Somehow, he brought Sylvester Powders to the house and introduced them. Sylvester was wanting to get married, but he was kind of shy, so Lula had to encourage him. She needed a husband, and he would do. Sylvester had a good job, wasn't bad looking except for his big ears, and went to church. But when she started showing, he decided he wanted no part of a baby that wasn't his, and told her he'd get a divorce as soon as he could afford it. She kept his name, though. It was easier that way, and for Topie.

Governor didn't like it, and he could have fired her, and nobody would have been the wiser. But Miss Bonita wasn't one to keep house by herself and two-year-old Zadie cried all night when Lula stayed at her momma's for a few days having her baby. Now there were two little girl babies in the house. Two-year-old Zadie was so happy to have Lula back that she didn't push the little dark-skinned baby away when Lula was feeding her at her breast.

Miss Bonita didn't mind the baby being there, as long as she kept quiet when her society friends came by or she hosted the Daughters of the Revolution club. Topie behaved herself. As she got older Topie learned how to help a little bit, but mostly she helped by playing with Zadie and keeping her out of Lula's hair.

That big old house on Clive Street wasn't the worst place in the world to raise her baby. It was always warm in winter. There was plenty of food. They had a room downstairs near the kitchen, so they could talk and laugh and not bother the Cleelands. No, it was a good life, as good a life as she was bound to get. Colored women had two paths in life: move up north, away from family, and find a job and maybe not be a maid. Some even got to go to school, even in big cities in the South, but she didn't know how they managed to do that, unless their daddies were preachers or undertakers. Or you stayed here, raising white babies and cleaning house. Or you did the shameful things, north or south, sleeping with all kinds of men for money or singing in a gambling house and bar.

Governor stayed away from her for a long time after Topie was born. But after a while he came around. She left the room if he was the only one in there. She only cleaned that room he called his study when he wasn't in there. She locked her door at night. He had a key, but it told him what she wanted and didn't want either way. She didn't want to have another half-white baby. She loved Topie more than anything she could think of, but she didn't want to have another baby unless she was married to a good man and able to stop being a housemaid. Anyway, it was bad enough loving on a man you weren't married to; she wasn't going to love on a man with a wife, not again.

Then Miss Bonita died. What an awful thing. Twice, maybe three times she let him take her to bed after that, and after every time she felt so dirty and low-down she wanted to hurt him and maybe herself. And it would be months before the next time. Until he brought home a new woman and married her within a month. That was the end.

Topie asked her one day, "Momma, why do I have green eyes? Zadie been making fun of me for having green eyes. She says colored girls don't have'em."

"Zadie don't know nothing."

"That's what I told her. I said, 'you don't know all the colored people in the world, so hush.'" Topie was proud of her sass. "But why are my eyes green?"

"Sometimes that just happens. Did you know my uncle had a hound dog that had one eye that was brown and one that was blue?"

"Oooh. That must have looked funny." Topie thought for a minute. "But I ain't a dog."

"It don't matter. Some black folks get born with red hair, too."

"Red hair?"

"Well, it's more like an orange, or leaves on trees in the fall."

Topie had to think about that. "I'm gonna have to tell her one of these days," Lula thought. "When she's older. When she's able to understand that sometimes we think we love somebody, or think that loving them is a good idea, even when it's not."

It was easy to put that off. Truth be told, she was scared. She didn't want to hurt Topie, and Topie could get a temper on when she thought she had a reason. Life went on. Hennie was born. Jessamyn died. It was a long death; it was like Miss Bonita's for the pain and crying out but took what seemed like months. Everybody was poor for all those years, or acted like they was. Then Zadie and Topie both getting married, and then Topie losing her babies. She thought Topie would die herself. Topie was a different woman after that. She looked like a sleepwalker sometimes, other times like a corpse in a coffin. Lula would find her staring off into space. But she woke up long enough to throw Lawrence Jackson out of her house. Oh, and Hennie ran off and got married. That was no surprise. Lula figured she was expecting, but she wasn't—not then, at least. And then Zadie's Eddie died. Oh, what a sad time. Sometimes there was so much grief to attend to that she forgot about what Topie didn't know. And it was easy to say that Topie was better off not knowing when so much sad was going on.

And then she always thought about Zadie. What would she do if she knew? There was no telling. Zadie acted like Topie was her best friend in the world, and that Lula was as close as a momma, but she was still white, and a Cleeland, too, and they were proud as peacocks, even if you couldn't tell why. Just having more money than other people, or thinking you do, can make a person real proud. She needed to hear the truth from her daddy. She wouldn't believe it from Lula. It would be crazy for Lula to even think about telling her. Zadie might go crazy when she found out what kind of man her daddy was. Or she might already know.

One warm day in the fall of 1953 Zadie came into the kitchen and plopped down. "Daddy—Governor—he's going to die."

"What you saying, Miss Zadie?" Lula frowned. "We all gonna die."

"No, he has cancer, probably. He's spitting blood. A lot of it. He won't go to the hospital. He's going to die. Soon."

"You sure about that?"

"Dr. Meese says so. And Daddy doesn't seem to care that much. It's like he's given up."

"Oh, Miss Zadie. I am sorry for you. You are so by yourself now. It'll be hard for you."

"Thank you, Lula. We just have to get through this. It will be like a different house without Daddy being here. But don't worry, I won't make it hard on you. I know you can't go up and down the stairs over and over again."

"I'll do what I can, Miss Zadie," Lula promised.

Now was the time, Lula thought. In a few days her real daddy, that old white man would be gone. No matter how Topie took it, Lula knew she needed to tell her now. And there was no way to do it polite-like.

"Topie, I have to tell you something. I should have told you a long time past."

"You gonna tell me that old man is my real daddy."

Lula's hand went to her mouth in surprise. "How did you know?"

"Momma, I done some dumb things in my life, but I ain't stupid. I am a whole lot more light-skinned than you, and I have green eyes. Green eyes, Momma. One day it all just came to me. That my real daddy was some white man, and it made just as much sense that it was Governor Cleeland as anybody else. Not that it made any difference. No matter who it was, he wasn't about to claim me as his daughter. That would never happen."

"Why didn't you tell me?

Topie shrugged. "I don't know. I guess I've had more on my mind than to worry about how that old man feels about me. We never wanted for anything, even when whites and coloreds all were hurting around us in the Depression. You and me had a house to live in. It wasn't my problem, Momma. It still isn't. He's gonna die, and he's not gonna leave me any money. He's not gonna put *my* name in the will. What went on was between you and him."

Lula wasn't sure what that expression on Topie's face meant. Topie looked like thinking of her momma and Governor together made her sick to her stomach.

"Topie, you ain't angry, are you?

260

"Angry? You asking me if I'm angry? I been angry for a long time, Momma. Angry goes with the territory of being me. But I ain't mad. I ain't gonna let things make me crazy, make me do crazy things. I lost four babies. Four babies, Momma. What did I ever do to God for him to do that to me? If I didn't go crazy, didn't go to hurting myself or other people over that, how would knowing about you and the old man change me?"

Topie saw the tears leaking out of Lula's clenched eyelids. She hated to know she hurt her momma, but Lula had to know this day was coming and that Topie would say meanness. Was she supposed to hug Lula and say, "Thank you, Momma?" Topie decided the best thing was to stop talking for a while and let her momma cry. This had to be hard for her, knowing Mr. Cleeland was passing on.

After a few minutes, Topie reached over and touched her momma's hand. "Momma, I'm forty years old, and I just found out I'm half white, for sure, that that old man dying upstairs got my momma with a baby but he would never admit it to the world. Do you think Zadie knows? Either of them wives of his? Maybe they did. Well, maybe not Zadie. She thinks he can do no wrong, no matter how bad he treats her. If we marched up there and in his room right now with him on that bed coughing out blood, and said, 'Tell the truth, admit I'm your daughter, or we'll tell the world,' what do you think he'd do? He'd deny it, he'd say, 'nobody gonna believe a colored woman.' Because no matter how much he slept with you or said he loved you or wanted to be sure you was taken care of, he don't think Negroes are worth the time of day. I ain't sure he thinks I'm worth the time of day.

"No, Momma, I'm angry, but I ain't mad, and I ain't gonna let him have control over me, like he did you. Anyway, I ain't getting a dime of his money, whatever he has left after spreading it around to cover up what Hennie done."

261

Topie was done. All those years of hurt were out now, and even though she didn't feel any better, at least it had been said.

"I think you wrong about him, Topie. He's the one who gave you your name. He asked me what I was gonna name you. I said Daisy. He said 'Don't give her a colored name like that. Give her a name that makes me think of you and how I feel about you.' Good place and happy. That's what he named you. So he does care about you."

"He didn't give me his last name. I ain't a Cleeland. I'm still Powders on the birth certificate, and I held on to Jackson because of my babies. I'll always have those names. That ain't gonna change."

"Topie."

"What, Momma?"

"I'm sorry, Topie. I can't change what's been done."

Topie was tired, and she looked even more tired than she felt. Forty years of living her life, of being herself, had just come out in the last ten minutes and spewed all over Lula.

"I know, Momma."

On September 2 Topie told an exhausted Zadie that she would sit by Governor's bed while Zadie got some sleep. They all knew it wouldn't be long now. Zadie couldn't bear the thought of someone in her house dying alone, so she wanted someone to be with her daddy all the time, but Lula suffered such pain getting up the stairs and Zadie didn't want Virginia to watch death taking over her grandfather.

His breathing was ragged and his body was too tired to cough fully, which meant pneumonia would set in if the cancer didn't take him first. Topie sat by the bed, ready to offer him water if he asked for it but not willing to hold the old man's hand or touch his forehead.

He opened his eyes. "Zadie."

"No, Mr. Cleeland, it's not Zadie. It's me, Topie."

"Topie."

"Yes." It didn't feel right on her tongue, but she said it anyway. "Yes, Daddy, it's me, Topie."

His eyes opened. Was it fear, after all these years, that she saw? Or questioning? Or was that just the look of a man seeing his grave?

"Yes. That's right. I know."

He died September 3. The house was now truly a house of women, for women. Lula, Virginia, and Zadie spent their days there until Lula burned to death and Topie, homeless and lost, took her place. The past stayed in the Governor's study for many months before Zadie could bring herself to begin to clean out his books and clothes. Slowly, the future started to live in the house.

When Topie heard that a Negro woman in Montgomery caused all the colored folks in that city to stop using the city buses, she took notice. She started reading the paper to learn about that young preacher from Atlanta who spoke so pretty about rights and what the Negroes wanted. He seemed to have a nice family and a pretty little wife. Then the state of South Carolina had to stop acting so low-down about Negroes voting, and even though she was more than fifty years old, she went and got a voter's card and cast her ballot. That felt good.

And when she heard that the church was getting up a bus to go hear that young preacher, Dr. King, speak down in the Lowcountry in a little bitty nothing of a town called Kingstree, she took a day off from work, seeing as the mill had to treat the workers better now so that the unions wouldn't get started. She put up with the miserable heat and the gnats and sat for hours waiting for Dr. King to come speak. She wrote it in her Bible, "May 9, 1966, the day I heard Dr. Martin Luther King, Jr., of Atlanta speak." What a proud day. Lula was smiling in heaven, Topie knew, if that was possible. She wasn't 100% sold on heaven and hell yet, but she'd give the Bible the benefit of the doubt and believe her sweet momma was up there.

Later she wrote "April 4, 1968, the day Dr. King was shot and killed in Memphis" in her Bible, so she'd remember.

For years Topie teetered over the brink of spilling the beans to Zadie, that she knew, that she called Governor "Daddy" on his deathbed. But when she thought about Dr. King, about voting, about what Negroes had been through, and about her cousins and aunts, about how Governor hadn't left her or Momma anything, she decided to keep the white part of herself a secret, even from Zadie.

At last Virgie Mae finally got around to having babies, and she and Zadie could play grandmas with Bethany and Matthew, two names from the Bible. Topie retired from the mill in 1978 at the age of 65, just like she was supposed to, and started to live as lazy as she could get away with.

When Zadie had a stroke, Virgie Mae, who always did like to run things, started working on them moving out of the big house on Clive Street. Topie didn't much mind. She was having trouble remembering how to cook, and how to wash clothes right, and the idea that somebody would wait on her from now on sounded pretty good. What would Momma think? Lula would have never thought her daughter would live in a place like St. Amber, or was it St. Ambrose? She liked her room, she liked having Zadie around, and she liked having servants, like she and Momma used to be.

She could watch the redbirds outside her window for as long as she wanted now, and think about her babies, and wonder about Governor, and miss Momma, and wait.

Chapter 22

September 1953

When the doctor proclaimed his body to be eaten up with cancer, Governor Cleeland took to his bed.

He knew it was the end, anyway, though those weren't the doctor's words. He figured old Meese pronounced the verdict in a hushed voice to Zadie, who told Governor herself. The doctor didn't have the courage to come right out with it, so he left it to a woman. The coughing, the blood on the handkerchiefs, the blood in the toilet when he made water these last few months, the pain in his gut. Food sickened him, and he could only eat enough to keep from starving.

Lula. She was still here. She was down in the kitchen, hobbled with arthritis that made the trip up the stairs a sacrifice. But maybe she would come. He'd had three women. That was better than some men, who didn't restrain themselves from anything in a skirt that looked good to them. He would have married Lula back during the Great War. They could have lived together as man and wife properly, even if it was a secret. They could have gone—where—to New York or Pennsylvania. Well, they would have had to travel separately in those days, back and forth, but surely some liberal preacher would have done the deed for them, and he would have given Lula some peace, some respectability, even if it was just between them.

But why Lula? His brother and sister-in-law, Lyons and Margaret, would not let up on him getting married again. "It doesn't look right," they kept saying. They introduced her to Jessamyn, through someone they knew. She was little, pretty. No one could gainsay she was a good-looking woman, even at almost forty. Jessamyn was almost as pretty as Lula.

Lula confronted him in his study the day after his and Jessamyn's engagement was announced. She entered, without knocking, closed the door and stared at him until he looked up. "You white son of a b--,"

"Woman, that is no way for a colored woman to talk to her employer. I could fire you in a heartbeat. I could have you slapped in jail for it if I were of a mind to."

"Try it. Try to deny whose baby Utopia is. I'll tell the whole world. I'll tell your family, your brother. I'll tell Jessamyn. Zadiah will know she has a little colored sister, not just a play friend. I'll have 'em put it in the paper that Governor Cleeland, the big man of the town, took advantage of a colored servant. Even in this town, that would mean something. And I was only seventeen."

"Lula, you're just mad."

"You're damn right I'm mad. You got no business bringing that white woman in here, and marrying her so fast. She might be crazy or somethin'. She may be one of them women who don't let you in her bed. She's got some money, that's all I see. And she's a Yankee, too. She's not going to fit in here in this town."

"She's a fine woman, and it's time Zadiah had a stepmomma. She's starting to act like she's colored."

Lula grabbed a book setting by her on a shelf and just missed him with it. "Better colored than a Cleeland, is what I say."

"Lula, honey--"

"Don't say 'honey' to me. You know what's going to happen. That woman—what kind of a name is Jessamyn anyway—is going to figure out that Topie is yours, and she's going to want me out of this house, and I'm going to be out of a job with a little one to care for."

"That's not gonna happen. And even if it did, you got a big

family . . ."

"I don't want to go living with my cousins. They's five kids to a bed, no running water, sharing an outdoor privy with other families. If you would leave this house and go over to colored town, you'd see how people live over there. Drafty houses, nothin' more than shacks. Is that how you want Topie living? You can say to the world she's just your colored housekeeper's young'un, but you know deep down she's yours and I seen you with her, you got some feelin' for her."

Lula was right about that. For all the thousands of years of African blood running through Utopia Felicia Powders' blood, for her wide lips and bronze skin, he saw his own mother's smile and cheekbones and his own green eyes when she played with Zadie. Zadie, who favored Bonita so much it chilled him, was never going to be a beauty, but she was a smart and steady girl.

"I'll figure something out," he said.

It had taken some money, but he got a builder to go in and patch up a decent house on the outskirts of colored town, far from the railroad tracks so the trains wouldn't wake Lula and Topie up at night. He had them install a pump in the house. They would still have to go outside and share a toilet, but most of the world still did. Lula nodded in approval when she saw the freshly painted dwelling with a kitchen, a sitting room, and a bedroom for herself and one for Topie. "One condition," Governor said. "You got dozens of kin. They are not to stay with you. It isn't supposed to be a flophouse for coloreds."

Sometimes, Lula told him, he acted like she wasn't colored herself, and said such ugly mean things.

After Meese came to the house and whispered with Zadie, he took to his bed. He knew it would not be long now. The pain grabbed him, every few minutes. He asked for morphine. In a clear moment, he asked for the lawyer to be sent in. He didn't want to see the doctor again, and he didn't really want to talk to that Father Bragg from the Episcopal Church, although he would have to give some directions for his funeral.

He just wanted to be sure that his two girls, and that granddaughter whose redneck daddy drove a truck and let Zadie raise the girl, would be all right. He wanted to be sure that no one else got any money. They'd all gotten enough when Hennie died. The town was $100,000 richer, probably more now. The town that laughed at him. As long as his blood was cared for, he could die, and he hoped it would be soon.

He tossed. He dreamed. He hallucinated from the morphine. He gritted and ground his teeth until his jaw throbbed. He didn't want to cry out. Zadie, who was too faithful for her own good, would jump up and be in there in a flash. His life paraded before him, in fragments. He could not remember yesterday, or last week, only twenty, thirty, forty years ago. Or more.

She was a beauty. Even in her fifties, she was small boned, but at sixteen and seventeen, she was perfect. She seemed to know how to walk like a princess and speak clearly, although where she learned it, he'd never known. She was working for the Draytons. She brought in the whiskey and crystal glasses on a silver plate after dinner over there one night. That was the first time he'd been there, back in those days when he was still considered important in town. People asked him over for dinner, him and Bonita. Bonita savored that life, being the town matron, the president of the Junior League and garden clubs.

He had wanted to be a college professor, early on. He went to the university and finished, but . . . why hadn't he gotten more schooling, earned the masters in history he loved so much, so he could teach at Clemson or Presbyterian College. He didn't remember now why he didn't. Maybe Daddy had said four years of college was enough, unless he wanted to study law? So he came home to run the business, or pretended to. The business consisted of collecting rents from the farmers who grew cotton and peaches and grazed livestock on the Cleelands' thousands of acres.

So that evening Butler and Mary Drayton invited them for dinner. The woman went to their gossip afterward, and he and Butler sat on the veranda and stared out at the orange sunset over the low ridge of mountains to the northwest and pretended to talk. Butler Drayton was a fool, but he knew how to marry money. Then Lula came out on the porch, delicate, with a light step, and settled the tray onto the table.

"Thank you, Lula," said Drayton, but not the way a white man would say it to a family's colored servant of several years.

"Yes, sir," she said, curtsied, and cut her eyes to Governor. "Ya'll enjoy your drinks."

This showed she had spirit, sass, he thought from the very beginning. "Where did you find her?" Governor remembered asking.

"Her momma works for us," Drayton said. "Fine-looking woman, isn't she?"

"Yes. Knows how to talk and walk."

That comment was not lost on Drayton. "You know, now that's she's of age, it might be good for her to start working for someone else."

Governor understood. Drayton's wife knew her husband to have a wandering eye, but she also wasn't cruel to her colored servants. She fancied herself a liberal when it came to the Negroes. "We could use another maid at our house," Governor offered. "Bonita has been complaining that our current housekeeper and cook is not keeping up." In Bonita's mind, all the best families of the

South had more than one servant. And this young girl could help with Zadiah, whom Bonita preferred to treat as a play pretty rather than as a child.

"That would work out real nice, if she agrees to it," said Drayton, taking a long and knowing drag from his cigar.

"What does she make now?"

"Nothing, she still lives with her momma here."

"I'll pay her fair wages . . ."

"Good," said Drayton. And that seemed to settle it.

I did, Governor thought, as the memory of that evening started to fade. Back then whites acted as if they could make decisions for the coloreds, at least in Abundance.

He writhed some more. How he wanted to sleep now. But he couldn't tell the difference between sleep, dreams, awake, memories.

Sometime that night he spent with Drayton, drinking too much whiskey, listening to his host tell a story about going to Louisville to see some horse racing, the girl appeared again. "Lula," said Drayton. "This is Mr. Governor Cleeland, a friend of ours."

She curtsied again. "Pleased to meet you, Governor. Are you the governor of a different state?"

"No, girl, that's just his Christian name." Drayton laughed, but Governor tried to keep from sighing. Why had he been christened with such a ridiculous name? "Anyway, he's been telling me he and his wife Miss Bonita need help at their house, and he's going to pay you a fair wage."

"That's mighty kind of you, Mr. Cleeland. Could I ask how much that is a week?"

He couldn't hide his astonishment at her direct question, but he wasn't offended. This pretty thing did have some sass.

"How much does your momma make? I'll pay you half of that, which is a lot more than you are making now."

Lula seemed to be thinking about it. "Where would I stay?"

"We have a big house. You'd be helping our housekeeper, Mattie. There's a room downstairs for you."

Lula narrowed her eyes in a way that made her look wise beyond her years. "What does Mrs. Governor Cleeland think about this?"

"Girl, it don't matter what his wife thinks," Drayton interrupted. "Do you want the job or not?"

"Yes, sir," she said, plainly, not betraying any enthusiasm.

"Good. Come to our house Monday morning at 8:00. Mr. Drayton here can tell you where we live."

"Oh, I know where you live. Everybody in Abundance knows the Cleeland house, sir. Thank you, sir."

She left, and he didn't see her again until Monday morning.

He didn't really plan on loving her. He convinced himself at first he was doing Drayton a favor, and making Bonita happy, giving her the extra household help her sense of social position demanded. Bonita was glad to have help for Mattie and a "nanny," as she called Lula, for Zadiah. Bonita was not an endearing mother. Neither was she turning out to be an endearing wife.

Lula didn't seem to be unwilling, not after the first time. He knew it was wrong. It was wrong for a man to have a woman in bed other than his wife. It was even more wrong that she was colored, although he didn't know why after the first time. Was it wrong because she was different, colored, or wrong because she was poor and would have a hard time saying no?

But Lula, who haggled with him about the job the first night they met, didn't have a hard time saying no. She did, plenty of times. She did all the time after Jessamyn came. He could count on two hands all the times they made love over the years. She said no much more than yes, but she said yes enough for him to get her with a baby, and enough for him to know how much he loved her.

The first time. It was months after she came to work with Mattie. He hid when she was doing her work, changing beds, dusting, cleaning the chamberpots, during the morning hours. He kept himself in his study, but when she served the meals in the dining room, bringing out the dishes from the kitchen, he felt electric, his blood quickened just to see her. If Bonita had been loving, would it have mattered? He let his hand linger on hers when she handed him a plate with dessert on it. He caught her eye and was not mistaken to see a slight smile, not a shy one, but a smile of awareness, eyes that met his and didn't turn away.

One day Bonita and Zadiah were out at some women's party or garden meeting. He went to his study to look at figures from the tenant farmers; this was his only work, his only real work, and after those were done every day, after he had made out and signed the checks for the agent who checked on the farmers and collected their rents, he could open his history books and begin to study why the states below Pennsylvania became the South and why the South insisted on its Cause and why the Cause was defeated and why the Defeat seemed to linger, fifty years later.

The door opened and silently she came in, with articles to clean his room with, to dump the ashes from the tray and dust the books and polish the glass and furniture.

"Oh, Mr. Cleeland, you're not usually here of a morning, when I clean. I beg your pardon, sir."

"Come in, Lula." He closed his book. "I do not have to leave for you to clean, do I?"

"I don't think so. I will just have to get around you a little bit."

"Just let me know when."

But he began to watch her as she moved lightly about the room. He did not return to his checkbook and ledger. "Am I botherin' you, Mr. Cleeland?"

"No, Lula."

She turned to him, fully. "You are watchin' me. Am I cleaning wrong?" Is something wrong with me?" she asked in a way that seemed to him, to say she both wanted to know his thoughts and yet she already knew the answer.

"You are beautiful, Lula."

"Mr. Cleeland, what a thing to say this morning."

But she approached him, and he reached his hand to her, and she sat on his lap, a weightless burden, soon in his arms.

Zadie came in and out. She didn't let the little girl, Virgie, come in. Virgie. Virginia Mae Cullins. Pretty little thing, just like Hennie. Zadie doted on her. Zadie had a real baby to raise now, in that little girl.

Waves of pain and dreams and memories and pain. Why didn't it just come? Zadie wanted to know he would be in heaven. He just wanted peace now.

Did he remember it, or imagine it, Lula coming in? No, it was

Topie. Topie came in, saying she would be there in Zadie's place for a while. They couldn't do anything now, but if he needed some water, she could place the glass to his lips.

Topie looked at him for a long time. She said nothing. He could feel her looking at him. He could never remembering being in a room with her, alone. All those years, someone was always in the room with them, Lula, or Zadie, or Jessamyn, or Hennie, or the little girl. How strange after all these years.

He let out a groan; the pain came deep from his bowels. Zadie had said something about cancer in his lungs. He knew better. It was engulfing him.

"Here, Daddy. Take a sip of water."

Who said "Daddy"? "Zadie?"

"No, Daddy, it's not Zadie. It's me, Topie."

"Topie."

"Yes. Yes, Daddy, it's me, Topie."

Daddy. Finally. It didn't matter who told her, or if anyone did. That last sin, the real sin, not the sin of loving Lula, but the sin of denying Topie, was over.

He tried to keep his eyes opened, but it was harder than drinking, breathing, speaking. He heard her. "I know." *I know.* .

Lula. He loved Lula. He loved Lula's child. Did Lula love him? She never said it. Never. But she stayed. The others left. She stayed. Surely that was love, after the kisses, after the embraces. He would be gone soon. *Topie knows.* It didn't matter if Zadie or anyone else did. Topie did, and she would now let the world know, and if the town laughed at him, at them, it didn't matter anymore. He had let the town tell him how to live, and he couldn't live that way, the way they wanted him to, and he couldn't live the way he wanted to. Why did they care? Why didn't the town, the other Cleelands, let him be? He couldn't marry the woman he really loved, and claim his daughter. Those were his crimes, and he would face God with them.

There was only one person living whom he had hurt. She sat there, waiting for him to speak. He tried to open his eyes. He couldn't speak. He glimpsed her for a second. Her face was set, hard, lips tight, eyes narrowed, like Lula the first night they met, Lula who could say no, Lula whom he loved, Lula who stayed with him.

"That's right, Daddy, I know," Topie said.

He closed his eyes. Death could not come soon enough.

Chapter 23

May 1998

Virginia's thoughts ran over her memories of her own life as she sat by Topie's bed. She had stopped noticing the beep-beep of the heart monitor. The clock said 5:30. She may have drowsed, but she sat upright in the aqua-covered chair that would stretch out to something like a chaise lounge. Right now that sounded like a good idea, so she pulled at the chair to elongate it and then settled herself into it again. Bethany had taken Zadie out to the ICU waiting area, where recliners were available, to rest. Zadie wanted to stay by her sister's side, but Virginia insisted, fearful that her vigil would only send Zadie to a bed in the next room. The ICU staff allowed Virginia to remain.

"Topie is my aunt. My real aunt. I have a black aunt." She started to laugh. "The craziest thing is, Zadie hid it from me and that was the last thing in the world that would bother me." But it bothered Zadie. Not for Topie's sake, whom she loved so much that she could not bring herself to tell Topie the truth about her parents. Virginia would have to find that out later. If Zadie never told Topie, now it was too late. Should Zadie have told her? Would it have made Topie's life better, happier? *Could* Zadie have told her? It would mean an admission that Zadie's own father was, if not a rapist, a seducer, a cad, who took advantage of a woman in meager circumstances but later tried to make it right, at least as right as his culture and time told him. But he was wrong. To his dying day Virginia knew her grandfather to be a bigot, a racist, despite his love for a black woman.

How strange and foolish and spacious the heart. Zadie loved Topie. Like those verses in Ruth that people quoted in weddings: "For where you go I will go, and where you lodge I will lodge. Your people shall be my people, and your God my God. Where you die I will die, and there will I be buried." Those words didn't really belong in a wedding ceremony. Those words were spoken by a woman to a woman, by a woman who chose that commitment even though the culture and circumstances around them would have split them apart. Zadie said them, in spirit and deed, to Topie long before she knew they were sisters. Yet perhaps Zadie still didn't love Topie enough to sully the reputation of Governor Cleeland and to do something that would, in her eyes, shame the family: admitting her father loved a black woman and fathered her child outside of marriage.

At 6:20 the heart monitor began making sounds that sent Ben the nurse in. He looked tired; he would be going off his 12-hour shift at 7:00. "I think this is it," he muttered. The pulse rate was quickly going down. "Do you want to get your aunt in here before Mrs. Jackson goes? It won't be long."

"Thank you, I'll be right back." She found Zadie, her head drooping, sitting with Bethany, who had clearly drunk too many cups of coffee. Her eyes were red with watching television and puffy from crying. She loved Topie, too. Virginia leaned over and gently nudged her aunt. "Zadie, Zadie, can you hear me?"

"Huh?"

"Can you get up? You need to come in and say good-bye to Topie."

Zadie looked up at her in a way that tore at Virginia's heart. But quickly Zadie summoned her strength to rise to her feet, and Bethany and Virginia guided her through the double doors to Topie's room.

Ben was right. Within five minutes, Topie's heart rate was at ten beats per minute. Her blood pressure was twenty over five; Virginia didn't know such a reading was possible. The doctor on call came in, said some soothing words, and they watched. The line on the monitor flattened.

"She's gone, Mrs. McCann, Mrs. Foster. I am sorry. Her heart was just too severely damaged from the attack."

"Thank you, doctor," Virginia managed to say, knowing he wondered why three white women were at the side of a black woman's death bed. "We were her family, as strange as it may seem. At least we could be here when it happened."

"Yes, ma'am." He turned to the nurse, "6:57, time of death."

After a talk with one of the nurses, who asked to which mortuary the body should be sent, Virginia, Zadie, and Bethany prepared to leave. Virginia realized only then that she had not thought about the festival in several hours. It seemed a distant memory, not the evening before. She would not be able to attend it today. She had to get Zadie back to St. Ambrose. She had to sleep in her own bed a while. She had to talk to Minnie and Deedra, who could contact the rest of Topie's cousins and the pastor at Zion AME. The festival would have to run itself. She had set in motion something that could have its own life now.

The funeral was held on Wednesday at Topie's church and managed by the mortuary that handled all the rituals for black families. "It's 1998, and we still separate ourselves in church and in death. Government laws haven't changed that. Maybe some day," Virginia contemplated as the service began. A respectable crowd showed up at Zion AME, where Topie worshiped for as long as Virginia could remember. When she was a teenager and Topie had moved in with them, Virginia would sometimes excuse herself from the Episcopal Church and go with Topie to the African Methodist Episcopal, figuring she was doing Zadie's church two names better. Virginia, the lone white face, liked it, the spontaneity, the fervor, the friendliness. The funeral reminded her of those times. She had as likely gone with Topie for purposes of rebellion against the formality of St. Michael's as much as a desire for worship, but it didn't diminish her enjoyment.

One time, when she was questioning her own faith, Virginia asked Topie if she believed the church's teaching. "No. I just go for the going. Sometimes that's the best you can do." Her frank, brutal, almost despairing answer shocked Virginia. Topie could tell. "I lost four babies, honey. It's mighty hard to sing about God loving me after that. But I figure if I go, I'll get some medicine for my heart and it will heal, one of these days. And I like the music, too." Virginia hoped that Topie had found the healing she wanted. She deserved it, of all people.

Sitting there, one of five white people in the church, Virginia thought about the Bible verse she learned as a child. "You shall know the truth and the truth shall make you free." She was not one to dispute the Scripture, but that one gave her pause. Would Topie have been free if she had known the truth all her life, that she was half white, that her momma's employer was her daddy, but that she was denied his wealth and station while her white sister got all of it? Was Virginia herself freer now that she knew the truth? Or did the truth just make a new prison of resentment? She hoped not. She truly hoped not.

The funeral was long, a celebration, the pastor said, of Topie's home going. Virginia understood what he meant, but in her thinking, Topie had been home, all along.

On May 20 she and Mack flew out of Greenville-Spartanburg airport and landed two hours later at LaGuardia. They took a cab to their hotel, a $250 per night disappointment. New York was as hot in late May as Abundance was, but they ate some fabulous food and saw *The Lion King* and *The Young Man from Atlanta*. Live theatre fascinated her, but she thought the young man should have stayed in Atlanta. On the flight home they decided it was time to take a trip out west; maybe Matthew would want to join them.

A few days after returning from New York, Virginia called the gang back together to evaluate the festival. She had the six of them over for dinner, no spouses this time. They sat around in a circle with beer and wine, perhaps flowing too freely, and read the evaluations visitors had filled out. They laughed until their breathing hurt at the sometimes outrageous comments. They then looked at the local reviews and decided to get serious. Each of them had something to be defensive about, but at the same time each had more to feel praised about.

"Was it a success?" Virginia asked.

"We'll know that when the bills are all paid," Daryl said.

"Oh, don't be an accountant. Did people have fun?"

"Yes!"

"Did people eat good food?"

"Yes!"

"Did people hear great music?"

"Yes!"

"Did people get sunburned and scream at their kids?"

"Yes!"

"So, I ask you, was it a success?"

"Yes!"

And they clinked their glasses together.

Good words continued to trickle in. When the bills were paid, Virginia had tangible proof that the festival was a success. Almost ten thousand people showed up in cars. The bank account read $45,477.28, only $4,523.72 less than the fifty grand the city council had allotted in January. 9,283 biscuits were consumed in Biscuit Central.

When the town heard about Topie's death, Virginia was forgiven for rushing off the stage in the middle of her big moment. In fact, Tally heard some women in the nail center suggesting that it was time Abundance had a woman for mayor and that Virgie Mae Foster made any of the men who might try for the job look sick by comparison.

On June 15 Kyung Motors put out an official announcement that they would be reopening their search for a plant in North America. Abundance had lost, but so had Macon and Jackson. Some of the shine of the festival tarnished with this news, but the next week an air conditioning manufacturer announced plans to open a new plant in Walkerburg County that would employ 500 workers. So things were looking up.

On June 20, Matthew and Virginia finally had their breakfast date. He handed her a printout of his grades. Three Ds, two Fs. Her heart sank. She wanted to remind him how much the wasted year had cost, how after eleven years of private school he should have been prepared for college. But she stopped herself from berating him.

"Matthew, what happened?"

"I gave up, Mom. I stopped going to class."

"Was it—because of. . ."

"No, Mom, believe it or not, no. Yeah, maybe some, but not in the end."

"So, where do we go? From here?"

"Not back to Charleston. They kind of, uh, sent me a letter asking me not to return."

"Oh. You mean you were kicked out."

"Let's just say released."

"And?"

"I want to stay here. I don't want to waste money at a college with a big name. Would it bother you if I went to Upstate Technical College and studied electronics? I think I could do ok in that."

"You want to stay at home?"

"Is there something wrong with that?"

"No. I think it's great. I just thought you were dying to get out of Abundance."

"I was last year. I changed my mind, for now."

"That's great."

"You don't mind, for real? Do you think Dad will?"

"He'll mind these horrible grades, but he won't mind you being here. I'll make sure of that."

"Thanks, Mom."

He was quiet for a while. "It's kind of funny."

"What?"

"A town by the name of Abundance. Where did that come from? Sounds like they thought they found a gold mine here in the old days."

"It used to be Rosy Dew. They changed the name because of a flour company, Abundance Mills."

"Oh. So that's where the biscuit idea came from."

"Yeah, sort of."

"The festival was great. People had a good time."

"Good."

"You're not going to run for mayor, are you?"

"Good grief, no. Your daddy would shoot me. But I will tell you this. I learned a whole lot more about me than I did running a festival. I'll tell you about it someday, soon, when I get it sorted out."

"OK. Is it about your own mom, and your granddad, and Miss Topie?"

"Some. But more about me. No, about *being* me. About me being here."

He looked at her as if to say he didn't understand the difference, but she changed the subject. "Can you help me get some bands for next year's festival?"

Later that day she drove through the town after a hair appointment. This time, she didn't ask for the girl to color it. She would see how the gray looked; it might not be so bad once it took over. She steered down the street that had held corn dog trucks and ice cream wagons and funnel cake tents, then turned on to the square where she thought she could still smell fresh biscuits. From there she went west on her way out to the countryside.

It was a day for putting flowers on graves. She had fresh arrangements, four, behind the front seats of the SUV. She would go out to Piney Grove first, and then make her way back into town.

She carried a dozen red roses to Hennie's grave at the far corner of the Piney Grove cemetery. They weren't appropriate for a grave, but she didn't care. Maybe if Hennie had gotten more red roses in her life. But she couldn't blame Daddy. She thought about her phone call to him a week after Topie's funeral. His wife, Mona, had answered. She and Mona had never met, just spoken politely and stiffly over the phone. She and Daddy had been together five years, meeting at a senior center.

"Daddy, this is Virgie."

"Hey, girl. What you up to?"

"About 5'6"." It was an old, silly joke, but one they always used to begin their conversations. "Oh, bunch of things. We had a festival here in Abundance, Mack and I did a lot of work in that. Bethany has a new boyfriend, I think she'll want to marry him, but I don't know if I like him."

"Nobody likes sons-in-law. I didn't like Mack, at first, but he's OK."

"I'll tell him you said that. Matthew is going to go to college around here. We're glad. Oh, and Topie died last week."

"I'm sorry to hear that. She meant a lot to you when you were growing up."

"She still does, Daddy. And that's really why I'm calling. It seems that I've learned a lot about the Cleelands in the last few months."

"You have?"

"Yes, sir. It turns out that Governor was Topie's real father."

"I'll be damned. Are you sure?"

"Yes, he told Zadie on his deathbed. She never told anyone else. I'm not even sure Topie knew. I just found out the night before Topie died."

"Well, think of that."

"I learned something else. I think you know where this is going."

Silence came from the other end. "Daddy?"

"Yes."

"I know about Momma. All about it. I know where she's buried. I know about the wreck, and the gun, and what happened, and how Zadie covered it up. And how you went along with it."

Another pause. "Then you know everything."

"No, I don't. I don't know why, Daddy."

Her voice choked. No, she didn't know why. She didn't know why Topie was not allowed to know the truth about herself. She didn't know why the adults in her own life conspired to deceive her. She didn't know why Hennie couldn't bring herself to love her child more than her desire to flee madness.

"Virgie. I probably didn't do the right thing. I did what seemed like the right thing. I truly did. That's all I can say."

"I know Daddy. And you know, Mack and I are going to come down to see you. And when I do, I'm not going to fuss at you. We're going to have a good cry, ok. Because I know you saved my life, too."

"Thank you, Virgie."

"Thank you, Daddy."

No, Daddy was not to blame. But Virginia loved to get a dozen red roses from Mack, and maybe that was something she inherited from Hennie.

Her next stop was the St. Michael's cemetery, where Governor was buried. Zadie had asked her to put flowers on his grave. She'd been in a nostalgic, weepy, sentimental mood since Topie died, understandably. She was lonely at St. Ambrose. "Maybe I'll talk to Mack about bringing her home to live with us now," Virginia thought. "It might be time."

She placed a bundle of wild flowers on Governor's grave. It would be a long time, if ever, before she thought of him with anything but disdain, as anything but a throw-back to plantation days, a man who held his privilege tightly and couldn't see beyond his status.

Her last cemetery stop was the Lakemont Memory Gardens where Topie had a plot next to Lula. The headstone had been delivered and installed two days before. She placed a bunch of tulips on Lula's grave; they had always been her favorite in the spring, although hard to come by now in June. She placed a potted plant of lilies at Topie's grave to the left of the headstone and stepped back to see the engraver's work.

Utopia Felecia Cleeland Jackson
November 1, 1913 to May 16, 1998
Our daughter, our sister, our aunt, our friend

She took a left out of Lakemont Memory Gardens to turn near home, but then changed her mind and did an illegal U-turn. She followed the road out of town again until Bosley Orchard appeared on the left. This land had belonged to Governor; he sold it to cover up Hennie's death. It stretched for acres and acres, straight rows of fifteen- foot-high peach trees, for as far as she could see to the horizon.

She pulled off the road and listened to the hot engine click after she turned it off. She pushed the button to open all the windows and the outdoor sounds of birds, cicadas, and a distant train rushed in. She savored it. This was Abundance. This was the town that made her. Why did she want to change it so much? It wasn't broken. All of her adult life she had seen her role as leading, pushing, cajoling, making decisions for others. Did that come from being a Cleeland, the town paragons, or from her own dissatisfaction? Now both of those truths of who she was seemed like the train whistle that was evaporating to the south.

She breathed in the sweet air of early summer. She opened the car door and climbed down and jumped over the ditch on the side of the road. She walked the twenty feet to a peach tree. They weren't quite ready; maybe in another week. But she reached up and picked one anyway. She bit into it. Yes, it was a bit too hard and tart, but not inedible. She took another bite and turned to her car.

In two weeks she'd stop at Bosley's stand and buy a basket. She wondered how they would taste on pound cake.

If you liked this novel, check out Barbara G. Tucker's other stories:

Traveling Through (Oaktara, 2008)

Cross Road (Oaktara, 2012)

Legacy (Oaktara, 2012)

The Unexpected Christmas Visitors (Amazon Kindle, 2012)

And her blog, partsofspeaking.blogspot.com

Made in the USA
Charleston, SC
23 June 2015